PRAISE FOR ERIQ LA SALLE

LAWS OF SOLOMON

"*Laws of Solomon* is a bracing, emotionally complex exploration of who we are and how the choices we make can define us. Eriq La Salle brings a deep reservoir of empathy and honesty to this story of a former hit man who finds his most dangerous enemy may be his own sense of regret. An amazing read!"

—S. A. Cosby, *New York Times* bestselling author of *King of Ashes*

"Eriq La Salle's *Laws of Solomon* is lush and brutal, a poem hiding out as a novel. I sped through this cinematic story that slashed and nursed my heart—and for me, that's the mark of extraordinary writing."

—Rachel Howzell Hall, *New York Times* bestselling author

"In this gripping addition to his Martyr Maker series, Eriq La Salle gives us a good reason to not spend time in New York with detectives Freeman and Cavanaugh—morally complex hit man Solomon Nangobi. La Salle seamlessly blends key moments from Solomon's past as a child soldier turned hit man with his precarious present trying to protect an innocent child from a brutal cartel kingpin. It's a story of sacrifice, second chances, and the unexpected bond of found family. You'll be cheering for La Salle's pitch-perfect anti-hero to finally get his version of a happy ending."

—Kellye Garrett, award-winning author of *Missing White Woman*

MARTYR MAKER SERIES

"Eriq La Salle's *Laws of Wrath* is all thriller; no filler—a white-knuckled treat."

—James Patterson

"Raw and gritty, with a careening plot and brisk dialogue, Eriq La Salle's satisfying new novel will especially appeal to fans of serial killer thrillers."

—Wendy Corsi Staub, *New York Times* bestselling suspense author

"A brilliant and bloody cop thriller from Eriq La Salle that Ed McBain himself would have been proud to have penned."

—Adrian McKinty, *New York Times* bestselling author of *The Chain*

"Eriq La Salle has crafted a pitch-perfect thriller that perfectly conjures the tension of a city at a boiling point. *Laws of Annihilation* is an exploration of racial conflict and personal turmoil and will have you flipping the pages at record speed. A startling and shocking and astute entry into the genre."

—Ivy Pochoda, author of *Wonder Valley*

"*Laws of Depravity* by Eriq La Salle should be on a fast track to bestseller status. It is the story of good vs. evil where it's not always clear who are the good and who are the evil. *Laws of Depravity* may be the most engrossing book you read this year, bar none."

—Lee Ashford, *Reader's Favorites*

"Eriq La Salle, in *Laws of Depravity*, has written an utterly compelling and riveting thriller with echoes of the dark master, Thomas Harris. Here, La Salle also adds a surprising twist by weaving in a spiritual component that raises the narrative to lofty and thought-provoking levels. It's a wonderful accomplishment."

—Leonard Chang, author of *Over the Shoulder* and *Crossings*

"Actor and director Eriq La Salle's intense debut is a modern-day parable cleverly masquerading as a crime novel. A muscular, gritty and spiritual thriller."

—John Shors, bestselling author of *Beneath a Marble Sky, Beside a Burning Sea, Dragon House, The Wishing Trees*, and *Cross Currents*

"*Laws of Depravity* will take you on a heart-pounding ride of vengeance, murder, and atonement, never letting you rest until you've reached the final page. Eriq La Salle deftly draws unforgettable characters who tangle with good and evil and seek spiritual understanding and forgiveness for some of the most dastardly deeds human beings are capable of committing. Drawing on his talent as an acclaimed actor and director, Mr. La Salle digs deep into his characters' psyches, delivering a group of bruised and tarnished individuals you won't soon forget."

—Neal Baer, coauthor of *Kill Switch* and former executive producer of *Law and Order: SVU*

"The surprises keep coming in La Salle's twisting debut thriller, in which good and evil aren't always black and white. In addition to the absorbing, fast-paced plot that will keep readers guessing until the end, each wonderfully sculpted character has a distinct lifelike personality. The plot offers catalysts for change while raising spiritual questions and blurring the line between good and evil, which propels the story upward from being merely a solid, entertaining thriller to being a gripping must-read that could have readers pondering right and wrong long after they've finished."

—*Kirkus Reviews*, Starred Review, for *Laws of Depravity*

"A serial killer known as the Martyr Maker is on his final round of murdering twelve clergymen once every ten years. Two New York City detectives and the FBI are on his trail, but maybe the dead clergy aren't as innocent as they appear. A gritty crime thriller, spiritual quest, and love story all woven into one compelling tale."

—*Publishers Weekly*

"Fast-paced… Characters are richly textured [and] none is without faults. Sets the hook for the captivating series."

—*Kirkus Reviews*

ALSO BY ERIQ LA SALLE

Laws of Depravity

Laws of Wrath

Laws of Annihilation

LAWS OF SOLOMON

ERIQ LA SALLE

Poisoned Pen Press

Cover design by Ellis Carson Jones/Sourcebooks, based on series design by *the*BookDesigners
Cover image © Chris Wynn Photography/Shutterstock

Published by Poisoned Pen Press, an imprint of Sourcebooks
1935 Brookdale RD, Naperville, IL 60563-2773
(630) 961-3900
sourcebooks.com

Cataloging-in-Publication Data is on file with the Library of Congress.

Printed and bound in the United States of America.
CR 10 9 8 7 6 5 4 3 2 1

This book is dedicated to the readers. Those who have been on this journey with me from the beginning and those who have discovered the series along the way. The bloggers, vloggers, book clubs, the voracious as well as casual readers. To the lovers of books from all walks of life. You all may not realize how much you actually keep authors going, despite the numerous rejections, naysayers, the difficulty of navigating the publishing industry, self-doubt, and paralyzing writer's block as well as a myriad of other challenges. Knowing that you all appreciate and support our efforts as loyal readers makes all the difference in the world. Thank you.

1

The Garden

As he did most nights, he waited for the ghosts to come. They came without fail, announcing their arrival first by song and tribal chants. The deep timbre of their voices lulled him to sleep like a child under the spell of a lullaby. Solomon Nangobi dreamed he died. It was in death that he'd finally found a good life. A simple life. Monastic even. A new life of absolution. The war with the Divine had ended in a stalemate. Ultimately, he'd found salvation neither in God nor another deity but in the land. It was the land that saved him. Moored him. The land was both his death and resurrection. For all the unanswered times it had beckoned him, he finally learned to heed its call. Even though it wasn't the land of his father or even the cradle of his birth, it spoke to him nonetheless. Made him feel human. Filled him with modest but meaningful purpose.

From the time he arrived in America as a teenager, most people simply called him "the African." His skin was immeasurably black, so much so that he still looked like a silhouette even in the unfolding sunrise. He started his mornings on his knees, inhaling deeply and smelling the dark earth. He sifted dew-damp clumps of soil through hands that were the color of coal. This was his predawn ritual. Smelling the earth. Touching it. Listening to it. It told him when to plant and what to plant. The flowers, trees, and shrubbery connected him to a life that was worth living. His father was a farmer, as was his father before him and so on. His veins flowed with the blood of seven generations of landmen. Had the soldiers not come all those years ago, he would have undoubtedly been the eighth generation of proud Nangobi farmers.

The ghosts felt too real to be just a dream. They came one after the other. The first of them were kinder spirits, heard but unseen. They whispered his name and sang to him the songs and chants of distant kin. It was the latter sect that troubled him most. They were the ghosts that came as uncountable faces, bringing with them unbearable memories. No matter how dark the night, he saw them clearly and knew what they came to demand of him. They took his sleep and left him instead with tremors and the clenching of dampened sheets.

The land was his only true respite. The hours in which he tilled, planted, or pruned somehow managed to keep the hauntings at bay. He rose before dawn, worked until dark, ate, read, slept what little he could, then began the cycle again. This was his fulfillment. It was the semblance of peace that had eluded him for more than five decades. The older he got, the less clear he was on the sum of all that was either lost or stolen from him. He only knew an estimate of his age. There were a number of irretrievable things taken from him in his youth, chief among them innocence and love.

Shortly after he started working for the old man two years ago, he was allowed to move into the storage shed, which he quickly converted into living quarters. The space was sparse. A used futon, a small space heater, a milk crate for the couple of items of clothing that he possessed, only the most essential of toiletries and a nighttime pee bucket. There were, however, several makeshift shelves for his many books. Morrison, Hemingway, Baldwin, Nietzsche, Fanon, Rand, Tzu (both Lao and Sun), Dickinson, King, Lehane, Winslow just to name a few. The shed was less than two hundred square feet, but it was his sanctuary. It was all his to call home.

Now that winter had all but faded, the inchoate spring granted him longer hours of sunlight. No matter the weather, he started each morning in quietness under the giant podocarpus tree just outside his shed. Even in the early morning chill, he toiled in the garden in his bare feet. As was the custom of his forefathers, he wanted nothing to come between him and the feel of earth.

The gardens located near the northern tip of Malibu were some of the many botanical gems in Southern California. From the late ’70s through the early ’90s the place belonged to the Hare Krishnas. The twenty-three acres of good land originally housed a four-thousand-square-foot temple that in ’94 had been converted to a public visitors center while the acres were divided into five sequential gardens: botanical, tropical, Japanese, English, and succulents. In the weeks following 9/11, the gardens were filled with Californians in desperate need of beauty and solace. Over the years, the crowds had thinned, and the gardens were no longer properly maintained by the corporate foundation that now owned them. Still, Solomon knew the instant he saw the place that there was magic, albeit dormant, in the land.

The old man who oversaw the place picked him up along with a couple of other day workers in front of Home Depot. Solomon outworked everyone, easily doing the workload of three. The old man took to him right away, admiring the care and passion with which he approached his work. He appreciated how Solomon handled the plants with the love and tenderness of a true landman. It was obvious to the old man shortly after meeting the man from Africa that he had a gentle spirit and special touch. Equally obvious was the fact that he also had the scarred hands of a once violent man.

It had taken Solomon two years, but he had finally turned the five gardens around, restoring them to their former glory. He was now even busier with the advent of spring. His days were spent fertilizing the grounds, replacing some of the deciduous plants, and doing the seasonal lacing and pruning along with the general prepping of spring's anthesis. After planting a half dozen pittosporum bushes along a pathway, he sat on a backless oak bench as the sunrise bathed the Zen garden in the warm hues of ocher rays. He was greeted by the sound of a steady trickle of water and the morning songs of waking birds. Just off in the distance, he heard the lull of intermittent waves breaking in the Pacific Ocean.

Of the five gardens, the two that were his favorite were the Zen and the botanical. Which garden he practiced his morning meditations in switched according to his moods. He woke up longing for the peace of being nestled among the Zen garden's bonsais, Japanese maples, giant bamboo, and eight-foot Buddha statue with water cascading from the top of its head. He loved the Zen garden not because he was a Buddhist or of any other religious persuasion. God by any name was nothing more to him than a distant memory. He was a Ugandan-born-and-raised Muslim who parted ways with Allah long before he made it to manhood. His deep connection to the Zen garden had nothing to do with any religious or spiritual implications but simply because it was a place where in his conscious stillness, the ghosts left him alone.

The old man, Uriel Tanaka, watched Solomon from a distance for a couple of seconds before joining him on the bench to partake in their morning tea ritual. Solomon and Tanaka drank their tea in silence as they watched two male hummingbirds fluttering around the waters that pooled at the base of the Buddha statue. The notoriously territorial birds uncharacteristically drank and bathed together in peace.

"Think lightly of yourself and deeply of the world," Tanaka said.

"Miyamoto Musashi, seventeenth-century samurai with a perfect dueling record," Solomon responded.

"Not bad. Fair warning, tomorrow the questions get much more challenging."

"So what exactly do you consider the ones that you've been asking me?"

"Just appetizers for a hungry mind," Tanaka said and smiled. "You might want to take advantage of this morning and start brushing up on more reading."

"Can't. I've got a bunch of pittosporums and a couple of plumerias I need to get in before it rains tonight," Solomon replied.

"You won't have time. The rain will be here shortly."

"Forecast said not until late tonight."

Tanaka sipped his tea. "You should know better by now than to doubt the aching knees of an old man."

Solomon was a serious man, not the type who smiled much, but Tanaka had such ease with him that he found himself occasionally bursting into wide grins in the old man's company. Despite having worked together closely for two years, they knew very little about each other. Neither asked the other much about his respective past. The three things that Solomon had gathered from snippets of conversation were that Tanaka had formally started studying gardening in his late sixties, he was now in his early to mid-eighties, and he was born in the Fort Meade internment camp during World War II shortly after his parents moved to the States from Tokyo.

Tanaka proved to be a great mentor to Solomon in many ways. He challenged his reading by testing him on his knowledge of historical figures. He taught him not just about gardening but also the power of meditation, the art of tea, and even what was called *wabi-sabi*, which was the practice of finding beauty in the imperfections in nature. He enlightened him in the ancient Buddhist teaching of the three marks of existence—impermanence, suffering, and the absence of self-nature. Solomon knew much more than most about suffering, but Tanaka's teachings had him at least for the first time in his life thinking about the possibilities of self-reconciliation and peace.

As they sat on the bench, they didn't talk much. They drank tea and listened to the calming waters flowing down the body of the Buddha statue. The men were serenaded with the morning coos of a courting dove. Two stranger friends who sat together for an hour with no real need for conversation, just the mutual appreciation of the other's existence.

Solomon looked upward at the slate-gray skies and felt the first raindrop on his face.

Just as Tanaka's aching knees predicted, the showers came early. Solomon spent the rest of the morning in his shed reading under the constant pitter-patter of the rain pelting the tin roof. The scent of petrichor lulled him to sleep for the briefest of naps until the screams of the children in his dreams woke him.

When the sun came out around 2:00 p.m., he went back to work. He enjoyed planting in wet earth. The soil was even more compliant. He worked until dark, until his muscles were sore and he was satisfied at having put in a full day's work. Solomon stripped naked just outside his shed and hosed off the mud and mulch from his clothes. As he rinsed himself in the brisk air, his dark skin shone in the moonlight like wet night. He changed into a pair of sweats and a hoodie, then prepared his dinner, which was two cans of tuna and a warm bottle of ginger beer. After he finished eating, he smoked half of a cigarette. It was one of the very few indulgences he still occasionally allowed himself. The nicotine somehow seemed to dull the abdominal pains he'd been experiencing, which of late seemed to occur with much more frequency and intensity.

Solomon sat on the corner of his futon and forced himself to read until his eyelids ceded all resistance and shuttered in silent defeat. His exhaustion was his best and often only defense against the ghosts that were intent on routinely waking him. He considered himself lucky on the nights that he was able to cobble more than three uninterrupted hours of sleep. Although the nights were consistently quiet, there was an uncanny stillness unlike what he had grown accustomed to. *Sketches of Spain* played softly in his headphones. The mournful trumpet soothed Solomon like warm milk to a baby. No one did melancholy quite like Miles. Many a night, Solomon drifted off to sleep to the plangent wails of the master and his horn. The times that his overactive mind needed extra calming, he found it through his submission to the music.

Solomon fell asleep much easier than he did on most nights. His head drooped in a heavy nod, waking him as his book fell to the floor. The crashing sound jolted him. Once he was fully awake and gathered his bearings, the realization dawned on him that the night would now feel eternal. He knew without doubt that he would have trouble falling back to sleep. And even if he could, he was certain that the ghosts would be there waiting for him. Each night before going to sleep, he wondered which would come for him first—the dead or the living. He closed his eyes, clutching a shiny Colt M1911 pistol.

The morning was cooler than it had been in previous days. The air, which was crisp and clear, still had the lingering, chaste scent of rain. The gardens smelled renewed. Pure even. The world was brilliantly green. Although at times Solomon doubted its very existence, the gardens after the rain left his soul feeling cleansed.

He chose to start his day in the botanical gardens, which he and Tanaka nicknamed "Angels by the Sea." They called it that because of the twelve statues of seraphs that were spread around the garden's rim. The perfectly manicured grounds sat just above a twenty-foot-high bluff with a magnificent view of the Pacific Ocean. The statues were each made of different materials and depicted in a variety of stances. Half had spread wings while the others were closed. One held a horn while the others carried swords or shields and spears. Some were made of alabaster while others were cast from bronze, marble, sandstone, or onyx.

Tanaka appeared, approached the bench, and handed Solomon a cup of tea as he sat beside him.

"Not what we have but what we enjoy constitutes our abundance," Tanaka quoted.

"Jean Antoine Petit-Senn," Solomon answered.

"That's pretty good."

"Like most poets, he died poor," Solomon offered.

"But nonetheless lived a rich life," Tanaka responded.

"How can you be certain of that?"

"Because two hundred years later, his words are just as relevant. Isn't that what really matters? Isn't it the impact and legacy that determine the quality of one's life?"

Solomon sipped his tea. "Not sure that I fully agree with that, but then again, of the two of us, I'm the one more apt to see the glass as half empty."

Tanaka smiled at him. "And after all this time, I thought I had taught you how much better tea tastes minus the dash of pessimism."

As Tanaka stood and gathered both their cups, Solomon couldn't help but laugh.

Tanaka waved and mumbled something incoherent as he walked off.

The crowds were light after the rains. The sodden earth kept the more casual spectators away. The few who came were the faithful and/or the true anthophiles. As a general practice, Solomon stayed clear of the visitors except in times of pressing repairs.

Tanaka stopped by the shed to tell him about some minor flooding near a row of monarch roses in the botanical garden. Solomon trenched the irrigation line until he found the spot where tree roots had broken a section of old PVC piping. He used a couple of connectors to stanch the hemorrhaging line, at least temporarily. As he toiled in the mud, he felt the weight of eyes on him. The curious scrutiny of an unannounced guest. Glancing over his shoulder, he noticed a small boy who was no more than eight years old watching his every move. The child, like most children, made Solomon uncomfortable. He regarded them as no more than the harbingers of unwanted memories. Of all the ghosts that came to torment him, and there were many, it was always the small ones that he found the most terrorizing.

The boy was dark like him. Maybe two to three shades lighter but definitely African. It wasn't just his complexion, the structure of the child's face with the full forehead and raised cheekbones, but his clothing as well that confirmed for Solomon that not only was the boy Nigerian but specifically of Yoruba descent. The aso-oke (handwoven cloth) he wore was that of a noble clan. He looked the part of a young prince in a flowing, sky-blue agbada (gown) and matching fila (hat). More than his elegant clothing or stately air, the thing that made him instantly unforgettable was that although his skin was the color of black acorn, the boy's almond-shaped eyes were a striking contrast of warm amber. Solomon stared at him because although he was certain he had never met a child with such eyes, the boy looked vaguely familiar.

"Do you know my father?" the boy asked.

"Excuse me?"

"Do you know my father?"

"Uh…I don't think so…no," Solomon responded.

"He owns the gardens."

"Well, I work here, but I've never met him. So no, I don't know him."

"Do you want to meet him?"

"Maybe some other time. I…"

Solomon saw an African man in a dark suit and tie approaching as he called to the boy. "Gaby, let the man finish his work. Your parents are asking for you."

The man was tall and wide with the gait and posture of a soldier. Fit build. Thick neck. Scarred hands. Solomon knew the type right away. He noticed the slight pull of the man's suit, a subtle sag that Solomon surmised was caused by a concealed handgun. Men like him were called many things. A *keeper*. A *minder*. A praetorian. A jacket. Those who were the most elite of their field were often given interesting nicknames such as the Long Winter or the Silent Wraith. The man was a bodyguard, which meant that his young charge was a boy of high standing.

As the man led him away, the child glanced one last time over his shoulder at Solomon.

Once the repairs were done, Solomon headed back to the shed. On his way, he passed the boy, two bodyguards, a tall, regal woman in expensive jewelry and clothing, and there at the center of the entourage a richly dressed African man who Solomon assumed was the boy's father. He heard one of the bodyguards address the man as Mr. Ramiel. Just off to the side, a photographer was snapping photos of the happy family. They were near the entrance of the botanical garden flanked by two statues as well as a myriad of flowers and greens. Tanaka, who often served as a personal chaperone to VIP guests, stood nearby. Solomon nodded at him as he passed.

Though the skies were still moist, the threat of more showers dissipated by the second. The sun beamed triumphant, parting the still-gray clouds. The air was made sweeter by the vernal rains. This was the time of year that Solomon felt the most alive. After the showers. After the ablution. As he walked the fertile grounds, he too felt renewed, temporarily purified even. He was simultaneously both grounded and lifted by the garden's serenity. He loved how the flowers smelled even more redolent in the rain's aftermath. He loved the inhalation and exhalation of the fresh air cooling his lungs. He especially loved the pleasant din of birdsong welcoming the early morn.

Just as he neared his shed, he passed two men in police uniforms walking in the direction of the botanical garden. They were both young, hard-looking Latinos. Solomon's acuity had always been a key to his survival. There were far too many times for him to remember how often his instincts had proven to be the difference between living or dying. He hated cops, but he most definitely knew enough about them to tell the difference between a real one and a fake one. He knew the men were impostors right away. Cops looked directly at the people they passed, not away from them as though trying to shield their faces. The men's uniforms hung on them more like borrowed articles of clothing than owned. It wasn't just a vibe or the way the men carried themselves; the biggest tell was that their guns were wrong. The Desert Eagle pistols that were tucked in the holsters of both men were most *certainly not* department issue.

As they walked past him and he turned to watch them, he noticed a tattoo of the letter *Z* engulfed in flames on the back of the neck of one of the men. Solomon had once killed a man or two who wore such a tattoo. They were popular among the newer recruits of the Zetas. All Mexican cartels were ruthlessly violent, but none more so than the Zetas.

Solomon, who was less than ten yards from his shed, sprinted to retrieve his weapon.

2

Scorched Earth

As he jogged back, he was only twenty yards from the botanical garden when he heard the first round of gunfire. There were screams and sounds of panic. Two terrified pedestrians ran past him toward the exit. By the time he arrived at the garden's edge, the mother and the photographer were both sprawled on the ground in dense pools of blood. The mother's lifeless eyes were frozen skyward as the little boy's desperate cries failed to summon her back to the land of the living. Solomon looked for Tanaka but did not see him. The bodyguard whom he'd met earlier shielded himself along with the boy and his father among a copse of white birch trees. His colleague was positioned behind a statue, firing at the two assailants who had him boxed in. The fake cops caught him in a crossfire and put him down.

It had been some time since Solomon last killed someone.

Although he slept each night with his weapon, the gun no longer felt the way it had years ago. It was now cumbrous in both feel and purpose. It was no longer the appendage that it had been in the past when he killed for a living. It felt different now from the way it used to when both his enemies and victims alike feared the mere whisper of either of his nicknames, the Black Reaper or the Darkness.

There were instincts, violent instincts that he thought he was done with that came back to him. Preternaturally so. He may no longer have been the best at what he used to do, but he was still better than the two shooters. They were too distracted by their prey. They never saw him coming. He fired four rapid shots, three of which hit their mark. One to the back of the head of the first shooter and two center mass to the second.

Although the men were down, Solomon remained safely positioned behind a statue. Even when the surviving bodyguard saw the two fallen shooters, he still pointed his gun at Solomon as a precaution. In a crisis situation, all strangers were potential threats. Before Solomon could warn him to stay in position, he saw the bodyguard attempting to quickly lead the man and boy deeper into the garden.

"Go back! It's not safe!" Solomon yelled.

In his previous encounter with Zetas, they were known for sending more than just one crew on kill runs. The first set of shooters were puppies auditioning to be *perros grandes*. They functioned as either decoys or sacrifices. If they happened to kill the mark, then they were instantly elevated to the coveted status of sicario. The fact that the target had two bodyguards meant that the man was a high-level kill. Both puppies and big dogs alike understood this was the quickest way to cement an impressive reputation. Solomon knew that they'd only seen the first wave, and more were soon to come.

Despite Solomon's warnings, the bodyguard led the man and the boy in the opposite direction from where the shooters had arrived. As he watched them pass a row of hedges, Solomon caught a glimpse of a bloodied Tanaka sprawled on the ground behind a tiny knoll. His heart dropped until he saw him move. Not much, but it was still proof of life. In his former profession, there were definitive rules to survive by. Key among them was never lead nor follow with emotion. The sight of Tanaka bleeding and in harm's way triggered more of a protective response than one of primal self-survival. There were risks that Solomon normally would not have taken, but Tanaka meant more to him than even his own safety.

Just as he hurried to the old man's side and glanced at his wound, Solomon saw not one but three pairs of additional shooters twenty-five yards away, approaching from both the east and west, essentially collapsing the field. Because he was obscured behind the knoll, he could see the pair who approached from the east, but they were unable to see him. He had less than a minute before the shooters passed within a few feet of them.

He felt Tanaka's hand gently squeezing his as the old man opened his eyes to look at him. Solomon quickly assessed the wound and remained calm for the old man's sake.

"Your gunshot is through and through. Didn't hit anything major," Solomon assured him.

"When you're my age, everything is major." Tanaka tried to smile.

Solomon glanced again in the direction of the approaching men. "I need you to trust me and do exactly as I say. Close your eyes, and lie here as still as possible."

Tanaka nodded at him and closed his eyes.

Solomon smeared his hands with Tanaka's blood and wiped a good amount of it on his chest. He positioned his body spread-eagled just a foot or two near Tanaka. They both played possum as they heard the crunch of gravel announcing the shooter's approach.

As the footsteps neared, then passed by them, Solomon rolled to a kneeling position and shot both men in the back. He then turned to check on the old man.

"Are you okay?"

"I'm fine. Go get the boy," Tanaka responded.

"But..."

"Don't worry. Death is not here for me today."

The clap of gunshots echoed in the distance.

"Please, save the boy," Tanaka pleaded.

Solomon followed the sound of gunfire until he came upon a trail of blood. At the end of the trail was the lifeless body of a Zeta as well as the bodyguard, who was dotted with bullet holes. He hurried past the dead men until he arrived at a set of stone stairs overlooking several rows of five-foot-high manicured hedges that formed a huge labyrinth. Spread throughout the garden were the dozen statues of angels. From his elevated position, he could see four Zetas, each headed in a different direction in pursuit of the man and boy. Two acres of the garden were intricately filled with numerous rows of dead ends and misleading turns. Solomon often referred to it as the maze of a thousand paths. No one, not even Tanaka, knew the gardens as intimately as he did. Solomon moved quickly to head off the shooters.

Mr. Ramiel used his body to shield the boy. As the gunman moved closer, the man begged not for his life but rather for the child's.

"Please, he's a—"

Three shots silenced his pleas.

As the shooter reloaded, he caught the boy's eyes. They both looked at each other vacantly, one seemingly with no regard for killing and the other with no regard for dying. The boy's blank expression was something akin to peace in the face of death. An acceptance. He stood his ground with no overwhelming signs of fear.

The killing was quick, loud, and bloody. The shooter never finished his reload. Solomon's bullets killed him where he stood.

Solomon hurried to the boy, grabbed him by the hand, and turned back toward the path from which he had come. The boy slowed as he looked over his shoulder at the corpse of Mr. Ramiel. Solomon took his eyes off the path for just a second to address the child.

"We have to hurry. If you want to live, you have to pay attention to everything I tell you to do."

Solomon looked up just as they rounded a corner of hedges and was met with the spray of automatic gunfire. He took two bullets in his upper body. One was a graze; the other was much more life-threatening. As he fell, he took the boy down with him. Solomon had been shot before, a few times in his life, some more grave than others. He measured the severity in terms of pain and blood loss. As he landed on the ground, there was quite a bit of both.

Solomon had played the details of his own mortality over in his head many times before. He'd long ago accepted the inevitability of his own violent demise. His only assumption was that it would have happened much sooner—in the spring of his life and not the winter.

As he lay on his back, he managed to keep his gun trained in the shooter's direction. He used what little energy and strength he had to prop himself up into a sitting position with his back against the base of a stone angel with outstretched wings.

He heard the shooter's voice calling to him in a heavy Latin accent, "This is not your fight, my friend. Not worth you dying over. We just want what we came here for."

Solomon nodded his head toward a small gap in the thicket of hedge trunks and whispered to the boy, "Go that way and just keep running straight until you see a white van near the gate. It's not locked. Hide on the floor in the back. You'll be safe."

"You have to come with me."

"I can't. You'll be fine, but you have to leave now."

"No, let me help you."

"You can't. Go."

The boy didn't move.

Although Solomon's voice was just above a whisper, he was much firmer. "Go!"

The boy reluctantly backed away toward the gap beneath the hedges.

As Solomon sat there, he focused on his breathing, fighting to tolerate the pain. Fighting to stay conscious. It took all that he had to keep his eyes open. He saw the tip of a weapon peeking just beyond the wall of bushy greens. Solomon managed to squeeze off several rounds into the hedges where he estimated the gunman's body to be. He stopped firing only after he heard the leaden thud of dead weight hitting the ground.

Solomon rested with his back against the statue. He could see the ocean and the beach below. He heard the calls of seagulls over the crashing of the ocean's waves.

Of all the wounds he had endured, he'd never felt such pain. He'd never felt being held so firmly in the clutch of death. As he sat in the soft grass, the thin blades still damp from rain and morning dew, he closed his eyes, or rather they closed on their own against his feeble will. In the silence, he thought of old man Tanaka's laughter. He thought he smelled the oolong tea from their morning ritual. Solomon was filled with an incredible sense of gratitude for all that the old man had taught him in their two years together. The imparted wisdom and the beauty of life itself. He felt most thankful for the fertile earth that reminded him of his real purpose in the world. It was this patch of land that had offered him protection. Even when he was certain that the ghosts would come seeking retribution, somehow the gardens kept them at bay. The gardens that he loved and that in fact loved him as well were his refuge that taught him peace and self-reclamation. Taught him to live the type of life that he presumed had been lost to him forever.

Nestled there in the bosom of his sanctuary among the stone statues and flora, Solomon heard the familiar baritone of his dead father's voice singing to him. Welcoming him. He thought he heard a chorus of chanting from unseen strangers. Although he could not make out the words, he was certain that they were chanting in his native Acholi dialect. Their voices soothed him and took his mind off his pain. There was peace in his heart because the garden whispered in his ears that there was nothing for him to fear. When he felt death's grasp tighten, he was surprised that it was more serene than he'd ever assumed it would be. The garden made it so. Solomon thought it only befitting; since the garden was in fact his den of surrender, he deemed it a perfect place to die.

The two remaining gunmen called out in vain to their fallen accomplices. Their voices grew nearer.

Solomon woke with a start, looking around, uncertain which world he was in. His head was cloudy; he felt like a man who had been abruptly awakened from the deepest of sleeps. He had no idea how long he'd been out. He did remember dreaming. His dreams amounted to no more than disjointed clips of his life. The thing he remembered most of his dreams was the faint chant of indistinguishable words.

Solomon's eyes fluttered when the sun that warmed his face was suddenly cooled by the heavy shadow of what he assumed was death hovering over him. When he finally looked up, he saw the amber eyes of the little boy staring down at him.

3

"Doc" Callan

Doc Callan dropped everything when Solomon called him to tell him that he'd been shot. He drove like a madman to the address Solomon mumbled to him over the phone. From the way he sounded on the brief call, Callan wasn't sure that his friend would still be alive by the time he got to him.

Callan missed the turn. The overgrown brush had all but obscured the cobbled driveway from the main road. He threw his Land Rover in reverse and turned down the winding path. A hundred yards later, he saw the white van peeking around a rear corner of a small, deserted, adobe-style chapel. As he turned the engine off, he gathered his things quickly. He had been a handsome man once, long before the onset of perpetual fatigue. His face was etched with the sunken lines of a hard life. The creases on his forehead ran deep like the striations of desert rock. His hair and beard were baby-powder white, and his eyes were bluer than noon in July. Doc Callan was only sixty but could easily pass for seventy-five.

He reached inside a duffel bag lying in the front passenger seat and pulled out a Mossberg 9mm. He placed the gun inside the shoulder holster he wore, then grabbed the bag and exited the vehicle. He stepped through the weeds and bramble, scanning his surroundings a few times as he slowly approached the chapel's entrance.

Just before Doc Callan entered the former house of worship, he looked up at the broken stained-glass window and the fang-like shards of Jesus in the garden at Gethsemane. As he slowly walked through the door, he saw the small boy holding Solomon's hand. Solomon was sprawled on a nearby pew. The scant lighting in the tiny church came mainly from the dappled rays of the broken stained glass. Because they were both so dark-skinned, they looked like two shadows gathering at twilight. Solomon was so still that it was hard to tell if he was alive or dead.

"Solomon. Solomon," Callan called to him but got no reaction.

Crossing closer, he watched as the boy gently shook him awake. Solomon, gun still in hand, opened his eyes and turned his head as the boy pointed toward the visitor.

"Thanks for coming, Linus," Solomon said, his voice thready.

"Don't thank me just yet. We need to hope that I have enough in my bag of tricks to make a difference. First thing first, let's get you in a better place for me to work on you. Can you move?"

Both Solomon's voice and movement were tentative. "Just a little at a time."

"That's all I need."

Solomon placed his gun in his waistband as Callan gently helped him up and crossed through the nave of the church toward the chancel, where he laid him on an altar stone. The boy held on to Solomon's hand the entire time.

"It's okay. You can let go now. By the way, what's your name?" Callan asked.

The boy just looked at Solomon, who nodded.

"Gaby," the boy muttered.

"That's a nice name. Gaby, would you mind giving us some room for just a little bit while I try to make Solomon better?"

Once again, the boy looked to Solomon, who simply nodded.

Gaby reluctantly released his hand and walked toward a corner of the church and sat on an overturned pew. He watched closely as Callan reached into his duffel bag and pulled out portable work lights and set them up. Callan gloved up and attached an IV, then laid out the necessary tools and drugs he needed to tend to Solomon.

"It's been over two years. I thought you were no longer in the business."

"I'm not," Solomon responded.

"And yet here we are."

"This came to me."

"Well, looks like a lot of bad came with it," Callan said as he inspected the wounds more closely. "One bullet is just a graze below your rib cage, but I gotta be honest, the one that's still in your chest looks bad. This is gonna hurt," Callan confirmed.

After cleansing the field with saline, he reached into the wound with a pair of forceps. Solomon's eyes went wide as the pain coursed through his body. Gaby flinched every time Solomon screamed. When the boy couldn't take it anymore, he slipped out the front door.

Gaby sat outside on an oak stump among the weeds, listening to the swelling chirp of crickets. Although it was a beautiful sight, he paid little attention to the streaks of clouds that looked brushed across the sky like wispy tendrils. Even in the meager light of a fading sun, as Gaby looked down, he could see that the beautiful aso-oke he wore was soiled with Solomon's blood. He lifted it over his head and sat in his undershirt, unfazed by the cool evening air. The boy inhaled deeply the sweet waft of evening primrose in bloom. He wrote his name in the dirt with a broken twig as splashes of Callan's lights faintly glowed through the shattered stained-glass window. Gaby then walked the large field behind the chapel, gathering a handful of various plants, herbs, as well as a few chrysanthemums and gardenias. The dim meadow was so expansive that he felt as though he were no more than a small silhouette against the backdrop of shoulder-high grass and the waning dusk. He toiled in the field after the sun had completely disappeared. As was his wont, he raised his arm and marveled at his dark skin merging with the black sky of a moonless night.

Doc Callan was finally able to remove a misshapen bullet, which he placed in a small metal basin.

"I'm not sure if you're just lucky or whether somebody upstairs is looking out for you, but a half inch in either direction would have made this a very different ending for you." As he irrigated the wound site, Solomon's eyes glazed over.

"So what are you hearing?" Solomon winced.

"Nothing much," Callan said as he reached for sutures and a needle.

"Don't lie to me, Linus. We've both been in the game too long for that."

Callan avoided Solomon's stare as he continued suturing.

"I hear that I'm working to save the life of a dead man. Jesus, Solomon, the Zetas? The name Cesar Quintero came up. That's nothing but bad news, trust me. How could you get mixed up with that?"

"I told you, this came to me, not the other way around."

"You shouldn't have gotten involved. They won't stop till they find you."

"I don't even know what it is that I'm involved in. Was it a political hit? Drugs? Was the boy's father in business with them?"

Callan finally looked Solomon in the eyes. "That's what I'm trying to tell you. The father wasn't the target—the boy is."

"What are you talking about? Why?"

"I have no idea. All I know is that there's a million-dollar tag on his head. After you called me, I reached out to one of my old clients, and that's all I got. I need you to hear me on this, Solomon, whether you like what I'm about to tell you or not. The only way you live is you turn over the boy. You of all people know what the

Zetas are capable of. Cesar Quintero is the worst of them all. This is not your fight. If it makes it easier for you, I can do the handover or even drop him at the police station."

"I'm not handing the kid over to the Zetas, and we both know that for a million dollars, half the cops in this city would give him up."

"Listen to me…"

"I'm *not* handing him over." Solomon winced again in pain.

"Take it easy. Neither one of us needs you making your injuries worse. I'll give you some antibiotics as well as something for the pain."

"I'm fine," Solomon responded.

"Don't be ridiculous. You're far from fine. The pain will get worse before it gets better. At least let me give you a shot of morphine."

As Callan picked up the syringe, Solomon rested his hand on the handle of his weapon.

"So, what? You're telling me you don't trust me now? Is this where we are?" Callan asked.

"I've seen people change for a lot less than a million dollars, so you tell me," Solomon replied.

"For Chrissake, Solomon, I came here to help you, not to hurt you. Do you really think I'm capable of something like that?"

"Men like you and me never truly know what we're capable of."

"You're wrong. Men like you and me know exactly what we're capable of."

Callan watched as Solomon removed his hand from his gun and nodded to him. The two men were silent as Callan wrapped the wounds in gauze. After he finished, he stood at the foot of the altar, discarded his gloves, and lit up a cigarette while he looked at a large, broken cross tilting on the wall above them. He took a puff and inhaled deeply. Pensive. The more he stared at the cross, the less certain of himself he seemed.

"I keep telling myself that smoking these things is gonna kill me one of these days, but then again, I should be so lucky to go out by my own doing and not somebody else's."

He looked back up at the cross, took another drag, then extinguished and fieldstripped the cigarette before tossing the remaining pack and matches back in the duffel bag.

He turned to address Solomon directly. "Let me ask you a question. If there really is such a thing as God, do you think He forgives men like you and me? I mean for all the horrible things we've done," Callan asked.

"I hope not?" Solomon answered.

"Why's that?"

"Because I can never forgive him for all the things he *didn't* do."

"You saved my life once, Solomon. So whether there is a God or not, I'd trade a stranger's life for yours any day. Even that of a child."

Solomon fell quiet. He suddenly felt the small hands of the boy take hold of his. As he turned his head, he saw Gaby staring at him.

Solomon addressed the doctor. "Thank you for coming, Linus. We'll be just fine."

"Have it your way. I brought you what I could. Medicine, food, water, clothes, and a bundle kit. There's some money and a burner in the bag as well. If I was you, I'd dump your phone as soon as possible. If they don't already know who you are, they will soon. When that happens, it won't take them long to connect you to me. If I try and stay off their radar, I can maybe buy you a day or so. As soon as you can move, you should find another hiding place. I can't give you up if I don't know where you are. And we both know if they come for me, they will make me give you up." He turned to the boy. "Gaby, right? I need you to change the bandage on his wound every four hours and make sure he takes his medicine so that he doesn't get sick, okay?"

Gaby nodded.

Callan's phone buzzed with an incoming text. Although he tried to mask it, as soon as he read the text, his mood shifted immediately.

"What's wrong?" Solomon asked.

"Nothing much. Just some business stuff."

"Linus, I need one last thing," Solomon said.

"What's that?"

"The old man that I worked for at the gardens, his name is Tanaka. He was down but alive when I last saw him. I just need to know he's okay."

"I'll see what I can find out and text you on the burner."

Callan patted Solomon's shoulder, then turned and headed toward the door.

Gaby used the book of matches to light three deformed candles that were still spiked on a rusted candelabra. Even in the dim light of the flickering candles, Gaby could clearly see the thin trail of a scar that ran from Solomon's temple to his mandible. There were in fact several old scars that covered Solomon's arms, hands, and torso like a series of intricate tattoos. He also saw the stub of two missing fingers on his left hand. Solomon's body was a living diary. One that was filled with pages of broader wounds. Each disfigurement chronicled a multitude of violent yesteryears. The markings whispered to the boy brutal secrets of the stranger who had saved him.

Gaby wet and mashed the plants, herbs, and medicinal flowers that he had gathered and placed them on Solomon's most recent injuries and then wrapped him anew in a fresh poultice. The boy didn't sleep. He nursed his protector as best he could. He used Solomon's wristwatch to make certain that the dressings were changed exactly every four hours as he had been instructed.

Solomon slept or at least attempted it. He seemed to do more coughing, moaning, and sweating than anything. When the nightmares took hold and violently shook him, the boy was at his side, holding his hand and cooling his skin with dampened gauze pads. Gaby held his hand through the night wars. Held it through the desperate fits while Solomon wrestled with the ghosts that came for him.

4
Idi Amin

UGANDA 1972
ACHOLI REGION

Solomon Nangobi came into the world during the violent years. He'd known the stain of blood on his hands from the time he was seven years old, when the bad men came and turned guiltless children into apathetic soldiers. They were the days of carnage when innocence, like so many other casualties of war, reddened the earth in brutal expiration. It was the time when the wide wings of vultures blotted the sun as they descended to feast on the human piles of carrion. From the mesas down to the rivers, valleys, and flatlands, entire villages in the Acholi region of northern Uganda were left decimated in the wake of Amin's barbarism.

Solomon was a child not unlike most other children. Maybe

a bit shyer and certainly wiser than the average seven-year-old. Beyond that, he laughed like other children. Played like them. Enjoyed sweets like them, particularly his mother's kashata as well as her sim-sim cookies. He adored his parents more than he could adequately put into words. He had more love in his heart for his mother, Miremba, than the night had stars. He worshipped his father, Moses, even more than he did Allah. He was Moses's world, and Moses was his universe. It was his father who taught him the ancient belief of Ubuntu, which was an old Bantu proverb that simply meant *I am because you are. You are because I am.*

Solomon was awakened just before seven a.m. by the melodious sounds of his mother singing as well as the delectable scent of cardamom and coconut. The sweet aroma of Miremba making kashata, a spiced peanut, coconut, and sugar candy, nudged him awake with a smile beaming brighter than the rising sun. He had barely slept the night before in anticipation of his special day. Later there would be dancing, clapping, songs sung to him, and gifts bestowed on him from the teachers and children at his school, especially the object of his schoolboy crush, Akika. Although Akika was Christian and Solomon was Muslim, the two had become inseparable shortly after Akika and her mother, Dembe, arrived in the township after having barely escaped the slaughter of their entire village, which claimed the young girl's father.

The thing that Solomon wanted most was that his birthday be perfect. He'd prayed the night before that the day would be filled with cookies, candy, and raucous laughter loud enough to drown out any mention of Idi Amin, the Butcher of Uganda.

Solomon's parents walked hand in hand as they chatted with Dembe. Solomon and Akika trailed behind the adults, their mouths watering as they savored the lingering whiff of the still-warm desserts that Miremba carried. Although she made it clear to both of them that they would have to wait to enjoy the treats with their classmates, Moses secretly slid them two pieces of kashata with a smile and a wink. Both children devoured the sweets like hungry cubs.

By the time they arrived at the dilapidated clay building with an aluminum roof, Solomon's nine classmates were waiting for him on the patch of red dirt that served as the schoolyard and welcomed him with claps and merriment. Their teacher, Mr. Mukasa, who was in his late sixties, had a dense white cloud of an Afro along with a set of eyes that smiled. He placed a crown made of straw and palm leaves on Solomon's head. A couple of the children danced as everyone started singing the Africana version of "Happy Birthday," which lyrically was the same as the English version, but the rhythm was slightly faster and more festive.

Although his classmates made the shy boy feel like a beloved prince, it was Akika's hug that exalted him. When she released him, he wondered if his legs would fail him. He wondered if the other children would hear his heart beating over their boisterous cheer. He blushed and looked toward his father, who smiled at him with a knowing look.

As Solomon took in all the love that was directed at him, he couldn't remember ever having been so happy. He muttered a silent prayer to himself, thanking Allah for answering his prayer. It wasn't quite 8:00 a.m. yet, and the day was already perfect.

It was a loud affair. Joyous. And though he smiled until his cheeks were sore, Solomon was the first to notice the red earth rumble beneath him and the approaching swell of dust swirling in the distance. The rat-a-tat-tat of gunfire followed by screams echoed as a small convoy of military trucks got closer. Solomon's father and Mr. Mukasa quickly herded everyone who was in the schoolyard inside the building where other students and teachers were already congregated. In addition to Mr. Mukasa and Solomon's classmates, there were forty students as well as one male and two female teachers. Outside, there was more gunfire and more screams. As the other children cowered in corners, whimpering uncontrollably, Solomon was calmer than most because of the presence of his father. The boy knew no matter what, his hero would protect them.

All they could do was wait. A long, unknowable wait.

Just as they started believing that the intruders had possibly departed, the doors to the school burst open as thirteen armed soldiers entered.

Solomon's father instructed the children to close their eyes as the angry soldiers approached rowdy and volatile, reeking of moonshine waragi—*cheap man's gin.* One soldier's voice bellowed above the clamor, demanding silence. Solomon obeyed his father and kept his eyes closed but had to steal a peek at the approaching footsteps of what sounded to be a giant. The floors shook with each step the man took, and the oak planks creaked as if they were on the verge of collapsing. When the man spoke, each child trembled from the thunderstorm in his voice. He sounded like a deep cave if in fact a cave had tongue and voice.

"Get up, all of you."

Those of the kids who hesitated were roughly snatched up by the soldiers as if they were no more than sacks of refuse.

Solomon waited for his father to do something, anything that would make the bad men leave, but instead Moses just bowed his head and huddled his family together along with Akika and Dembe. Solomon didn't understand why his hero wasn't more… heroic.

As Mr. Mukasa stepped forward, Solomon saw his father reach out a hand in a vain attempt to intercept his reproach of the soldier. "They're just children. You have no right to scare them this way. They've done nothing wro—"

Mid-sentence of Mr. Mukasa's protest, Solomon jumped from the sudden crack of gunfire. His eyes burned from the warm splatter of red mist and pulp that landed on his face, neck, and bare arms.

After the boy wiped his eyes, he gazed upon the lifeless body of Mr. Mukasa. His teacher was sprawled on his back on the floor, an odd tangle of limbs and blood.

Solomon and his classmates saw things that day, things beneath the flesh that were never meant for the eyes of children. More than half the man's face was missing. His tight, white Afro, which had always reminded Solomon of baby lamb's wool, was now mostly red in a bucket's worth of blood.

As the children wailed, their dark cheeks glistened under the steady stream of tears while the soldiers laughed at their beloved teacher, who now lay before them in crimson ruin. Despite the five adults having huddled the children as best they could, there was neither a line of defense nor length of arms to adequately comfort the young and inconsolable.

Solomon held his mother's hand, but all the while, his eyes were locked on his father. As Moses kept his head bowed and positioned himself between the soldiers and his family, Solomon was confused by his inaction. The boy was too young to comprehend the often brutal tariff imposed on an errant act of courage.

5

The Horn

When the morning light woke him from his dream, Solomon opened his eyes and was greeted by the innocence of Gaby's smile. The boy had been the calm and the much-needed truce even through the night terrors of unseen wars. Gaby played the role of both protector and nurse who loyally stayed by his ward's side even as Solomon occasionally cried out from his dreams. It was Gaby's presence that had allowed Solomon to sleep semi-undisturbed for ten hours. Not since the years of his youth had he slept through the night.

The inside of the small church was aglow in the tawny rays of early sunlight that snuck through the broken window. Considering all that he'd been through, Solomon woke feeling relatively good. Despite the pain and uncertainty, he was simply grateful to be alive. Grateful for the boy's smile, which welcomed him back among the living.

Solomon looked at his watch, amazed that he had slept as long as he did. "Would you hand me some water, please?" Solomon asked.

"Yes, sir."

"Call me Solomon. Don't call me sir."

"Yes, sir."

"Solomon!"

"Yes, Solomon."

Gaby reached into the duffel bag, grabbed a bottle, unscrewed the cap, and handed him the water. Solomon downed the entire bottle as though he had just run a marathon, then gestured for more. He sat up gingerly and asked Gaby to hand him the collarless shirt and windbreaker that Doc Callan had left for him. It took him some time, but he managed to change his clothes by himself. Once he was done, he slid off the altar stone and tested his weight before fully standing. Although he winced a few times, he waved Gaby off, who instinctively moved toward him when he staggered a bit.

"I just need to get some fresh air," Solomon said.

Despite his initial reaction to the boy's attempted assistance, Solomon walked closely alongside Gaby and rested his large hand on the child's small shoulder as they slowly walked toward the door.

"Can I show you something?" Gaby asked.

"Sure."

They took their time as Gaby led him outside and to the rear of the chapel where he showed Solomon a small pond surrounded by a field peppered with patches of jasmine, briars, and a half dozen jacaranda trees. The sun was still low in the sky as though it were taking its time in waking. It may not have been the type of dawn he had grown used to over the past two years, the beautiful gardens and tea with Tanaka, but Solomon cherished the morning for a multitude of reasons. He breathed in deeply, grateful first and foremost for his survival and even surprised that his pain was much more manageable.

Solomon and the boy sat in the field among the tall grass that rimmed the boggy pond and listened to the occasional croak of a lone bullfrog. Gaby leaned back on his elbows and pointed up at two massive clouds stacked atop each other, resembling an alien spacecraft. A pair of red-tailed hawks soared flapless above them, effortlessly riding the thermals in graceful wonder. He seemed particularly preoccupied by a gray-and-cinnamon-colored Douglas squirrel that stood completely upright on its haunches like a meerkat keeping watch. Gaby even laughed and commented on how the curious animal looked out at the pond as though it were actually enjoying the view.

Solomon found himself staring at the boy as much as he did their surroundings. He wondered how sheltered Gaby's upbringing had been because everything seemed fascinating and new to him. Solomon had never seen a child so obsessively observant of nature. One so enchanted by all her offerings.

When they got hungry, the boy ran back inside the church and dragged out the half-empty duffel bag. As Solomon riffled through the bag, he pulled out a couple of Subway sandwiches and bottles of water, bags of chips, a burner phone, a roll of a few hundred-dollar bills, four full magazines, and even a suppressor for his gun. Solomon handed his old cell phone to Gaby and nodded in the direction of the pond. The boy ran to the edge of the water and threw the phone as far as he could. The echo of the splash silenced the bullfrog. Gaby stood frozen and watched the ripples spread, then fade until the water was placid once again.

After they ate, Gaby changed Solomon's dressing and added the last of the medicinal plants to his wounds.

"Where did you learn to do that?" Solomon asked.

"My father taught me."

"I'm really sorry about what happened to your mother and father. Do you know why…"

Although Gaby turned slightly from Solomon and looked toward the pond, Solomon could feel the profound sadness in the boy's demeanor. He rested the questions that he wanted to ask and allowed the boy to mourn in peace. They sat quietly for several minutes.

Gaby was still looking in the direction of the pond when he finally spoke. "They weren't my mother and father."

Solomon was a little confused. "But I thought the man that you were with said they were your parents."

"They were my foster parents. I've been living with them since around Christmas."

"Where were you before that?" Solomon asked.

"I was with my real father."

"What about your mother?"

"It was just me and my father."

"Do you have any idea where your father is now? I can take you to him."

"No, you can't. He's in heaven."

"I'm sorry to hear that."

"It's okay. Everyone says he's happy there."

"Do you know why those men wanted to hurt you?"

As Gaby slightly nodded his head, his eyes watered, and the tears made his cheeks shine like the lit side of an eclipse.

"Because they're bad men."

"Yeah, I know but… Is there anyone I can take you to? Someplace you'll be safe?" Solomon asked.

"I'm safe with you," Gaby replied.

"No, you're not. We have to get you somewhere where the bad men can't find you."

~

They drove on the grim side of town. The white van crept past the blocks of urban decay. This section of downtown Los Angeles was a pocket of the city that was nothing more than littered sectors of dwelling spaces for the forgotten and widely disregarded.

As they stopped at a red light, Gaby looked out the window at the block-long stretch of homeless encampments. Dull eyes and broken souls gazed back at him. The stares directed at the boy were filled either with yearning or contempt and in some instances a simultaneous combination of the two.

Solomon, looking for a specific building, slowed even more

when they were two blocks past the outskirts of the encampment. As he stared out at the derelict streets and all their blight, he couldn't help but think how he and the neighborhood had at least two things in common—they were both rough and tumble, and both were in need of healing from their respective wounds.

When Gaby saw that they were parking in front of an old thrift store, he asked, "Why are we stopping here?"

"While I try and figure out what to do with you, we at least need to get you a change of clothes," Solomon responded. He moved slower than usual as he exited the vehicle and walked in measured steps toward the store.

Like the majority of its inventory, the small shop felt worn. There seemed to be very little care given to its upkeep. For the most part, everything about it felt random. Clothes were strewn in bins, and the few that hung from racks did so in no particular categorization. Along with the clothes, there were knickknacks, musical instruments, toys and board games, cheap art, and even a lawn mower. The plastered ceiling was water-stained, and peeling paint clung to the walls for dear life. The place smelled of tuna fish and wood rot.

An older woman with long, white hair sat behind the counter, eating a sandwich and listening to a gospel station on an old-school transistor radio. She was a petite woman, a four-footer with a sizable smile.

"Hello," the woman greeted them.

"Hello. Where would I find children's clothing?" Solomon asked.

"Your best bet will be the two bins closest to the window. Everything is kinda mixed together though."

As Solomon crossed over to the bins and started digging through them, Gaby walked around the shop, looking at the eclectic collection of items. The woman couldn't stop staring at the boy's beautiful black skin and almond-shaped amber eyes. She simply smiled at him even as he touched almost everything he saw, including an antique salt and pepper shaker set that he picked up and put back down.

Solomon looked in his direction and admonished the boy when he saw him pluck at the strings of the broken upright bass near the rear of the store. "Gaby, don't touch that."

"It's okay," the woman interceded. "That's what all this stuff is for."

Before Solomon could respond, he felt his burner phone buzzing.

"Hello?"

"How are you feeling?" Doc Callan asked on the other end.

"Hold on." As Solomon walked toward the front door, he called toward the boy, "Gaby, I just need to take this call quickly. I'll be right outside. See if you can find anything to wear, but don't touch anything else, okay?"

"Okay," Gaby replied as Solomon stepped outside.

Even though the streets were empty, Solomon instinctively looked around as he talked on the phone. His hand was never far from the gun in his waistband.

"I'm good," he said. "Still a little stiff and sore but actually feeling better the more I move around. Tell you the truth, when I got hit, I didn't think I would make it. This was the first time I actually thought I saw white lights." Solomon laughed.

"Not quite yet. Glad you're feeling better, but you've still got a lot of healing to do. Still not sure how you're managing the pain with no meds."

"I just need to stay sharp," Solomon said.

"So the old man Tanaka is over at St. Joseph's. I spoke to a nurse who told me he looks like he'll be fine."

"That's good news. Thanks for checking for me."

"Well, that's the only good news I've got. Someone from the Zetas reached out to me, which means they've more than likely figured out who you are. I'll tell you the same thing I said earlier: Just give them the kid, Solomon."

"I already told you that's not an option."

"Well then, you've fucked us all."

"What did you tell them?" Solomon asked.

"Nothing yet. They left two messages, the last one about twenty minutes ago. They want me to meet them."

"Are you going to?"

"You know how this plays out. I got no choice. I'm too old and tired to run, and besides, they'd just find me anyway, the same way they will eventually find you."

"I'm sorry that I dragged you into all this, Linus. I still don't even know what it is exactly."

"At the end of the day, does it really make a difference?" Callan asked.

"I guess not, because no matter what, I'm not turning the kid over. Let me ask you a question. Do you know if McKinty is still running illegals up through Canada?"

"He's still got his hands in a few different jars, but I don't think McKinty will help you."

"He will for the right amount of money," Solomon responded.

Solomon rested his hand on the grip of his gun and stared at a car that drove by slowly. He relaxed a bit as he saw the driver of the car was an elderly Asian woman.

"Makes no difference where you send the kid or even where you go. They won't stop until they find you both. Being hunted is not what you do. Hunting is. You know how they think. You're gonna have to use that to your advantage if you wanna get to the bottom of whatever's going on."

"What about you?"

Callan hesitated, a telling pause that belied his usual air of confidence. "Don't worry about me. I'll be fine. You know what I'll need you to do for me, right?"

"Yeah. Consider it done."

"This settles everything between us, Solomon. All debts are cleared."

"Yeah, and then some."

They were both quiet, as though there were still unsaid things between them. Callan was the first to break the silence. "You ever think about your first kill, Solomon? I do, every day. Well, at least every night. I think about how my life could have been different. I could have been a real doctor. As smart as you are, who knows what you could have been?"

Solomon was quiet, reflective for a moment or three before he finally spoke. "Maybe I see it differently. Maybe we were born to do what we do."

"Born or molded?" Callan asked.

"It's all the same thing. The circumstances of our lives mold us into what we were born to be."

"You really think we were born to be guns for hire?"

"I can't speak for you, but my path was laid before me a very long time ago."

"Whether we agree or disagree, it really makes no difference. We are where we are. Such is the life we've chosen. You take care of yourself, my friend. I'll be seeing you."

"Thank you, Linus," Solomon said before hanging up.

After he hung up the phone and watched the occasional car pass, his mind was still on his conversation with Doc Callan. He lit a cigarette, smoked half, then fieldstripped it, sprinkling the remains in the gutter. He looked at his phone, knowing he had a difficult call to make.

Gaby was in a pair of jeans and a white guayabera shirt and holding a Dodgers baseball jacket when Solomon reentered the shop. The boy was standing next to the woman, who was opening an old, beat-up trumpet case that was held together by duct tape and twine. She pulled the dented trumpet from the case. Though the aged brass was oxidized and speckled with black and green blotches, Gaby looked on in awe at it as if it were one of the most fascinating things he'd ever seen. As Solomon approached them, she cleaned the mouthpiece with an alcohol wipe and handed the horn to Gaby. "Go ahead. Give it a try," she said.

Gaby blew several times, but nothing was heard but the sound of strained air. He blew harder until a small vein pulsed in the center of his forehead and even his dark skin turned a slight shade of plum.

The woman laughed. "Well, you're certainly no Miles, but I've got faith that you'll get the hang of it one day."

"Gaby, put the horn back. We have to go. How much do I owe you for the clothes?"

"Just give me twenty for the lot and we're square."

"Thank you. Gaby, grab your old clothes."

As Solomon paid the woman, Gaby walked behind a hanging curtain in the corner of the shop and came back with his old clothes balled up.

"Thank the nice lady for everything," Solomon nudged the boy.

"Thank you, ma'am."

"Well, aren't you quite the gentleman. I've been called many things around here but never ma'am. I should be the one thanking you for making my day. I do believe you have the most beautiful eyes I've ever seen."

"Thank you again, ma'am," Gaby said and blushed.

As he and Solomon turned to leave, the woman called after them, "Don't forget the horn."

"No, no, we're not taking that," Solomon said.

The woman saw how Gaby looked up at Solomon with pleading eyes.

"Please let him have it. No charge. It's a gift," the woman replied.

"No, that's fine. We couldn't. He doesn't need it."

"Please," the woman insisted. "It would be my honor, and you'd be doing me a favor. This thing has been here longer than me, and I've been here forever. He's the first person I've ever even seen touch it."

Gaby jumped in. "I promise to only play it when you say I can."

As the two continued staring at Solomon, he finally relented, then turned and headed toward the exit. "Okay fine, but remember your promise."

The woman put the horn back in its case and handed it to an elated Gaby, who grabbed it, smiled at her, and waved as he hurried out of the door after Solomon.

When they got back into the van, Solomon's mind was elsewhere, mired in rumination of all that Callan had come to mean to him. Besides Tanaka, Doc Callan was the closest thing Solomon had to a friend. He couldn't shake the foreboding thoughts that he had seen the last of him. The uneasy feeling made him think back to the first time they met.

6

The Diner

FOUR YEARS AGO

Solomon had been a hunter of men long enough to know that he himself was now being hunted. Although he never saw the face or even the make of car, he knew he had been followed for the past two days. He could feel it everywhere he went. He hid in plain sight and stuck to what little routine he had. The fact that his pursuer had revealed themselves as nothing more than an uneasy feeling was evidence enough for Solomon that he was being targeted by a professional. Like himself, the most gifted of killers were the unheard and the unseen. They moved through space as invisible as a draft of wind, there one moment and gone the next. The only thing he wasn't certain of was why they hadn't already killed him. All he could do was wait and see if there was a countermove to be made. Solomon was, if nothing else, a pragmatist. In the end, the trailing shadow would either kill him or he would kill them.

The list of those who might have wanted him dead was impossibly long and equally old. After spending the last forty-plus years in New York, he had thought the move to California might offer him something of a fresh start. During his tenure as bodyguard and fixer for Harlem crime boss Clay Freeman, he had stacked plenty of bodies and incurred the hatred of many enemies on the East Coast. After he had healed from a particularly violent clash with a nemesis of his former boss, an encounter in which by all logic and account he should have died, Solomon retired and decided to head west to see if there was peace for him to be found in the back nine of his life.

He'd only visited California once, twenty years ago, when he accompanied Clay Freeman on a business trip to Beverly Hills. It was neither the mansions nor the fancy cars and restaurants that impressed him but rather the land. He was born of farmers, so it was the topography that spoke to him the most passionately. The trees and swaths of green were the closest thing he had seen to home since leaving as a teenager. The plush hills, skinny boughs of palm trees, and the waxy sheen of their fronds reminded him of his childhood. Even the snowcaps of the distant San Bernardino Mountains made him think of the glaciers of the Ruwenzori Mountains that bordered the Congo. It was the abundance of sunshine and beaches that warmed him with the memories of how he and his family had played on the shores of Lake Victoria. He thought California was beautiful, even more so in person than what he'd seen on TV and in the movies or what he'd read in books. In his one-week visit to Los Angeles, Solomon had only had a few hours to himself here and there to explore the pride of the left coast. It wasn't much time, but the place made a deep enough impression that he often thought about it throughout the years.

He came to California with the best of intentions, ready to put a violent epoch of forty-plus years behind him. He made a promise to himself to lay down his guns forever and seek what little peace and possible love the world might still have to offer. Though his *forever* lasted only five years, he honored his vows and, in doing so, learned what happiness was. It was easier than he thought it would be. He found a quiet life, and it was good. For a while. His weapons lay untouched, gathering dust on a shelf in a storage unit. Now he spent his days wondering who had tracked him down to the small town of La Cañada. Although he tried to busy himself with daily activity, it was all nothing more than attempts at distraction from the indeterminable wait.

He pulled his guns from storage and cleaned them the way he used to when they were inseparable allies. He was somewhat surprised at how different they felt in his hands. They no longer felt like the extensions of himself that they used to. He reacquainted himself with them at the outdoor gun range that was ten miles from his tiny apartment. It took him a week to find the old comfort that he used to take for granted. Each day that he went to the range, he stayed for an hour, one eye always on the target and the other always on the other shooters that came and went. On his daily drive, he circled blocks and made unexpected U-turns, but he never saw the shadow that he could feel trailing him.

Solomon went to the same diner each morning and sat with his back toward the wall, sipping his coffee, eating his two over-easy eggs with smoked salmon and dry toast while watching every customer who entered its doors. There was nothing special about the diner. Both food and decor were average at best. There was a long, curved countertop with swivel stools, and the tables and booths were accentuated with red-and-white-checkered table-cloths along with oxblood-colored benches and chairs. There was a sense of blandness to the place that passed as Americana, but the service was great, the coffee was hot, and Solomon appreciated the comfort of having a morning tradition.

The second the stranger walked into the diner, Solomon knew. He pegged the man at six three with a weathered face that put him in the nebulous age range of anywhere from mid-fifties to sep-tuagenarian. He was easily two hundred and twenty pounds. His sun-kissed hair, shoulder length, was a thick mop of white tresses. His bronze tanned skin had the leathered look of an aging surfer. He was fit and looked every bit the part of a ripe California native. No doubt this was a man who spent his fair share of time lounging on the sands of shimmering beaches. Even his eyes were the same blue as ocean and sky.

Declared or undeclared, a cop knew when they were in the presence of another cop. So too did soldiers. The same could be said of killers. For a seasoned professional, it was all in the read.

Everything from one's gait and movement to the hang and/or subtle bulge of clothing that confirmed whether a subject was carrying. To the untrained eye, there may not have been any telltale signs, but Solomon knew right away that the stranger was definitely carrying. At least two weapons.

The thought crossed Solomon's mind to kill the man mid-approach with no questions asked. He had made clean kills in crowds before when he was at the top of his game, but five years of rust and inactivity as well as the assessment of the potential collateral damage made him loath to try his luck with the stranger.

As the man walked past the dozen or so customers and made his way over to the table, Solomon continued sipping his coffee while he rested his free hand in his lap.

"I figured it was high time that we formally met." The man gestured toward the empty seat. "You mind?"

Solomon didn't speak, but the man sat anyway. An attractive Latina server came over right away.

"Can I start you with some coffee?" she asked.

Before the man could respond, Solomon intervened. "That's quite all right. He won't be staying."

As the server walked away, the man sighed. "That's too bad, because I'm assuming the food here is pretty good if you come here every day. You can relax. If I wanted you dead, I would be viewing a corpse right now."

From underneath the table, there was a very distinctive click of the hammer of a handgun being pulled back.

"I could easily say the same," Solomon said.

"Based on your reputation, let me guess. A Colt M1911."

"Since you know your weapons, I don't have to bother to explain to you what it will do to you and your manhood this close up."

The stranger smiled, revealing the top row of perfect teeth by way of expensive veneers. There was another click with an ever so subtle difference in sound from under the table.

"At this angle, I'm sure you know what a Mossberg nine will do to you," the man said. "So we can either blow each other's balls off, or we can talk like the two professionals that we are."

"You get five minutes," Solomon said.

They both kept one hand on the table and one under.

The man waved the server over with his free hand. "I've decided I will take a cup of coffee after all."

"Anything else?"

"No, that's it, thank you." He watched the server walk off in the way that men watch attractive servers walk off.

"What exactly do you want?" Solomon asked.

"When I was a kid, my father used to warn me that not all legends were born the same. He said most were only 30 percent truth and 70 percent exaggeration." The man glanced down at Solomon's left hand and the two missing fingers as he continued talking. "I was just a freshman at NYU the first time I heard about a young African boy in Brooklyn who had two of his fingers cut off by drug dealers. When I heard the tales of his retaliation, I mean how he... Well, let's just say I became an instant fan. Supposedly that same African boy went on to help rule half of New York under his boss, Clay Freeman. Funny thing is, the story about the drug dealers went the way most stories go. The details became more fantastical every time it was told. Truth is, I personally never felt it needed any embellishment because the reality was more brutal than fiction. So yeah, you can call me a fan of your work 'cause I've always wanted to meet the New York legend."

"It's not good practice to believe everything you hear," Solomon responded.

The server came over and put a cup of coffee in front of the man. Again, he watched her walk away.

"A year ago, I heard the cops over in La Verne questioned a man who sounded a lot like you who beat at least one man to death with his bare hands. The last nine months, I've made it a little hobby of mine to scout these quiet towns, curious to see for myself if the New York legend had settled out west."

"Hate to disappoint you, but you've got the wrong man," Solomon said coolly.

The man sipped his coffee and started laughing. "I was born and raised out here in Cali. This is the place the talentless usually lie and take credit for the things they haven't done. Hard pressed to find someone out here with true skill who actually denies it."

"Five minutes is up, and you still haven't told me what you want."

"I'd like to offer you a job. Well, actually more of a position."

"I already have a job."

"What, fixing people's toilets? Or wiring their lights? How long do you think that will be enough for a man with your talents? I'm sure it made more sense to you when you were doing the family thing but…"

Solomon looked at him hard.

"Yes, I know all about what happened, and I'm sorry."

"Don't talk about my family," Solomon said.

"I meant no disrespect. And for the record, I'm talking about you, not them. In some ways, you and I aren't that different. When I went to NYU, I was actually there as a med student. More for my family than anything. After two years, I finally dropped out because I knew I was just lying to myself about who I was and who I wasn't. Took me several years to find out what I'm really good at."

"And what's that?" Solomon asked.

"Same as you. I'm good at killing."

Solomon started to speak but decided not to. He just looked at the man and thought about the simplicity of his declaration.

The man continued. "I have a pretty good client roster here on the West Coast. People who are willing to pay quite a bit of money to have me eliminate problems for them. I could definitely use a man with your talents. Not as an employee but as an equal. If there's a particular job you decide you don't want to do, no problem. No questions asked."

"I'm happy for you that you found your calling, but we're not the same men."

"Of course, not the same, but we're more alike than you might imagine."

"I beg to differ. And for your sake, I hope you've said all that you've wanted to say."

"Why for my sake?"

"Because if I see you again, I'll kill you."

"I highly doubt that. As a matter of fact, when you finally get around to accepting that we're more alike than you're willing to admit, I have a feeling we'll be seeing a lot more of each other."

The man finally put his second hand on the table sans weapon. He slowly reached into his jacket pocket and pulled out a pen and wrote his number on a napkin and slid it across the table to Solomon, who ignored it and never took his eyes off the stranger. The man took a last sip of coffee, then stood and placed a couple of dollars on the table.

"By the way, my name is Linus, but everyone calls me Doc Callan."

Solomon watched Callan walk toward the door, flirt with the server, then leave.

7

Payback

THREE YEARS AGO

The reflection of the low-hanging sun on the sea glittered so brilliantly that Doc Callan had to put on his sunglasses to better enjoy the view. The ocean looked as though its surface was blanketed in a layer of sequin. Although his love for the water was dictated neither by time nor climate, he regarded the spring light of dawn and dusk as near to divinity as he would ever get. He was surprised at how quiet the marina was. How thin even the late-afternoon crowds were. He had expected more admirers, larger gatherings of people who appreciated the splendor of a sky laden with streaks of fire and magenta.

Doc Callan was a punctual man. He always showed up at least fifteen minutes early to appointments. Even though he was already five minutes late, he took his time as he strolled the pier past the small shops and eateries. He needed every moment he could get to play out the possible scenarios that awaited him. Worst-case scenario, he was walking into a trap that could end with him being killed.

As Callan lumbered toward his meeting, he looked every bit the part of a hapless Atlas, a man slowed under the weight of the world. Solomon had warned him not to go, but Callan was determined to get what was owed to him, even if his own death proved to be an unwanted bonus.

The small outside café with its tables just twenty feet from the water was all but empty save for Dominic D'Abbrizzi and four of his men. As Doc Callan approached and removed his sunglasses, he was intercepted by two bodyguards who frisked him, removing the Mossberg 9mm from his shoulder holster as well as a backup Walther PPQ Sub-Compact from an ankle holster. Dominic sat alone at a table for eight, eating a large bowl of clams and a side of oysters, as Callan was escorted to him by one of the bodyguards.

A few things crossed Callan's mind as he approached and watched the big man eat. Somehow Dominic D'Abbrizzi hadn't yet gotten the various memos that (a) his comb-over wasn't fooling anyone, (b) Columbus was actually more villain than hero, and (c) the West Coast mob was now nothing more than a toothless tiger desperately grasping for relevancy. He was an old-school holdover from the eighties, when the word "Mafia" demanded respect and instilled fear. He now teetered on the thin line of arrogance and delusion that he could single-handedly restore the family business to its former glory.

He was a big man. Huge in fact. At nearly four hundred pounds, he looked like a baby whale in an overpriced suit. Callan wondered if Dominic knew or even suspected that not only his enemies but even some of his own men laughed at him behind his massive back and branded him with belittling sobriquets such as the Thin Man or Skinny Dom. Based on his dealings with the big man, Callan knew that Dominic was determined to have the last laugh. Now that he had successfully eliminated the head of the Russian family, things would begin to turn in his favor. Callan did the math and suspected all that was left for Dominic to do was make sure that there was no way to tie him to the hitter he had hired to make the kill.

Dominic barely looked up as he continued eating. "Have a seat. Do you do clams or oysters? These are the best in town. They do their clams with this whole white wine and garlic butter sauce that's insane."

"I'm good," Callan said as he sat.

"Trust me, you're missing out."

"Yeah, I seem to be doing that quite a bit these days."

Dominic looked up at him quizzically.

"You hired me to do a job, which I did, but I seem to be missing out on the payment that you and I agreed on," Callan clarified.

Dominic chuckled. "Straight to the point, huh?"

"Anything less keeps me here longer than either one of us wants me to be."

"Relax, you'll get your money. The only reason I didn't wire it into your account like we agreed is because the more I thought about it, the more I decided that it's best for both of us if there's no possible paper trail connecting us. The Russians have contacts inside the banks. You'll get paid in cash."

"That's not what we agreed on, and that's not how this works," Callan said, baiting him.

Though there was the instinctual flash of anger in Dominic's eyes, Callan paid closer attention to the instant suppression of it. Dominic D'Abbrizzi was not the type of man to be instructed and certainly not by hired help on how things did or did not work. He was known to have a legendary temper. He was from the school of thought that the louder bosses yelled, the more powerful they were.

Dominic stopped eating and looked at Callan for a beat or two, then simply smiled. It was the smile that was the most telling.

"This might feel like a pain in the ass for you and all, but you gotta trust me that this is the safest way for both of us. Look, I've got some business downtown to handle, but you can go with Lenny now to my office, and he'll get you your two hundred k. If it makes you feel better, I'll throw in an extra 5 percent inconvenience tax."

Had he gotten indignant and pitched the predictable tirade, Callan might have believed him, but the fact that he was calm and even made the strained effort of what could pass as pleasantness spoke volumes of consequence. It was the second he smiled that Callan knew Solomon was right: Dominic D'Abbrizzi was going to kill him.

Callan glanced over his shoulder at the bodyguards and saw it right away, their veiled attempts at normalcy. When he turned back around, Dominic refused to meet his gaze as he occupied himself with dabbing pieces of charred bread into the sauce and slurping at the bowl of clams. Callan didn't know if it was intentional or coincidental, but save for the tiny oyster fork, there were no utensils on the table, not even so much as a butter knife. Even if he wanted to take Dominic out in a desperate blaze of glory, there were unfortunately no viable options. He was weaponless and outmatched.

"So was this the play all along?" he asked.

Dominic looked up from his bowl. "Whaddaya mean?"

"You hiring me to kill the Russian, then you taking me out. Is it economics or strategy? You can shoot straight with me. You at least owe me that."

Dominic did little to mask the hint of malevolence in his smile. In fact, he was quite pleased with himself. He was the type of man who never forfeited an opportunity to show people how impressed he was with his own cleverness.

"That's part of your problem, Callan, making assumptions that I owe you anything. But to answer your question, it's both. I can't afford a war with the Russians, but I sure as shit can't just sit back and watch them take over everything we've built out here. Once they get the tip that you did a couple of big hits for the Colombians back in the day, the Russians will assume it's them covering their asses when your body turns up. They beef it out with a high body count, and then I get to step in and clean up both sides. The Irish prick McKinty who hired you for me is the only connection between us. After we're done with you, we'll make sure he joins you. Look, I know it doesn't end well for you, but you gotta appreciate the play."

As Dominic stared at him and basked in the brilliance of his plan, Callan caught the subtle movement of a thin red ray of light in the bowl of clams. As he started laughing, Dominic looked at him, completely confused.

"What the hell's so funny?" Dominic demanded.

"You are. Did you really think it was a good idea to cross a man who kills for a living? The question is rhetorical. You don't have to answer. By the way, I think I will try one of your clams."

Callan reached over and picked up a clam, smelled it, then tossed it back in the bowl.

"Eh, too much garlic, and I think there's some mold on your bread."

Dominic's face turned red with anger. "What the hell are you..."

He followed Callan's eyes. As the big man looked down, he was cut off by the red laser light he saw in the bowl of clams. The light traveled from the bowl up to Dominic's chest. The bodyguards drew their weapons and moved closer.

"Your men might want to rethink their next moves right now. Unless of course they want your blood on their hands."

The confused guards stopped in their tracks and looked at Dominic.

Callan spoke very casually. "Part of your problem, Dominic, is making assumptions. Did you really think I'd come in here without covering my ass? You've got your army. I've got mine. Just a friendly suggestion. If I were you, I definitely wouldn't make any big moves right now. You're a hard target to miss. Not sure how much you or your boys here know guns, but you've got a McMillan TAC 50 pointed right on your chest. A fifty-caliber rifle will drop an elephant. No insult implied."

The fear and sweat were immediate. Dominic looked in the direction of his bodyguards in frozen panic.

As one of the men instinctively took a step toward the table, Callan stopped him with his voice. "Your boss dies, it's on you."

"Stop fucking moving, Lenny," Dominic barked at his man.

It was now Callan who smiled triumphantly. "So this is how we're gonna handle this situation that we find ourselves in. You're gonna slowly pick up your phone, keyword being 'slowly,' and then you're going to transfer the two hundred k that you owe me plus a 25 percent inconvenience tax," Callan warned.

The red dot stayed fixed on Dominic's chest. He moved in slow motion as he reached for his phone. He made a phone call, and as it rang a few times, he input several numbers. On the sixth ring, someone answered on the other end.

"Hey, Shaeffer, this is Dominic. Listen, I just texted you a routing number and amount that I need transferred right away. I don't really care about bank protocol right now. Unless you plan on trying to explain to your boss and the feds about the accounts you've been skimming from, I need it to happen, and I need it to happen now. This is an emergency."

As he hung up, Callan couldn't help but chuckle. "There's nothing like proper motivation to get things done, is there?"

Dominic sat quietly, seething at Callan, who was enjoying the situation thoroughly.

"Relax, Dominic. Even though this doesn't end well for you, you gotta appreciate the play."

Although he knew better than to raise his voice, Dominic was so angry that tiny drops of spittle spurted out as he spoke. "No matter what it takes, Callan, this ain't over. Not by a long shot."

"Actually, if I were a betting man, I'd say it was definitely over for you."

Callan took his phone out, fiddled with it a bit, then pressed playback of the recorded conversation.

"…it's both. I can't afford a war with the Russians, but I sure as shit can't just sit back and watch them take over everything we've built out here. Once they get the tip that you did a couple of big hits for the Colombians back in the day, the Russians will assume it's them covering their asses when your body turns up. They beef it out with a high body count, and then I get to step in and clean up both sides."

Dominic's eyes went wild, and his bodyguard raised his gun in Callan's direction until Dominic yelled at him.

"What the hell are you doing, Lenny? Stop!"

"Listen to your boss, Lenny. I've already group texted the recording to a couple of my associates. Just to make sure I walk out of here. So now is a good time for all of you to put your guns down."

No one moved.

"Tell them, Dominic. Or if you want, I raise my hand and have both you and Lenny dropped before he gets off a shot. Tell them!"

"Everybody put them down," Dominic ordered.

Lenny lowered his gun to the floor along with the rest of the guards. He just stood there, both enraged and defeated.

Callan looked down at his phone as he got an incoming ping.

"Looks like your guy at the bank was sufficiently motivated. The wire just came through. Thank you. I'm going to leave now and let you finish your meal. By the way, just to show you that there are no hard feelings, I'm gonna see that you get a head start. I'll wait maybe an hour, maybe less before making sure the recording ends up in the hands of both the Russians and the Colombians. Can't wait to see what happens when they both come at you. A little free advice—pack light, you fat fuck."

As Callan got up to leave, Dominic and his men remained motionless, each staring at the red laser dot still trained on the big man's chest.

~

The ocean was predictably more beautiful at eventide. The sky was a canvas awash with the vibrant colors of raw sienna, deep blues, and even a hint of lilac. Both the clouds and water looked as though they had been set ablaze by the drooping sun. Save the lulling sway of the surf at dusk, all else was still. Quiet. Doc Callan sat on a dune on an empty stretch of beach. With his gun nestled in his lap, he drank a cold Dos Equis and watched the sun sinking into the water. He heard the barely perceptible approach of soft footsteps in the sand. Callan ever so subtly rested his hand on his weapon. As he turned, Solomon was at his side looking out to sea.

"You can go ahead and say it now," Callan said.

"Say what?" Solomon asked.

"That you told me so."

Solomon laughed as he sat beside Callan. "I've never been the gloating kind, so you thinking it is enough for me. You know, if Dominic had actually pulled it off, it would have been a smart play."

"In our line of work, the words *if, woulda, coulda, shoulda* don't count. If my aunt had balls, she'd be my uncle," Callan retorted. He reached into a plastic grocery bag and pulled out a bottle of ginger beer and handed it to Solomon. "Still cold."

"Thank you." Solomon smiled.

"You do realize that a real beer every once in a while won't kill you."

"One man's pleasure is another man's poison."

"Thanks for having my back, Solomon. I already wired the extra 25 percent that I made on the deal into your account."

"That wasn't necessary. I didn't do it for money."

"I know that, but I definitely owe you."

"I wanted the last thing I do in this business to at least mean something to me."

Callan looked at him, slightly confused. "What are you talking about?"

"I'm done. Call it retirement or whatever you want, but this time, I'm really finished."

"And what do you plan on doing?" Callan asked.

"No idea, but whatever it is, it'll be something quiet."

"Maybe you should go see the world."

"That sounds overrated. From what little of it that I've already seen, I'm not impressed."

Callan laughed. "In case you haven't heard, cynics are usually the first ones to miss the point. You can't look at this ocean and tell me there's not beauty in the world. You just need to find yours. I'm sure you've got enough money tucked away to do whatever adventures you want."

"If I need to use blood money to find my happiness, then maybe you're the one missing the point. Besides, no matter where I go, there'll always be men there like you and me."

Doc Callan sipped his beer and looked out to the ocean, momentarily silenced by Solomon's simple truth. The two men quietly drank until the sun disappeared and an evening wind stirred. Callan looked at his watch, then jumped up quickly, gathering the bag of drinks.

"Oh shit, I'm late. Look, I know I already owe you, but tonight I could definitely use your backup one last time."

"Is this something else to do with Dominic and the Russians?" Solomon asked.

"No, this is ten times more dangerous than that. My sister's cooking and invited me over."

The two men laughed as they walked back to their cars.

Margaret certainly was not a good cook. Callan knew it, her two daughters knew it, and Solomon found out the hard way. She piled his plate with overcooked brisket and undercooked rice swimming in a sea of lumpy gravy. Solomon was happy that there were two extra ginger beers left over from the beach. They at least helped things to go down a bit smoother, even the corn muffins, which were the driest he'd ever had.

Whatever she lacked in culinary prowess, she more than made up for in personality. Margaret, simply put, was a joy to be around. She inspirited the house with her big, contagious laughter even in her self-deprecation. She poked the most fun at herself and her cooking. She was a kind woman with two kind daughters. The eldest, Chloe, who was seventeen and the family athlete, gushed about the multiple soccer scholarships that she'd been offered. Adele was the shyer fifteen-year-old honor student who already had her heart and mind set on becoming a veterinarian. Doc Callan was the affectionate brother and uncle who beamed with joy and pride for the loves of his life.

Though the food was terrible, the evening turned into a risible affair nonetheless. *Family* wasn't a word that came easily to Solomon. From the time he was eleven years old, he'd navigated the world as no more than a kithless wanderer. His wasn't the type of life that consisted of bonding meals (good food or bad), tear-inducing laughter, or love so palpable that it ricocheted from one person to the next.

At around ten thirty, after unending rounds of laughter and slightly burned pound cake, Solomon bid his farewells. Just before he left, he thanked Margaret, Callan, and the two girls for one of the best meals of his life.

8
The Underpass

Solomon looked over at Gaby in the passenger seat, clutching the trumpet's case as though the horn were the best present he'd ever received. After leaving the thrift shop, Solomon drove a few miles down streets that grew more and more scarce of life until he pulled over and parked under a desolate overpass. He got out of the van and paced among the giant, decaying pillars. Gaby eventually exited the vehicle and quietly watched him walking back and forth, deep in thought. Similar to when they first met, Solomon felt the boy's eyes on him, studying him. When Solomon looked back at him, Gaby turned away slightly and looked sideways as though he hadn't been staring. The child's profile in sunlight made Solomon think for the briefest of seconds that there was something in Gaby's features, his cheekbones, his chin, the slope of his forehead that made him look even more familiar. When the boy finally turned and looked in his direction, smiling, Solomon determined that the hint of recognition was just a blur of his imagination and fatigue.

He waved him over. "Gaby, I need you to listen to me. You have to tell me everything you know about the man who was your foster parent. Whatever you can think of. I need to know everything I can."

"The people from the foster agency said he knew my real father from a long time ago. He brought me home to live with him just before Christmas. He was really nice to me. He had a big house, and he said he had made a promise to my father that he would look after me."

Solomon pulled out his cell phone. "What was his name?"

"Mr. Ramiel."

"What was his first name?"

"Joseph-Malaika."

Solomon googled Joseph-Malaika Ramiel and pulled up a couple of different pages on him. He read how the man was Nigerian born but raised in Botswana and had made millions of dollars in construction and was one of the leading telecommunications providers in several African nations. He was a philanthropist and devout Christian who sat on the boards of a few different human rights organizations. Nothing in Solomon's search shed any light on what the intersection of him and the Zetas might be and how that junction involved the boy. They were by all accounts polar opposites.

Solomon looked up from his phone and addressed Gaby. "Are you sure there's nothing else you're not telling me?"

Gaby looked at him, confused. "Like what?"

Although Solomon was growing impatient, he did what he could to hide it from the boy. He spoke to him as calmly as possible.

"I don't know, Gaby, but I can only really help you if I know everything. There has to be a reason why they killed Mr. Ramiel and his wife and why they want to hurt you."

"But I don't know anything."

"Even if you think it's small or unimportant, I just need you to think." Solomon's frustration was slowly creeping in.

"I can't think of anything."

"Did you ever hear Mr. Ramiel mention the name Cesar Quintero?"

"I'm not sure. I don't remember."

"What about Zetas?"

"I don't know what that is."

As Solomon started getting more desperate, his voice got louder.

"When you were living with Mr. Ramiel, did you see or hear him on the phone arguing with anyone?"

"No. Like I said, he was a very nice man."

Solomon breathed in deeply, trying to manage his growing impatience.

"Are you mad at me because I don't know anything?" Gaby asked.

"I'm not mad. I just…I need to figure out what's going on."

Gaby seemed as if he were on the verge of tears as he looked at Solomon. "I'm sorry."

"Look, it's not your fault. I…uh…I just need some help understanding exactly what's happening, that's all. I didn't mean to raise my voice at you. I'll see if I can find anything else on Mr. Ramiel. Why don't you just go wait in the van? You can play with the trumpet if you want to. You can't get great at what you love if you don't practice."

The boy pepped up slightly as he nodded and walked back toward the van.

Solomon took out his half pack of smokes and lit one as he leaned against the charred carcass of a minivan and did a deep dive on his phone, trying to find more information on Joseph-Malaika Ramiel. He inhaled deeply and immediately felt his body relax as he filled his lungs with the soothing comfort of warm nicotine.

Gaby sat on the back bumper of the van with the rear doors open. While Solomon continued scanning the web, he looked up from time to time at the boy and heard the empty hiss of futile breaths as he blew into the horn.

After Solomon felt he had done an exhaustive search on Ramiel, which yielded nothing useful, his thoughts turned to Cesar Quintero and why he might possibly want to hurt an innocent child.

9

Cesar Quintero

SIX MONTHS AGO

There was no greater pain between heaven and hell than that of a parent watching their child die. Slowly. Helplessly. Cesar thought leukemia was the cruelest of diseases created by the most callous of gods. Though he was only a casual believer in things like fate and karma, he couldn't help but wonder if somehow the universe had conspired against him. If there was in fact some God Almighty, he couldn't think of a more merciless punishment.

Cesar never made excuses for the horrible, violent things he'd done. He only saw them as necessities of his trade. Still, he wondered how it was possible that something so pure and good was of his seed. From the day his son entered the world, Cesar was awed by how the child actually glowed like an angel born of man. The boy still shone despite the cancer doing everything in its power to dim his light. The hardest thing Cesar ever faced was watching his *almost* eight-year-old son wilt before his eyes like an unwatered rose. Unless the doctor came bearing good news, the boy would be lucky if he made it to his eighth birthday, which was less than a month away. Although he was already heartbreakingly frail, he still seemed to waste away a little more each day. His skin was whiter than the hospital sheets that enshrouded him. His head was as smooth as an egg. Gone were the thick, curly locks that he inherited from his mother. His eyes, which used to sparkle with happiness, were now just dull reminders of the boy's former joyfulness.

Cesar died a little each time that he saw his son. He died even more when the boy's mother, Camila, looked at him not with the loving eyes of a wife but rather with a cold emptiness. He knew she blamed him for their son's condition. Camila had been decimated from the very beginning of their son's diagnosis. She stopped eating. She stopped speaking. She prayed incessantly for miracles that never came. Although she wept enough to make fertile even the most fallow of fields, her tears could neither heal nor give life to what mattered most. Cesar listened each night as her plaintive cries lulled her to sleep where she cried even more in her dreams. She woke each morning with renewed defeat from a heart overflowing with unanswered prayers.

Camila no longer saw Cesar as a husband or grieving father or even a man for that matter. All that she saw of him was that he was the object of God's wrath. Surely God had cursed him for the wickedness of his ways. She in turn was punished for letting him father her child. It was Catholic guilt by association.

Camila refused to see her son. She couldn't bear to witness his daily decline. Although it was a difficult choice, she decided that the best thing that she could do was to stay steadfast with the barrage of prayers that she sent up to heaven. Even though there was no evidence at all that her prayers were even received, let alone considered, she still prayed and wept, then wept and prayed more. As she sank even lower in her despair, she tried negotiating with her Heavenly Father. She asked Him to take her life but spare her son's. Nothing changed except that the boy's condition continued to worsen.

Cesar sat at the bedside of his dying son and gently held his brittle hand. The boy was a shell not just of who he used to be but also of what he could have been. Cesar came every day and stayed for hours, although his visits amounted to not much more than one-way conversations and long stretches of deafening silences. Even when there was no longer meaningful interaction between them, it was the memory of better times that got Cesar out of bed each morning.

As his son got worse, it was difficult to look at him. There were days when Cesar thought he could actually glimpse the dark shadow of death hovering in the corner of the hospital room. He knew enough about death to smell, hear, and feel its nearness. Every moment spent at his son's bedside filled him with fear that it was quite possibly his last.

The boy was awake, but his eyes were fixed in a distant gaze. His mind drifted in and out of worlds just beyond his father's reach. Cesar lived for the sporadic moments of lucidity and connection, no matter how few and far between they may have seemed. His son was everything to him. Nothing mattered more than his family. Those closest to him knew that he was family first, business second.

Cesar oversaw a Zeta drug enterprise that generated several hundred million dollars a year. Despite the fact that he'd killed many men and ordered the deaths of even more, he didn't consider himself to be like most narcos. He killed or had men killed only when necessary to protect profit or reputation. He ran his business like a nine-to-five. He was home for dinner every night, and his weekends were devoted to his woman and child exclusively. Camila and Cesar Jr. were his world. He had never taken mistresses or fathered other children out of wedlock. He never indulged in the perks granted to men of his status. In Mexico, men like Cesar were treated like gods. Whatever gods wanted, gods got.

Although he wasn't particularly fond of America, he didn't hesitate to move the family from Sinaloa to San Diego for the best possible medical treatment as soon as his son was first diagnosed. Despite his wealth and tenacity, none of the American specialists gave his son a good prognosis. Dr. Tarver was the only one who was willing to at least try experimental treatment to help the boy. Knowing that he had sought out and found one of the top specialists in the world and was still unable to make any significant strides only devastated Cesar more. Each day, he watched the erosion, knowing there was nothing he could do to stop it.

Although Cesar was a powerful man feared by both wise men and fools alike, there was no amount of money or influence that could change the course of Cesar Jr.'s decline. For all the power he wielded, his son's condition leveled the playing field. Cesar was rendered helpless with the same anguish as that of lesser men. He lost bits and pieces of his son daily. He lost his wife more rapidly. Camila still lived in the same house and even shared the same bed, but she had forsaken him months ago, leaving in her stead mere fragments of the woman who had once loved him. He was left only with his sorrow. He wore it like a heavy cloak that had somehow become inseparable from his skin.

Cesar's eyes grew heavy as he held his son's hand. He nodded off and dreamed of happier times when the boy was whole. He saw his son smiling and thought it was ten times more beautiful than whatever others defined as heaven. Camila was there in the dream as well, attentive and affectionate the way she used to be before their son's cancer changed everything. In the dream, neither of them could stop laughing. They were loud and carefree. Camila shouted out how much she loved them both. When she reached out and touched Cesar, it was a moment that felt as if it would last forever, but then he was awakened to find Dr. Tarver hovering over him, gently shaking him by the shoulder. The second Dr. Tarver asked him to step outside to discuss the results of the latest rounds of tests, Cesar knew what was coming.

Good news required neither preludes nor strategy. Good news

would not have bent the good doctor's body in a defeatist posture. Bad news, on the other hand, required privacy and discretion. There were of course the telltale signs of averted eye contact and obvious gestures of stalling.

Cesar could tell Dr. Tarver was trying to mask his nervousness with talk of inconsequential things like baseball scores and the weather as they walked down the hall to a private office. Once the door was closed and Tarver finally looked directly at him, Cesar saw everything in the doctor's eyes before he spoke a word. The formal announcement simply felt redundant. Dr. Tarver was a lanky Texan with the hint of a southern drawl.

"Unfortunately, the results of the tests didn't go the way we would have liked. I'm so sorry, Mr. Quintero, but your son is simply not responding to anything we've tried, and I'm afraid we're all out of viable options."

Although Cesar thought he had prepared himself for the moment, when he opened his mouth to speak, the words were imprisoned in the bottom of his throat. He was not the type of man to cry, but raw grief was abiding to neither reputation nor demeanor. Cesar had no defenses against the flood of tears that came gushing forth. He cried like men whom he had deemed weak. Everything inside him cracked into a million little pieces of jagged edges that shredded whatever he thought he knew of his heart and soul. There were several failed attempts at composure. It took both time and determination to finally ask the one question that still mattered. "How long?"

Despite his education and power, Cesar still spoke in the cadences of a chinola peasant.

His question made Dr. Tarver even more nervous, "Well… uh, at this point, we're talking days. To be quite honest, he's fought longer and harder than most kids at this stage."

"How many days?"

"Well, it's hard to definitively say when…"

"How many days?" Cesar demanded.

"Uh…two to three. Four max. I think right now the most important thing for us to focus on is—"

Cesar silenced the doctor with a hand gesture. The doctor's southern drawl was now grating to him. He didn't want to hear the man's voice anymore. Every sound from that point on was just a reminder of his son's death sentence. He dried his eyes and made himself as presentable as he could, then crossed to the door and spoke with his back to the doctor. "Thank you for doing your best."

Before Tarver could respond, Cesar was already out the door. As he walked back down the hall, he noticed the families of other children in the rooms that he passed. He could tell those of them who were genuinely happy and optimistic as well as those who were desperately putting up fronts with the hopes of miracles happening. It was the same mask he had worn from the time of his son's diagnosis. Dr. Tarver, who was considered one of the top pediatric oncologists in the world, had given him hope only to have it dashed by his latest news. Dr. Tarver's fatal flaw was that somehow, he had forgotten that although they were in the States, men like Cesar were to be treated like gods. Whatever gods wanted, gods got.

When Cesar was just a few feet from his son's room, he made the decision that the exact day that Cesar Jr. died, the doctor's life would end as well, because gods were fickle and often punished failure with death.

Just as Cesar approached his son's room, he heard the sound of a child laughing. When he entered, he saw a boy around his son's age with incredibly dark skin standing at the bedside laughing loudly. Cesar Jr. was too weak to laugh but strong enough still to smile. It was a bold, beautiful smile that had been absent far too long. The dark boy wore a sharp, cream-colored suit and shiny black shoes. When he turned toward the door, Cesar asked, "Who are you? What are you doing here?"

"I'm Gaby. I was just walking by and saw him alone, so I came in to say hi."

Cesar crossed to the opposite side of the bed and smiled at his son. Gaby watched how gentle the man was with the boy.

"Are you his father?" Gaby asked.

"Yes, I am."

"I'm sorry if I'm not supposed to be here. I didn't mean to do anything wrong."

"No, you didn't… I just… You're not here alone, are you?"

"No, I'm here with my father."

The more Cesar looked at how his son stared at Gaby, he was taken even more by the dark boy. The two youngsters were similar in age and size, but the thing that stood out to Cesar the most was that when Gaby smiled, he shone brightly the way his son did. He saw in the stranger the same thing he saw in Cesar Jr.—pureness. He hadn't seen his son light up in a while, but Gaby brought it back. Seeing Cesar Jr. smile may not have changed the course of his fate, but even if it was only a temporary victory, it lifted his father. He leaned down and kissed his son's forehead and rubbed the boy's hand.

He turned when he heard a deep voice with the heavy accent of a foreigner coming from the doorway. There was a tall African man standing there.

"Gaby, I've been looking for you. I've told you many times before that you are not to just walk off. I hope he hasn't…disturbed you in any way."

"No, no, not at all. We're actually both glad he came in. My name is Cesar, and this is my son, Cesar Junior."

The man crossed and shook hands with Cesar. "I am Joseph-Malaika Ramiel. I am sorry to meet you under such circumstances."

"Is Gaby a patient here as well?" Cesar asked.

"No, I am a donor to the hospital. Once a month, we tour the different wings."

A large, fit man suddenly appeared in the doorway. Cesar immediately pegged him as a bodyguard.

"Excuse me, sir, but if you're going to make your meeting in LA, we should leave now," the man said.

Mr. Ramiel looked down at his watch. "You are right. I completely lost track of the time. Gaby, we need to leave."

"Can I just stay for a little while longer?" Gaby asked.

"I'm afraid that is not possible. If traffic is bad on the way to the airport, I'll be late for my meeting."

"Please."

"Gaby, I said—"

Cesar interrupted. "Would you mind if I spoke with you for just a moment or two out in the hallway?"

Mr. Ramiel glanced once again down at his watch, then back at Cesar. "Certainly."

As the two men headed toward the door, Cesar glanced back over his shoulder and saw that his son was still smiling.

"I know we met just three minutes ago, and I certainly have no right to…uh…impose on you in any way, but I'm wondering if it is at all possible that you and Gaby could stay for just a little while longer."

"I really do have to…."

"My son is dying. The doctor just told me it's only a matter of days. Before seeing him with Gaby, I can't even remember the last time I saw him smile. I don't mean to insult you, but I could pay you for your time or inconvenience. I would make it worth your while. Please."

Men who were used to being treated like gods were not made to beg. But beg Cesar did, because when it came to his son, he was not afforded the luxury of pride.

Malaika was genuinely moved by Cesar's words. It was obvious that he was struggling with his obligations and Cesar's request. The men heard Gaby's laugh spilling into the hallway.

"I'm truly sorry to hear about your son. I will certainly keep you both in my prayers. Unfortunately, I have eleven board members waiting for me in Los Angeles. They're in from all over the world. I apologize most sincerely, but regrettably I couldn't delay or reschedule the meeting even if I wanted to. I truly am sorry." Malaika crossed back to the entrance of the room. "Gaby, we really must leave now. Say goodbye to your friend."

Cesar stood behind Malaika and watched Gaby whisper into his son's ear. Gaby hooked his little finger around Cesar Jr.'s in the shape of a pinkie swear. Cesar Jr. managed to smile again just before Gaby and Malaika exited.

After they were alone, Cesar sat at his son's bedside, holding his hand as the boy's smile slowly faded away.

10
The Beach

Doc Callan was exasperated that he couldn't convince Solomon to turn the boy over. Now that he had gotten involved, there was an inadvertent target on his back as well. Callan may not have believed in God, but he was certain that the devil was real. Evil went by many names; Cesar Quintero was surely one of them. The multiple messages that he had gotten on his cell phone left very little doubt that there would be no avoiding the inevitable.

Even from a block away, Callan heard it clearly. The beckoning of the ocean whispering to him louder than it had in the past. From the time he was a boy, the sound of rolling waves soothed him even in the most turbulent of times. He rolled his window down to better smell the sea air and feel the faint mist of salt on his skin. The ocean was his wall-less temple. It was the place he felt the most connected to nature and the universe. This was his peace. His stillness. The haven of his surrender.

As he parked his car in the sand, Doc Callan took out his wallet and looked at a photo of his sister and two nieces smiling and hugging each other. He placed the wallet under the front of his seat but pocketed the photo. He then reached inside his jacket for his weapon, released its safety, then stuffed it back into its holster as he opened his door and walked toward the water, which called him even louder.

Four men were waiting for him. Three were oversize, but ironically the alpha of the pack was the smallest of them all. Cesar Quintero.

As Callan approached the men, Cesar greeted him. "Thank you for meeting me, Mr. Callan."

"Your name and reputation don't really offer the option of a choice," Callan responded.

"We always have choices. That's what defines us."

"So what can I do for you?"

Cesar smirked and locked eyes with Callan as though the two were competing in some undeclared staring contest.

"We both know why I reached out to you. If you insist on starting this conversation by pretending otherwise, then the day is not going to go well for either one of us. But much worse for you."

"How did you know he would come to me?"

Cesar smiled at him. "I'm not the only one here who's known by name and reputation. Does he still have the boy?"

"No, he was alone."

"I'll ask you again. This time if you lie to me, I'll start by taking pieces of you."

"Yeah, he's got the boy."

"So where are they now?"

"I don't know, and that's the God's heaven truth. He let me work on him for about twenty minutes, I hit him up with some antibiotics and pain meds, he dumped his phone, and then he and the kid took off."

"I'm sure you've heard that there's a million-dollar tag on the kid, yet you want me to believe that you just decided to let them go?"

"I didn't really have a choice. It's hard to say no to a man who's got a gun pointed at your head."

"Like I said before, we always have choices. So you're saying that not only do you not know where Mr. Nangobi is but that you have no way of contacting him?"

"That's correct."

"So why don't I believe you?"

"Because you *choose* not to. Why do you want to kill the kid anyway?"

Cesar smiled. "Your only concern should be your own mortality, not the boy's. You and I are both professionals. True, neither one of us is remotely close to being a saint, but I'd still like to believe that there is such a thing as honor among thieves. Yet you insist on insulting my intelligence."

"Look, I've told you everything I—"

"I was told you and Mr. Nangobi go back a few years and that he even saved your ass a time or two. So that we're clear, I actually respect you for trying to protect him. I really do. I'll find him with or without your help, but please understand my dilemma now. I can't let you walk away from here thinking for a second that it's okay for you to be dishonest with me. That's bad for my business."

The ocean behind them stirred restlessly as the wind chopped the water in small, violent outbursts. Scores of whitecaps appeared and disappeared on the backs of waves that surged, then retreated.

"I've answered what you've asked of me," Callan said.

"You and I actually have something in common."

Callan looked at him oddly.

Cesar nodded his head. "It's my understanding that you did a couple of years of med school before deciding it wasn't for you. Not sure how you ultimately ended up here, but I guess we both started in different directions from where we are now. Would you believe me if I told you that I started out life wanting to be a priest? Went to seminary and everything. Learned a lot about souls during that time. Do you believe in that sort of stuff?"

"Never gave it much thought one way or the other."

"You should. I believed in God until I found something better. Something more real."

"Anything is real if you choose to believe it is."

"Exactly. Unfortunately for both of us, you chose not to believe me when I said that if you continued lying to me, I would take pieces of you. For the record, I didn't mean that physically.

That's too easy. I meant something much deeper. Pieces of your soul, for example."

"I don't—"

"Shh—9255 Lanewood Road. That's where your sister and your two nieces live, am I right?" Cesar asked.

Callan quickly pulled out his gun and pointed it at Cesar's head. Cesar calmly waved off his three henchmen, who had pulled out their weapons and pointed them at Callan.

"You go near my family and I'll..."

"You'll what, kill me?" Cesar sneered. "Do you really think that would change anything? What would you do if you thought my brother and two of his associates were parked a block away from your sister's house in anticipation of you trying to play the misguided hero? What if they were just waiting for my phone call? Which if they don't get in ten minutes, then they know to pay a visit to your very pretty sister and her two young daughters. I'm talking about men short on patience and long on perverted imagination. What would you do? Hmm? What would you do to protect them?"

"If you touch them, I swear to God..."

"He can't help you. This is between you and me, one professional to another."

Callan yelled as he pressed the barrel of his gun against the center of Cesar's forehead, "Fuck you!"

Cesar, who didn't flinch, spoke calmly, "You've already attempted that, and look at how that's working out for you. The only question is will you fuck your family as well? Even though you dare raise a gun to me, it's still not too late for you to do right by them. You want to save them? Start by biting down on that gun and going out with at least something that could pass for professional dignity."

Callan was reduced to a combination of sweat, snot, and tears.

"How do I know that my family stays clear?"

Cesar laughed. "You don't. You're just going to have to hope like hell that there really is such a thing as honor among thieves."

"Whether there is or isn't, I'll be waiting for you."

"You won't be the first or the only."

Callan took the gun out of Cesar's face, then backed away toward the edge of the water. He quickly glanced upward as a small flock of squawking gulls passed overhead. He squinted at the brightness of the sun. His eyes were a mirror of the pale blue skies on which they rested. He looked out toward the rimless sea and the rays of shimmering white sunlight shining down on the offing. As he listened to the waves crashing, he placed the muzzle of the gun under his chin.

The last thing Doc Callan heard before pulling the trigger was the calming rumble of the ocean calling him.

Cesar stared at Callan's corpse for a few seconds, then turned and walked away, throwing a couple of orders toward his men in Spanish. "Check him for his phone. Look at the call logs and texts for the last twelve hours. Call Emilio and tell them to kill the sister and the girls."

Over the years, Emilio had lost count at around forty of the bodies he'd put into the ground for his brother Cesar. From the time they were both young teenagers, he knew that he was not nearly as smart or enterprising as his younger brother. Despite his limited skill set, he took great pride in the two things at which he did excel—hurting people and/or killing them. Although his brother was definitely capable of great violence and never hesitated to kill for professional purposes, Emilio needed very little reason other than he simply relished the kill. It made no difference to him: young men, old men, women, children, pets. They were all interchangeable cogs. Blood was blood. Death was death.

Doc Callan's sister Margaret lived in a good old-fashioned American craftsman. From the low-pitched gables and hanging eaves to the patterned windowpanes and covered front porch, it was a suburban gem. Most of the homes on the street were similarly built as though Frank Lloyd Wright himself was the president of the HOA. It was a quiet enclave where the homes had deep setbacks from the street and quite a bit of side yard that gave them ample space and privacy from their neighbors.

The black Ford F-250 with tinted windows eased down the quiet street like a steel panther entering a field of prey. Emilio looked the part of a Mexican Elvis, complete with pompadour and angular sideburns. He wore a black-and-gold Versace shirt with a Grecian print. It was unbuttoned down to his solar plexus, revealing a shiny silver necklace of the Virgin Mary nestled among a thick forest of chest hairs. He was silent as he rode shotgun. It was all a part of his pregame ritual. Once he was in the kill zone, he was equally engrossed in all the moments—the before, during, and after. The immeasurable high for him was the omnipotence of determining the when and how of someone's final moments of life. It was nothing short of God-like.

As the truck stopped in front of the house, Emilio reached for the machete on the seat beside him. Blades more often than guns scripted the most effective narrative. The sheer brutality was just the type of messaging that enemies and would-be enemies feared most. With *publicity kills* such as this, Emilio always ordered his men to bring their knives and machetes. They were his personal preference because he savored the intimacy of feeling a person's last breath or seeing up close the final dimming of their eyes.

He got out of the truck, followed by his two underlings, Gael and Alejandro, both of whom sported tattoos of the letter *Z* engulfed in flames on the backs of their necks. Emilio nodded to Alejandro, who made his way to the rear of the house as he and Gael climbed the stairs of the front porch, picked the lock, and entered.

The inside of the house was warm, understated, and undeniably feminine. Pastel colors, frilly throw pillows, and an array of candles and tchotchkes. The overmantel was filled with various framed photos. Prominent among them was an eight-by-ten version of a familiar photo of Margaret and her two teenage daughters hamming it up for the camera. There was also a solo photo of a younger-looking Doc Callan.

Emilio and his two men cleared all the rooms on the first floor and were heading upstairs when they heard the soft thud of footsteps just above them. As they ascended the stairs, they slowed and froze at times when the old wooden steps creaked, announcing their advance. Once the men made it to the second-story landing, they split up and headed to different bedrooms.

The sound of a running shower could be heard behind a closed bathroom door. Alejandro eased the door open and saw a faint silhouette that was mostly obscured by a thick fog of steam. As he raised his machete, he was surprised by the two muffled sounds that were quickly followed by a world of pain in his upper body. He was confused even as he fell back and lay crumpled in the doorway, blood seeping from his chest. He first thought the figure was a shadow until he realized it was actually Solomon's black skin. The last thing that Alejandro saw was the Darkness.

Gael heard the thud and moved quickly toward the bathroom. As he rushed and knelt at the side of his fallen colleague, he didn't notice the shadow that emerged from the linen closet directly behind him. Solomon was quiet as air. He clamped his hand over Gael's mouth and took his life with Alejandro's machete, then eased the corpse to the floor. The two bodies lay mere inches from each other, joined together in death by the convergence of the two streams of blood pooling beneath them.

Emilio exited the master bedroom at the far end of the hallway and roared like an angry lion when he saw the arms and legs of his men sticking out from the bathroom's doorway. He raised his machete and rushed toward the shadow disappearing around the corner to one of the bedrooms.

Solomon knelt and waited. Although his body may have only been operating at 70 percent, his mind was still his most lethal weapon. One of the first lessons he had learned in the art of killing was that emotion was ultimately the greatest liability. He knew one could compensate for physical compromise such as weakness or lack of speed, but a mind clouded by emotion made even the fiercest of warriors *defeatable*.

Emilio blindly rushed around the corner and was met by the swing of Solomon's machete, which split both flesh and tibia. The pain and shattered bone dropped him as his blade skidded from his hands and slid across the tiled floor. He writhed on his back as he instinctively grabbed at his bloodied and broken shin. Solomon stood and hovered above him.

"Why are you after the boy?"

"Fuck you, pendejo," Emilio cried out in agony.

"Whatever pain you're in, you have to trust me when I tell you this is just the first chapter. The story ends with you dying. The only two questions left are how badly and how quickly."

"Do you really think I'm afraid to die?" Emilio asked, smirking to hide the pain.

"Whether you are or aren't is ultimately irrelevant to me. The only thing of consequence to you should be how much pain do you actually think you can endure before telling me what I need to know?"

The rise of fear in Emilio came not from the threat of death, not even from the sight of his blood dripping from Solomon's blade. The fear came when he looked into Solomon's eyes and saw the same mercilessness that he himself had shown to the countless victims in his past.

Solomon was two years removed from his role as a professional killer. He had thought, hoped, that the call of violence was long behind him, but it reattached itself to him like a familiar shadow. The business of killing simply refused to let him go. He lifted the blade and started with Emilio's hands and feet.

Emilio lasted seven and a half minutes, which was about six minutes longer than most. In the end, he didn't have much to tell. He went on and on about how his brother would avenge him in the most brutal of ways. Cesar had given clear instructions that the boy had to be brought back to him alive so that he could be the one to kill him.

Solomon wasn't sure if Emilio had gone into shock, but as he tried to fight through the pain, he babbled about a couple of things that made no sense, especially his dying words. The man muttered something about "the skinny lady," then drew his last breath.

11

McKinty

Having called Margaret right after his final conversation with Callan, Solomon made sure she and her daughters were nowhere near the ambush he planned for her would-be killers. After killing Emilio at Margaret's house, he walked the block and a half to where he had parked the van and got in. He looked in the rearview mirror and asked, "You okay?"

Gaby, who was hiding on the floor in the back, sat up and answered, "Yes."

They drove about ten miles in silence. Solomon was so deep in thought that he completely ignored Gaby. The more he tried to figure things out, the less sense their predicament made. It frustrated him to no end that he was still no closer to understanding why the boy was being hunted and consequently why he was as well. He had assumed he would gain more clarity from his encounter with Emilio, but he was wrong.

Solomon had only heard the name Cesar Quintero a few times in passing. What little he'd heard was all bad. The body count from any cartel was astronomical. The number of people killed at Cesar Quintero's behest was obscenely high even by those standards.

~

Solomon and Gaby drove out to Simi Valley to a mostly deserted industrial park that rose up like an urban monolith in the desolate flatlands. Gone were the dozens of businesses that once flourished in the four redbrick constructions that were erected in the late '50s. The buildings were decades removed from their glory days and were now defeated by graffiti, deterioration, and rusted signage. Only one of the structures was still operational, with just a handful of functioning offices.

As they got out of the van and Solomon was momentarily obscured by the hood of the vehicle, he discreetly checked his weapon before leading the boy up three flights of stairs to the one active office on the entire floor. The sign on the door read McKinty Consulting. The inside of the office fared much better than any of the building's decrepit exterior. It was a loft-style open floor plan with eighteen-foot-high ceilings. The space was one large room subdivided into three different sections by two partitions. There were exposed wooden beams and gray-painted steel girders.

As soon as Solomon and Gaby walked in, a short reed of a man who sat behind a large desk that dwarfed him stood up and made his way over to them. The man's name was McKinty. He stared at Gaby and as best he could tried not to look at Solomon directly.

"Mr. Nangobi, uh…what are you doing here?" McKinty asked.

It was immediately clear to Solomon that his arrival made the man very ill at ease.

"I need to talk to you."

"Now is not a…not a good time. I'm sorry I…"

"I just need five minutes, that's all," Solomon said, more as a command than a request.

The small man tried to be calm, but Solomon's mere presence raised his blood pressure. Although McKinty had brokered a couple of Solomon's hits back in the day and there had never been issues between them, he found it impossible to ever be comfortable in the presence of a man who at the peak of his game was reputed to be the coldest of killers. McKinty may have tried his best to act calm, but the truth was he was a web of frayed nerves because of the unexpected visit from the man infamously called either the Black Reaper or the Darkness.

"Uh, yeah sure, but I've got an important meeting that I've gotta get ready to leave for."

Solomon nodded in the direction of McKinty's desk. "Let's talk in private," he said as he locked the door. "Gaby, grab a seat. I'll just be a couple of minutes."

Gaby sat on a wooden bench by the front door as the two men made their way back to the desk. McKinty sat while Solomon remained standing. The place reeked of heavy cigar smoke even though Solomon noticed that one of the large windows was wide open, its long, white sheets gently undulating from the morning breeze. The two men spoke in lowered voices so as not to be heard by the boy.

"There's a lot of heat on you right now. Jesus H. Christ, how did you get tangled with Cesar Quintero? I'm telling you for both our good, you can't be here. I can't get involved in any of this." McKinty was insistent.

"How much exactly do you know?" Solomon asked.

"I know he wants the kid and that he's looking to make an example out of you. They've already reached out to me and even showed me what would happen if I in any way tried to help you."

"What are you talking about?" Solomon was confused.

McKinty picked up his cell phone off his desk, opened up a text, and showed a photo to Solomon.

Throughout his life, Solomon had done quite a bit of killing, maiming, and torturing. He was well versed not just in the inhumanity of men but equally in the depths of his own depravity. In the realm of violence, there wasn't much he hadn't seen. The victims of death, no matter how horrible the manner, had very little if any effect on him, but seeing the photo of Doc Callan with part of his head blown off weakened his knees.

"They said they gave him a choice. Either he did it or they'd do it. Please just leave and keep me out of this, I'm begging you," McKinty pleaded.

It took Solomon a minute or two to bounce back from the sight of Callan's death. "Look, I don't have much of a choice here.

I'm calling in all markers. You and your entire family would have been killed years ago if Callan and I hadn't stopped Dominic. You owe both of us and you know it. I'm here to collect. You do one thing for me, and I'm out of your life."

"Please don't..."

"Just one thing, and I'm willing to pay."

"What good is money if I'm too dead to spend it?" McKinty retorted.

"We play this the right way, there's a good chance we both live. You get to name your price. I'm talking about the kind of money that helps get you out of the game completely. Go retire anywhere you want."

Solomon saw the subtle spark of interest in McKinty's face.

"You know the type of money that you used to wire into my account. I never touched it. It's all just sitting in my bank with the bulk of the money I made in New York over the years," Solomon persisted.

"What's the ask?"

"Smuggle the kid to Canada, and put him with one of your rich families looking to jump to the head of the adoption line."

"How much is it worth to you?"

"I'm sitting on just over two mil. It's all yours."

"You're telling me you're willing to spend two mil on a kid you just met?"

"It's all blood money. It might as well go to doing something decent. You want a way out so that you never have to deal with people like me or Quintero ever again? Well, I'm giving it to you."

McKinty looked at Solomon for a few seconds, then glanced back in Gaby's direction. Although he seemed to be vacillating, Solomon already knew the decision had been made.

"Let me work on getting him some ID as well as making some phone calls up north to find a family."

"I need you to make sure it's a good situation for him."

"I will. You got my word. Meet me back here at nine tomorrow morning."

"I can wire you the money at 9:05. One last thing. I need some clean plates for my van. Mine are hot."

McKinty got up and crossed to a row of filing cabinets, opened one, and pulled out a gym bag filled with license plates. He put the bag on the desk in front of Solomon.

"Don't show me which ones you take. It's best if I don't know," McKinty said.

Solomon grabbed two plates and turned to leave. "I'll see you tomorrow at nine."

If anyone could find Gaby a good home, it was McKinty. Every child deserved love and safety. Solomon just wanted the boy to have the opportunity to grow up happy. He wanted him to be raised by parents who were at least half as loving as his.

As they exited McKinty's office, Solomon thought about the day the soldiers came and when he saw his parents for the last time.

12

The Boy King

UGANDA 1972
ACHOLI REGION

After the soldiers killed Solomon's beloved teacher, Mr. Mukasa, they segregated the boys from the girls as well as the two male and four female adults. Akika stared back at Solomon as they were separated. The boy cried when he was snatched from the bosom of his mother. It took two of the armed men to restrain Moses. It was only after the man with the cave of a voice placed the muzzle of his weapon to Miremba's temple that Moses ceased to resist.

Solomon had never before seen hatred in his father's eyes. He never imagined that the same eyes that had always looked on him and his mother so lovingly were capable of such contempt. As the boy stared at his father, all that glanced back at him were two wet, black stones that were even more empty and cold than those of their captors.

The soldiers were rough with his mother, as they were with all the women. Rough even with the weeping girls. Solomon looked toward the floor when he saw one of the men dishonor Akika. They laughed as they brazenly fondled the private parts of the women as well as the *not-yet* women. When Miremba and Dembe resisted, three of the soldiers ripped their blouses, exposing their breasts. Miremba spat in the face of the man who had most violated her. When he struck her, Moses broke free and grabbed the offender from behind in a choke hold. They beat him savagely with the butts of their rifles until he lay in a heap of broken bones and a web of nasty gashes. Solomon rushed to the side of his barely conscious father. The pitiful wails from Miremba filled the entire school yet rang loudest in Solomon's ears. Aside from Akika, who sobbed steadily for her mother, the cries from the rest of the children rose and fell like the waves of a storm at sea.

As Solomon held his father, the man with the thundering voice knelt across from him.

"Is this your father?" the man asked.

Solomon nodded.

The man pointed to Miremba. "And is that your mother?"

Once again, the boy nodded.

"So what do they call you?"

Solomon said nothing.

Miremba interrupted her crying long enough to plead with the man. "Please, leave him alone. He's just a boy."

Solomon looked past the man toward his mother, who was being held by two of the soldiers.

"Look at me. I'm the one speaking to you, not her. Tell me your name, boy!"

Solomon recoiled back a foot as the man's voice boomed like cannon fire.

"Solom… Solomon."

"So are you a prince or a king?" the man asked.

Solomon just looked at him, frightened and confused.

The man pointed at the crown of palm leaf and straw that still rested on Solomon's head.

"You're wearing a crown, so you must feel that you're either a prince or a king. So when exactly did the Acholi people start thinking they were royalty?"

"He's just wearing it because it's his birthday. Please, sir, leave him alone," Miremba pleaded.

"Is that true? Is it your birthday?"

Solomon slowly nodded.

The man looked back at Miremba. "So is it because the boy pretends he's a king that you and your husband think you're allowed to spit on and attack my men?"

"Please, sir, I…"

He silenced her with just the raising of his hand. He then looked back at Solomon and asked him, "Do you have any idea why a king's crown is so heavy?"

The scared boy shook his head no.

"It's because the man who wears it carries the fate of his

people. The burden of impossible choices is never an easy load. Since you wear the crown, you must learn these things. For example, if you had to make a choice between…killing your mother or killing your father so that everyone else in here could live, what would you choose?"

The man unholstered his sidearm and admired it as one would a favored heirloom. It was a shiny Colt M1911 pistol. He regarded it with much more respect than he did the captives under his charge.

When he gently offered it to Solomon, the boy's mother pleaded hysterically, "Please, sir, leave him alone. I'm begging you…"

The man gave a slight nod to the soldier whom Miremba had spat on earlier. The soldier's dark lips parted, revealing even darker gums with teeth the color of rancid butter. He stripped Miremba completely naked and paraded her before a frightened audience. Moses, who was still on his back, stirred and struggled to rise, but the most his injuries would allow him to do was to raise himself up on his elbows.

Over the ruckus of the drunken soldiers' jeers, Solomon cried ferociously at his mother's humiliation. She was fondled, slapped, and cursed by each of the soldiers. Every violation was greeted with vile cheer. They then brought her closer to Solomon and forced her on her knees. She was made to kneel next to her husband, putting them both directly in front of their son.

The man in charge knelt behind Solomon and bade him to take the weapon. As the heavy metal sagged in the child's grasp, the man put his hands around Solomon's to help him steady the gun.

He was oddly gentle with the boy, patient in the preparation of an execution. Although he bore the brunt of the weight, he pinned Solomon's finger under his so that they were both one with the trigger. He casually alternated aiming the weapon at Moses and then Miremba. Each time the muzzle rested in the direction of either parent, Solomon cried and pleaded more. It was all cheap sport to the man and his soldiers. A victory-less game in which the threat of taking human lives was bartered for laughter.

"Either you choose, or I'll shoot them both along with everyone else in here. So tell me, young king, which one shall it be? I'm sure my men would prefer that you spare your mother. At least she could be of use to us. Your father, on the other hand, is nothing more than a wounded dog. An Acholi mutt at that. Surely a king has the courage to put a dog out of its misery."

Miremba held Moses's hand much tighter than he was able to reciprocate. Though his father was not much more than a bloodied sequence of welts and cuts, Solomon still saw the piercing hatred in the slits of Moses's eyes. When he spoke to his son, his voice was a ragged whisper.

"Better by your…hands…than at the…paws of animals."

The soldier with the yellowed teeth struck Moses twice to the side of his head with the buttstock of his rifle. Miremba and Solomon both cried out.

"It's…okay, Solomon. I'm…not…afraid to die. Allah…will protect…you and…your mother."

His father's words only added more confusion to Solomon's fear. He couldn't understand why Allah hadn't already protected them.

Why did the blood of Mr. Mukasa lie freshly pooled but ten feet in front of him? If Allah hadn't protected any of them thus far, then his father's words were nothing more than fruitless lies. The truth was simple enough even for a child to understand. Allah evidently despised the Acholi people as much as Idi Amin did. Solomon had heard the rumors from neighboring townships about just how lowly his kind were regarded. He'd overheard Dembe whispering to his mother about the beatings, burnings, and killings. He'd heard the horrid things they did to women. Solomon knew his mother's only use to them was fodder for their unspeakable hungers.

The calloused palms of the man completely enveloped the boy's trembling hands, forcing him to hold the gun tighter. He put his lips next to Solomon's ear and spoke words that only the two of them could hear.

Miremba's cries punctured the air. Solomon felt the rattling not just in his head and chest but piercing even the smallest parts of him. He was blinded as much by tears as he was the dripping beads of sweat that stung his eyes. His parents were blurs. The man continued whispering atrocious secrets into the boy's ear, detailing the graphic violence that awaited whichever of his parents was spared. Miremba wailed more. A high-pitched, searing wail.

In imagining the things the men would do to her, Solomon knew that her woes were only a precursor of more bitter days to come. And still the man was unrelenting in whispering the unthinkable. Solomon closed his eyes and squeezed his small finger against the trigger.

Moses flinched, then cried. For the briefest of seconds, it was the only sound, the lonely bawl of a husband's anguish. Some of the soldiers laughed as Miremba's body toppled backward from the bullet in her chest.

Unprompted by the man, Solomon pointed the weapon in the direction of his father's agony and pulled the trigger twice until he heard the cries no more.

As Solomon's body sagged, he released the gun into the man's hands. The man simply smiled and patted the boy's head as if he were an obedient pet. "Maybe you have the makings of a king after all. I guess we'll just have to wait and see."

The man put his hand on Solomon's shoulder and led him toward the door, pausing slightly after one of the soldiers asked, "Sir, what would you like us to do with the rest of them?"

"The same thing you would do with any pack of treacherous dogs."

Just before exiting, Solomon looked back over his shoulder at the sprawled bodies of his dead parents as well as a soldier raising his weapon at a weeping Akika and her mother. As the door closed behind him, the screaming began, muffled by the thudding echo of gunfire. He was too overwhelmed to be certain, but he thought somewhere among the panic and cacophony, he heard the distinctive cries of Akika and Dembe.

13

Lake Arrowhead

Gaby sat in the front passenger seat and looked out the window at the world whirring by as they drove down the freeway. Solomon glanced at the gas gauge and saw that they were in the red. As he pulled into an empty gas station, he looked again at Gaby, who was doggedly trying to clean the oxidized blotches off the old horn with the sleeve of his discarded outfit. Solomon sat for a moment, scanning his surroundings before turning toward Gaby.

"Do you need to go to the bathroom?" Solomon asked.

"No."

"We've got an hour-and-a-half drive ahead of us. Are you sure?"

"Yes."

"Okay, then I need you to stay here. Do not move, and keep the doors locked. Do you understand me?"

"Yes."

"You want a Coke or anything?"

"Soda is not good for you," the boy replied.

"Well, then how about a bottle of water or juice?"

"I'll have some water, please."

"Don't forget what I said. Keep the door locked and don't move."

"Okay."

Amar the clerk, a Mumbai transplant, was stocking boxes of cigarettes when Solomon entered. Solomon immediately noticed the security camera hovering hawklike above them. The local news played on a small TV that was suspended from the ceiling in a corner by the front door.

"Hello, sir, how are you?"

"I'm good, thank you."

Solomon walked straight to the back and got a couple of bottles of water and picked up some chips and cookies.

As he placed his items on the counter, he pointed to some disposable phones displayed next to the rows of cigarettes. "Let me get three of those, and you can ring me up for seventy on number two."

Amar tapped in the items for purchase on the cash register, "Okay, that'll be $211.23," he said. After Solomon handed him cash, Amar pointed at two stacks of baseball caps on display. "By the way, you get a free Dodgers or Angels baseball cap with purchases over a hundred. Would you like blue, white, or red?"

"It's okay. I'm not really a baseball fan," Solomon responded.

"Well, they're free, so you can just give it away to somebody if you want."

"Fine. Just put one of the white Dodgers caps in the bag," Solomon said, relenting.

Solomon went back outside, put the bag in the van, then placed the pump nozzle in his tank. As he refueled, he looked up to see Gaby smiling at him from inside the car. He thought about all that the boy had been through and was impressed at how he still managed to smile. As he turned to put the pump back in its station, his shirt felt like it was sticking to his wound. Solomon turned and reentered the mart.

"May I have the key to the bathroom?"

"Yes, sir," Amar said and handed him the key.

As soon as Solomon entered the small bathroom, he opened his shirt to examine his bandaging. Although a small amount of blood had seeped through, it was nothing to cause concern. Solomon used the bathroom, washed his hands, and left. After he returned the key to Amar, who was now watching TV, he headed for the door until he made a quick pivot, walked to the back of the store, and grabbed a bottle of peroxide. When he stepped back to the counter to pay, he noticed that Amar seemed on edge and evaded looking at him. Solomon turned just in time to see video of himself on the news as a suspect in the garden's shooting. Amar sat trembling, still trying to avoid his eyes but panicked more when he saw Solomon taking his gun out.

"Please, sir, you never came here. I don't know what you look like. I'll swear I've never seen you. You have no cause to harm me. Twelve years in this country and I've never given anyone cause. Believe me, sir, I'm a good man."

Solomon raised his gun and pointed it at Amar. "This has nothing to do with how good or bad you are. It's not personal."

"If you take my son's father from him and my wife's husband from her, it is definitely personal. It's not just *my life* you'll be taking," Amar pleaded.

Solomon knew the clerk was right and that the ripples of death reached far beyond the shores of a single kill. He had long ago made peace with the simple truth that the killing of one was in fact the annihilation of entire generations. In his lifetime, Solomon had looked in the incalculable eyes of pleading victims. For reasons he himself couldn't understand, Amar's were some of the most difficult he'd ever faced.

"Turn around," Solomon ordered.

Amar was crying now, knowing that his fate had been decided.

"Please, sir, I'm begging you. You don't have to do this."

"I said turn around!" Solomon bellowed as he tightened his finger on the trigger.

When the door suddenly opened, Solomon swung his gun and found it pointing at a startled Gaby.

"I have to go to the bathroom," Gaby muttered apologetically.

"Go back to the van."

Gaby stood frozen, looking from Solomon to a weeping Amar. He jumped when Solomon yelled at him.

"Go back to the van, now!"

Gaby turned and slowly walked toward the van, his face twisted in angst. When he glanced back, he saw two quick flashes of gunfire inside the mart. He stood frozen on the pavement as he trembled and cried.

The bullet-riddled surveillance camera dangled by its cables as a terrified Amar cowered underneath it.

"Give me your driver's license," Solomon demanded.

Amar reached in his pocket and put his wallet on the counter. Solomon took out the license and pocketed it.

"For the sake of you and your wife and son, if I were you, I'd forget any of this ever happened."

"Yes, sir. Thank you, sir. God bless you."

Solomon hurried out of the mart carrying the surveillance camera's console along with the bottle of peroxide. He scooped up Gaby, put him in the van, then sped off.

As they drove down the freeway, Solomon kept his eyes glued to the road before him, avoiding the stares from Gaby, who sat next to him.

"I thought I told you to stay in the van."

"I had to go to the bathroom."

"I had just asked you ten minutes ago if you had to go and you said no."

"I didn't have to go then. Why did—"

"Look, I don't want to talk about what happened back there. I told you to stay in the van, and you didn't. So if I tell you to do something, is that what I should expect? Because that's not going to work. When I tell you to do something, you do it. No discussion. No talk back. Are we clear?"

"You shouldn't hurt people. That's not good."

"We're not talking about that. We're talking about whether you're gonna listen to me or not. Are you?"

"Yes."

"Yes what?"

"Yes, I'm going to listen to you."

"Good."

"You still shouldn't hurt people."

"Look, kid, I'm doing whatever I have to do to keep us both alive. Whatever. I don't know who or what you think I am, but let me make something very clear. I'm not the good person that you've dreamed up. I've done plenty of bad things, and I'm pretty certain before this is all over, I'll be doing plenty more."

"Are you bad like the men that want to hurt me?"

Solomon looked at Gaby for the first time. "Yes, I am."

~

They were an hour east of Los Angeles, heading toward the San Bernardino Mountains. Besides the one request to pull over so that he could relieve himself behind a tree, Gaby hadn't said a word since the incident at the gas station. The boy's sadness weighed heavily in the van. The echoes of his silence spoke loudly. Even in the absence of words, Gaby's indictment was implicit enough. So too was the quiet protest and rejection of who Solomon admitted to being. Solomon had never been one to apologize or make excuses for who or what he was, but neither had he ever been confronted by eyes that were filled with such profound disappointment.

Traffic on the 210 freeway was light. Solomon listened to a smooth jazz station while Gaby counted passing cars to himself and continued giving the silent treatment. After they exited the freeway, they started the twenty-minute trek up the mountain toward the unincorporated community of Lake Arrowhead, which was over five thousand feet above sea level. Solomon periodically glanced at the boy, who still refused to look in his direction. Three-quarters of the way up the mountain, he saw how Gaby was awed by the incredible transformation of the sky. As they literally drove above the clouds, they witnessed the dramatic shift from the dull taupe hue of California smog to perfect azure. The skies were now bluer and the foliage more verdant.

Gaby sat forward, much more attentive, and looked out his window at the scenic landscape unfolding before him. His head swiveled at the pastures replete with the wide stretch of yellow and purple petals of crocus in bloom, which represented the official start of spring. The boy gently rocked his hand back and forth as he emulated the sway of tall, golden field grass that blew in the mountain gusts. Although Solomon could only see the side of Gaby's face, he saw the beam of his smile as the boy gaped at the tall pines and the smooth red trunks of giant manzanita. He seemed genuinely riveted by how the sunlight shone on the silken black backs of a dozen crows that scavenged for food in a narrow meadow. Solomon had never met a child quite like Gaby. The boy's eyes widened with joy at even the simplest of things. He seemed to process much more intently than an average child his age. He made Solomon think of the words that his father used to say about him: "Some children are just born with old souls."

Solomon understood immediately why Doc Callan had nicknamed the mountain retreat "Lake Heaven." Callan used to brag about how Lake Arrowhead was the go-to getaway in the 1920s and '30s for Hollywood stars and California power brokers. The area was a mixture of charming cabins, modest homes, and even sprawling estates that still bore the names of famous families such as the Mulhollands and Dohenys. From the architecture and charm of the idyllic community, it felt like a throwback, a hidden gem from days long gone.

Solomon rolled down the windows, inviting in the sweet mountain air. He breathed in deeply and felt his ears pop from the change in altitude. He enjoyed the feel of the fresh air washing not just over him but through him as well. When he turned toward Gaby, the boy was staring at him, but unlike before, it was neither in judgment nor accusation.

Solomon pulled into the gravel driveway of an unassuming A-frame cabin that was nuzzled in the hills just above the lake in an area called Cedar Glen. He parked behind a white Land Cruiser, and he and Gaby got out and both looked around before approaching the door and knocking. Solomon was aware that they were being watched from the subtle movement of the curtain in a corner window. A few seconds later, Doc Callan's sister Margaret opened the door and greeted them. Her face was puffy, and her eyes were bloodshot from crying. She seemed a shell of the vivacious woman whom Solomon so fondly remembered. Margaret looked hollowed by her mourning.

As she let them in, Solomon gave the place a quick once-over. The cabin was quaint. Simple. One story, two bedrooms, no television, no luxuries or distractions save the four nature paintings that he recognized as the works of Thomas Kinkade from previous photos that Callan had shared with him. It was a house in which to think, to disconnect and commune with nature. The main highlight of the place was the twenty-foot-wide floor-to-ceiling glass wall that looked out onto the beautiful lake below.

Solomon made the introductions. "Margaret, this is Gaby. Gaby, this is Ms. Margaret."

"It's nice to meet you, Gaby," she said.

"Nice meeting you as well, ma'am."

"Gaby, how would you like to go down to the lake? My daughters are down there. I need to talk to Solomon."

Gaby looked up at Solomon, who nodded.

"Is it okay if I bring my horn down to show it to her daughters?" Gaby asked.

"Sure, go get it out of the van. Look in the bag that I got at the gas station. There's a baseball cap in there if you want it," Solomon answered.

Gaby's eyes lit up.

As soon as he headed out, Margaret turned back to Solomon. "You gotta tell me what's going on. All I know is I get a frantic call from you telling me to drop everything and bring the girls up here. Why didn't my brother call me?"

"I told you, because he didn't want your number to be on his call log in case he needed to buy you time."

"Buy time for what? Something's happened to him, hasn't it? He's dead? I already know it in my heart, so you might as well just tell me the truth."

Solomon lowered his head. "I wish I had better news, but yes, he is."

The confirmation cut through her like a blade through shallow water, sending her into a crying fit.

"I'm so sorry, Margaret," Solomon said. He waited until the tearful waves had passed and she had somewhat recomposed herself. "What have you told the girls?" he asked.

"Nothing much, but they know something bad is going on. You still haven't told me what it is."

They stopped speaking when Gaby walked back through the door carrying his horn in the case. He sported the white Dodgers cap, which contrasted heavily against his dark skin.

Margaret turned her face away to hide the fact that she'd been crying. "You can take the back stairs down to the water. You'll see them on the dock," she said.

Once Gaby was gone, Solomon crossed to the back door and looked out the window. When he turned back to Margaret, she was trembling, teetering on the verge of new tears. He waited patiently until she regained control.

"How much do you know about what your brother did for a living?" he asked.

"Linus and I never lied to each other, but the fact that the most he would ever say about his work was that he was in security let me know that whatever he was doing, he wasn't comfortable telling me more. So will you tell me now?" she asked.

"No. It's not my place. But he made me promise that if anything happened to him, I would make sure you and the girls were safe. That's what I intend to do." Solomon handed her a piece of paper with a series of numbers on it. "He wanted you to have this. It's the account numbers and passwords to all his holdings. There's enough there to take care of you and the girls for the rest of your lives. I know it's of little consolation to you right now, but it was important to him that all of you were taken care of."

"How long are we supposed to stay here?"

"Just long enough for me to figure things out. I'm hoping just a few days…a week at the most. Linus said the cabin is under an LLC that can't be traced back to him or you."

"Traced back to him by who?"

"The people responsible for his death. Those same people will try and do harm to you and your daughters. I need you to believe me when I tell you that I'm not going to let that happen, okay? You just have to trust me and be patient right now."

"What am I supposed to tell the girls? I had to send them down to the lake so that they would stop asking me questions. They're already beginning to freak out."

"I don't know what to tell them, but you have to do exactly as I say. Did you leave your cell phones at the house like I asked you to?"

"Yes, but I don't understa—"

"Don't worry. I picked you up some disposables. If you want to protect yourself and your daughters, it's not safe for them to be on social media for any reason or speak to any of their friends."

"You clearly don't have teenagers."

"No, I don't, but none of you can let anyone know where you are. Until I get a better handle on this thing, the three of you are still in danger."

Margaret was overwhelmed by all that he said and launched into a spontaneous crying fit. Solomon just stood helplessly by until it subsided.

"I know this is hard on you and the girls, losing your brother, then having to uproot yourselves like this, all the while feeling left in the dark on what's happening, but I plan on doing everything I can to help you get through this."

"Get through what, Solomon? What exactly is going on?" She was growing more frustrated and desperate.

"I'm being completely honest with you when I tell you that I'm really not sure yet."

"But you know more than you're saying. Please, I'm begging you," she pleaded.

"What I can tell you is this—I just met Gaby yesterday. Someone very powerful is trying to harm him for some reason. I got wounded trying to make sure that didn't happen. Your brother came to me when I needed him and helped me." Solomon's words got caught in his throat. "He…uh…died because of it. All of this…is my fault. That is the truth, I swear to you. I can't bring your brother back, but I can and will protect the three most important things in the world to him. I owe him, I owe you, and I owe the girls that."

Margaret cried more. Much more. For the next half hour, she was on and off again. When she felt all but cried out, she and Solomon made their way to the back deck and sat in two Adirondack chairs watching Chloe and Adele unsuccessfully trying to teach Gaby how to make sounds with his horn.

"I thought he was your son when I first saw him," Margaret said.

"No, like I said, I just met him yesterday at the gardens where I worked."

"Do you have family, Solomon?"

Though it was a simple enough question, Solomon found it difficult to answer. He staggered in the memories of the two families he'd lost.

When he didn't answer, Margaret assumed he hadn't heard her, so she repeated herself. "Do you have any family?"

"Not anymore," he answered.

"I'm sorry to hear that. My family is everything to me. Those girls are my life. My brother was my rock. Would you do me a favor?"

"Anything I can."

"Would you stay and help me tell the girls that they won't be seeing their uncle anymore? I can't do it alone."

"I…uh…"

"Please. You and Gaby can crash on the sofa. You don't want to drive down the mountain at night anyway. I know it's not ideal, but it would mean a lot to me, and I know it would have meant a lot to Linus as well."

Solomon looked down at the children on the dock, knowing the unavoidable pain that awaited Callan's nieces. "Sure, we'll stay. We'll have to leave first thing in the morning though."

Margaret tried to smile as best she could. "If it makes you feel better, I promise not to cook tonight. We'll order pizza."

Solomon couldn't help but laugh at even a sliver of her old sense of humor.

As she got up to go back into the cabin, she stopped at the door and turned back to Solomon. "By the way, it's not your fault. There's never any blame to be had when it comes to saving a child. And if that's the reason my brother died, then at least it meant something."

~

The night was long, filled with the tears and unanswerable questions of the young and wounded. The girls weren't the only ones. Solomon was a bit surprised at how much even Gaby cried for a man he'd only met once. Solomon had heard stories but couldn't recall ever meeting a true empath before and certainly not one in the guise of an eight-year-old child. Their pain became his pain. When Margaret and her daughters were in desperate need of con solation, his arms, though small, were offered in compassion.

By nine p.m., the cabin was quiet. Inert. It was only after that Margaret and the girls, exhausted from the day's events and the toll of grieving, finally surrendered to the night. After Gaby finished washing up for bed, Solomon offered him the couch while he took the floor.

"I think it's time to change your bandage," Gaby said.

"I did it just before dinner, but thanks."

The boy nodded, then knelt on his knees and turned toward Solomon.

"My father said I should always pray before going to sleep. Do you pray?" Gaby asked.

"No, I don't."

"Why not?"

"Because I don't believe the same things your father did. People are different, Gaby. Everybody has a right to decide what works for them and what doesn't."

The boy turned around and closed his eyes and bowed his head and said a long, silent prayer. Whatever words he offered to God, Solomon suspected they had a lot to do with Callan's sister and nieces. He prayed for at least ten minutes. Although Solomon had much more of an indifferent opinion about God, he couldn't help but wonder what the things said in the lengthy prayer of an eight-year-old were.

When he was done, Gaby lay on the sofa and stared up at

the ceiling. Despite his stillness, Solomon could feel that the boy was nowhere near falling asleep. The mountain night was infinitely black. Save for the tinkle of a distant wind chime and the melancholy deep hoot of a lonesome owl, it was incredibly quiet. A night so serene that one might think it possible to actually hear the whoosh of falling stars.

"Did your friend die because of me?" Gaby asked.

"No, he died because of me."

"I'm sorry you got hurt helping me, and I'm really sorry about your friend."

"Yeah, me too."

The boy was quiet for a moment before he spoke again.

"Maybe you were wrong though."

"About what?" Solomon asked.

"What you said before. I don't think you're like those bad men who tried to hurt me, because if you were, you wouldn't be helping me."

"Get some sleep. We have to leave early."

Solomon had lived numerous lives. The winding path of fate had led him down many a violent road. In addition to having been a child soldier, a mercenary, an errand boy for the Russian mob, a longtime bodyguard and fixer for a Harlem gangster, he had even hired himself out as a freelance hitter in his later years. Gaby refused to see him for who he truly was. To see the horrible things he was capable of. To acknowledge the *unwashable* blood of others on his hands. The boy couldn't begin to comprehend the atrocities he had perpetrated against others. How his entire life had in one way or another been a construction of violence. No matter the darkness that defined Solomon, Gaby chose only to see his light.

There had been only two other people in Solomon's life who saw him for more than he saw himself. Two strangers who thought him worthy of clemency. They were a grandmother and granddaughter who in different ways came to mean the world to him.

The granddaughter's name was Aisha.

14
Aisha

TEN YEARS AGO

As funerals went, it was a pleasant enough affair. Solomon had actually never attended one. Although his work had filled both the coffins and coffers of many an undertaker, he never had need to ceremoniously mourn the dead. He came for the old woman because he felt it was the least he could do. Ida Gant was the closest thing to a friend he had made when he first landed in New York. He was unclear on exactly how old she was because, be it her female modesty or vanity (he wasn't versed enough on women to quite know the difference), she had always evaded telling him. All he remembered for certain was that when he first met her, she was already old but still possessed the spirit of a young, vibrant woman.

Even after he had moved to Harlem and gone to work for Clay

Freeman, he still kept in touch with his former landlady. As often as his schedule permitted, he tried to maintain the tradition of their Sunday dinners together. It broke his heart that she couldn't speak and that she pureed her portion of the meals. Although he tried not to, whenever he saw her, he couldn't help but think about the fateful night that he lost his fingers and she her tongue. She was a reminder of things both good and bad. Mostly good. After their near-death encounter, like him, she too was instantly mythologized in the eyes and mouths of Brooklyn. She became a living legend in her own right. No one dared cross her. Drug dealers steered ten blocks clear of her. As the children of the neighborhood passed her in the streets, they spoke her name only in whispers. They called her the Silent Queen.

Solomon was a man of few words and even fewer expressions of emotion. Although they never discussed it openly, he often wondered if she knew the profound impact she had made on him. Intentional or unintentional, she had played a significant role in his life. She had been both surrogate mother and grandmother to him. Although she came to know the violence he was capable of, Ida Gant was the first to see and treat Solomon simply as a man.

It was a small gathering, just sixty or so. It was mainly family and a few old-timers from the neighborhood. Ida had always been frugal with her money and pretty astute with her investments. Despite the fact that her family was in no way in need of any financial assistance, Solomon still offered to pay for the coffin, but they flat out refused.

All he wanted to do was honor her with a gesture of his eternal gratitude for her having been a source of light in an oft dark world.

Ida looked in death as she had in life—noble. She was outfitted in her favorite lapis-colored dress. Her coffin was modest, a cherry veneer shell with white satin lining and chrome handles. Like her, it was elegant in its simplicity. Ida looked to be sleeping, a soul incarnate resting in peace.

As Solomon looked down at her, he was impressed that her skin was smooth and absent the expected wrinkles even for an old woman of indeterminable age. Her hair, more salt than pepper, hung in thick, hoary vines of beautiful dreadlocks that rested three to four inches past her shoulders. Even in the still countenance of death, chapters of her life were still legible to the likes of Solomon. He saw in her face a life of both love and hardship, strength and tenderness. The smooth terrain of her skin implied that she had basked much more in the glow of victory than the shadow of defeat. He saw in her the peace of a woman who lived her life on her own terms.

From the first day of meeting her to his final glimpse of her displayed in her coffin, Solomon had always seen Ida as a woman of dignity. Though highly skeptical of either existence, Solomon thought if somehow there was in fact a God and/or heaven, then he hoped Ida was being received with all the pomp and circumstance of a royal head of state.

After the church viewing of the body and the short drive to the Holy Cross cemetery for her burial, the mourners gathered at Ida's apartment for the repast. Solomon stayed for what he felt was a respectable fifteen minutes. He was in fact heading for the front door when the woman intercepted him.

"You just made me lose a bet with myself," she said.

"How's that?" Solomon asked.

"I was certain that you would only last ten minutes, but you managed to hold out for a full fifteen. You don't remember me, do you?"

Solomon took the woman in from head to toe. He stared at her, trying to recall who she was, but he was unable to.

"I apologize but I don't. When I saw you earlier, I thought you looked a little familiar, but I couldn't remember if and when we had met," he offered.

He watched her intently as the corners of her mouth turned upward and her full lips parted, gifting him with the most beautiful smile he'd ever seen. He couldn't help but think of sunrise. She reminded him of home and the spectacle of dawn over the Ayugi River. Just like with sunrise, the longer he looked at her, the more he saw her beauty unfold. Her skin was the rich, brown color of cassava root. He thought she had the innocent eyes of a doe, and when she looked at him, she somehow left him feeling absolved.

"I'm Ida's granddaughter. I met you once shortly after you started renting a room from her. I think I was eight years old," she said.

"Thin Mint?" Solomon laughed.

"Oh God, I loved my grandmother to death, but I can't tell you how much I hated that nickname."

When she joined in his laughter, the two of them were loud enough to warrant a few stares from some of the other mourners.

Solomon couldn't take his eyes off her. He was confused because the simple nearness of her made it impossible for him to be himself. He had never known the slight buckling of knees from the presence of a woman. He had certainly never been the type of man who was made weak from the flutter of butterflies in the pit of his stomach. The more she smiled, the less he recognized himself. He had long ago accepted the tragic markers that defined him. He was an island unto himself. A barren stretch of violence and indifference. He was a taker of lives. A killer nicknamed the Darkness for both his complexion as well as the abyss from the presumed absence of a soul. He was mystified by the ease with which she immediately made him feel alive in beautifully awkward ways that he had never considered possible.

They sat in two chairs in a corner of the apartment near a window overlooking Nostrand Avenue. She brought him food and drink, but it was her undivided attention that sated him most. Although he had never experienced it personally, he'd heard tell of instances when one person made another feel as if they were the only one in a crowded room. He had always dismissed the notion as nothing more than romantic hyperbole. She proved him wrong. She looked at him in a way that made him feel as though he were the sole light of her sky. He wondered if her smile was sculpted for the singular purpose of his redemption. He loved how her eyes rested on his. They were welcomed rain to a lifetime of drought. They talked for hours as their food grew cold and their drinks warm. Though he was self-conscious about his amputated fingers, he tried not to conceal them from her. He saw her glance quickly at them as he sipped from his glass of water. He appreciated that not only did she seem unfazed but later as they shared a laugh, she gently put her hand atop his.

They huddled among themselves with the occasional interruption from her parents and other random relatives. There was something about her name that made him think of music each time he spoke it. It was like a difficult aria that he had conceded long ago was far beyond his breadth of pitch. She told him the Arabic translation of Aisha meant both *living* and *prosperous*. He immediately thought about how alive she made him feel. How rich in ways he never thought achievable. He had never met anyone quite like her. She was a living, breathing shape-shifter, a woman who deftly switched identities right before his eyes. He watched her indiscriminately alternate between being a willing captive of his gaze one second and then an abductor of his most primal senses the next. With no apparent effort on her part, she made him want to know everything about her. She was ten years younger than Solomon. He learned that she was an only child, born in Brooklyn, but when she was nine, she and her parents moved to Southern California. She started out as a public school teacher who eventually attained the position of a tenured professor of African American studies at a college in the small town of La Verne, California, which was thirty-five miles east of downtown Los Angeles. She had been married once for four years to a fellow academic before they both found the courage to admit to each other that they were better friends and colleagues than husband and wife. Solomon saw the subtle flash of sadness in her eyes when she confessed to him the regret of not having children. Like him, she too was the last of her bloodline.

"My grandmother used to mention you when she wrote. She brought you up all the time. She adored you," she said.

"She was a tough old woman. She never really came off as the adoring type," he laughed.

When Aisha laughed as well, Solomon weakened a little more in the realm of her smile.

"She was definitely tough, but she had the biggest heart I've ever known. There was nothing she wouldn't do for the people she loved. She most definitely loved you, Solomon."

Although he didn't say it to Aisha, he loved Ida as well. She was in fact the first person he had loved since the deaths of his parents and Akika. It was the thought of never having told the old woman how he truly felt that made him hang his head in sadness. When he felt the warmth of Aisha's hand on his, he raised his eyes even though his lids were made heavy under the weight of his own regrets.

"Don't worry. She knew. She told me in her letters. She wrote me once that having you in her life gave her joy. She said if she had ever had a son or grandson, she would have wanted him to be you." Her hand lingered on his even after the consolation.

Aisha extended her stay in New York. They spent the week mainly doing things that Solomon had never done. Simple things.

The types of events that most people take for granted. Solomon was by no means most people. He was used to being on guard for unseen foes, real or imagined. When he took her to the movies and even a Broadway play, he sat each time either in a corner or in the very last row so that he always had the vantage point. The same was true each time they went to a restaurant, where he always sat with his back to the wall. Solomon managed to keep one eye on Aisha and whatever activity they were enjoying and the other on the rest of the world and any potential threats. Old habits never died easily.

Although he was a man who could never give himself completely to the moment, Aisha at least made him want to try. He found himself at times, despite his efforts not to, surrendering to her whether it be there in the movies or theater, at romantic dinners, or on casual walks along the water, holding hands. She filled him with so much joy and optimism that it often left very little room for his natural sense of cautiousness.

On the last day of her trip, Aisha scheduled their visit to the Central Park Zoo to coincide with the feeding of the sea lions, which happened each day at one thirty, followed by the feeding of the penguins at two thirty. Solomon didn't realize just how much he hated zoos until he went to one. He pretended to enjoy himself for Aisha's sake, but seeing the animals up close in cages left him feeling a bit sullen.

As they headed toward the Great Lawn, which was considered the epicenter of the park, Aisha hooked her arm in his and leaned her head on his shoulder.

"You okay? You've been pretty quiet since we left the zoo," she asked.

"Yeah, I'm fine. When I was a child, my father took my mother and me once to an animal reserve in Uganda where we saw everything from lions to monkeys, impalas, rhinoceros, you name it. After you've seen them in their natural habitat, it's difficult to appreciate them caged."

"I understand, and I apologize."

"There's nothing for you to apologize for. I didn't even know I would feel that way myself until you and I were standing there looking at them."

"Had you never been to a zoo before?"

"No. There are a lot of things I've never done before meeting you." Solomon looked away from her as though he were trying to hide his embarrassment. "You must think I'm..."

"I think you're an interesting man, Solomon Nangobi. All kinds of interesting." She smiled.

Although he smiled back at her, there were other things on his mind besides caged animals. As they approached the thirteen acres of the flat oval field, he looked at the sunbathers, revelers, and lovers littered like wildflowers across the Great Lawn. He took it all in, the dog walkers and carriage pushers, the picnics and the Frisbee games. He saw the smiles of mothers and babies as well as the pride of fathers tossing balls to sons. Just spending time with Aisha changed the lens through which he saw the world. The things that he observed as they sat hand in hand were nothing new in content, but her presence made them feel new in context. They resonated in a manner in which they had never before. Aisha made him feel like much more than just a witness to life being lived in ways that he never felt himself worthy of. He was now a present participant.

They sat in a sward of freshly cut grass under the canopy of a tall elm that shaded them from the warm spring sun. He saw the tiny white petals of blooming dogwoods as they fell to the earth like windblown confetti. As Solomon looked out at the skyscrapers sprouting above the tree line, he felt her eyes on him. He could tell that she was waiting for him to speak. To let her into the thoughts that quieted him. They sat for moments in silence, listening to neighboring laughs and other interactions around them. When he finally spoke, he continued staring straight ahead.

"I'm sure if your grandmother didn't tell you, then you've at least heard from others what kind of man I am. Whatever you've heard, you need to know I've done worse than the whispers and rumors that follow me like so many shadows. You're a good woman, Aisha, the kindest I've ever known, but there are men in this world, men like me who are more deserving of being locked in cages than any animal in a zoo."

"You're not an animal, Solomon, and you certainly aren't lower than one. Do you really think you're the same man you used to be?"

"Before I met you, I thought I knew who I was. I accepted that. Now I'm not so sure." He sounded confused.

"My grandmother as well as my parents told me all about that night in Brooklyn and what everyone assumes you did in the aftermath. They even told me of later rumors, big and small. My grandmother had a gift. She was an amazing judge of character. She saw things in you, Solomon, that even you don't see. My family teases me all the time that I have the same gift as my grandmother. I see and feel things in you that tell me what type of man you truly are. Down in your core where it really matters. Before I was born and even before he met my mother, my father spent time in prison for what he said were his wild days. Fortunately, I never got to see that side of him. All I've ever known was the good man who my mother trusted he had the potential to be. So even knowing the things I know of you as well as the things I don't, I'm still here because my heart keeps telling me to trust you."

There beneath the shading of the elm, he bared to her a soul darkened with a history of violence and iniquity. Solomon told her the painful truth about his past. The deaths of his parents, Akika, Dembe, and Mr. Mukasa. He told of the unimaginable things he did as a child soldier. He told her of the lives he'd taken or ruined under the profit of war. He spoke of her grandmother and the night in Brooklyn that he mercilessly avenged them both. Solomon confessed the litany of crimes he'd committed on Clay Freeman's behalf. He held nothing back even as she cried and trembled from the magnitude of his offenses. Through it all, she never let go of his hand. She never recoiled or ran away as he feared she might.

They talked for hours even as the park emptied and night moved slowly toward them. As he walked her back to her hotel in Times Square, they were once again silent. Solomon finally found the difficult words he'd been searching for long before they arrived under the bright lights of the hotel's awning.

"I know the things I told you today are scary. It certainly wasn't my intention to unburden so much on you, but you more than anyone I've ever met deserve to know me for everything that I am. It's the only honest way for me to say goodbye to you. I just wanna thank you for this week. You'll never know how much it's meant to me. Somehow, you've managed to give me a lifetime of great memories in just seven days."

Aisha stared at him as though searching for the right words. "The only thing that scares me about you, Solomon, is that I see light in you where you only see darkness. I see the love that's still in you, but it only really matters if you see it in yourself. You can't change who you were or what you've done, but you can change who you choose to be now. First thing you have to do is forgive yourself. If you ever plan on being happy, then you can't let the enemies from your past determine your future. They only truly win if you allow them to rule your heart." Even as her eyes watered, she tried to smile. "I've gotta admit this certainly wasn't the way I imagined us saying goodbye. Let me know if you ever decide that you're ready to live on more than just a week's worth of memories."

Aisha kissed him, then turned and headed inside the hotel lobby, leaving Solomon under the pale glare of the awning's fluorescent lighting.

He headed down Broadway among the herd of springtime pedestrians. Solomon ambled along with neither purpose nor destination. He simply walked. He walked from one avenue to the next. Up one street and then down another. There were blocks that he walked, then circled back aimlessly. He just needed to keep moving. Even at midnight, the streets of New York were still pulsating. Solomon walked for hours. He walked until time was nothing more than an afterthought. He would have walked forever if he could have because he knew the only thing awaiting him was a lonely apartment crowded with ghosts ready to steal his dreams of Aisha.

~

Even two weeks after she had returned to California, Solomon stumbled about in a sensate overload. The more he attempted to go about his days, the more he realized that the smells, sounds, and energy of the city all colluded with her hold over him. Everything summoned yet another memory of her. The distance that separated him and Aisha was ultimately inconsequential. Despite the fact that there were two thousand four hundred and fifty miles between them, he was still subject to the tyranny of her touch. Aisha was ever present, a constant reminder of her ownership over him. Every step he took and every corner he turned, he heard the echo of her final words to him. He saw her not just in the reflection of store windows and windshields but also in the face of every woman who passed him. Solomon felt the deepening void from the absence of her laughter. The vacancy of segments that only she had been able to fill. The sparkle of city lights was all but dimmed by the longing for her smile. He heard Aisha's voice over the honk of taxi cabs and street vendors. He smelled her in the air. Solomon still felt the warmth of her hand and her skin claiming his. Her head resting peacefully on his shoulder. He still tasted their last kiss.

In the very short time that he had known her, she had become the unimaginable. The unforeseeable arrival that disrupted the defective life that he had long ago accepted as his norm. Aisha left him wanting more for himself.

15
Michael

The minute Solomon opened his eyes, he was immediately reminded why Arrowhead had been such a special place for Callan. The quiet, mountain air allowed him to sleep much deeper than he was used to. It was the first time in years that he actually *enjoyed* his dreams. The memory of Aisha woke him with a smile. He had no idea what the day had in store for him, but he felt rested and somewhat at peace.

Solomon wasn't good at goodbyes. He knew that the morning would bring more questions hungry for greater details. Questions that he was uncomfortable answering. He hadn't bothered to mention to Margaret the fact that he'd left three corpses at her home and that the police were looking for him in connection to the shooting at the gardens. He hoped that there would be time enough later to explain everything to her.

He and Gaby left just before six when the dawn was still yawning and before there was any stirring in the cabin. After they made it down the mountain, Solomon connected to the Cajon Pass for a few miles before opting for street traffic instead of the freeway. The slower route added forty minutes to his drive, but he needed to take every precaution possible. The important thing was making it to McKinty's by nine. Once he was certain that the boy was safely on his way to Canada, then he could move more freely.

Callan was absolutely correct about Solomon being much better at hunting than being hunted. If he was in fact going to get to the bottom of whatever was going on, then he first needed to get the boy to safety so that he would be allowed to do what he did best. Solomon needed to avenge Doc Callan. He needed to give Margaret and her daughters back their lives. He cared very little what happened to himself after he accomplished those three things.

He arrived just after eight thirty, scouted the neighborhood twice, then parked a block and a half away from McKinty's office in an abandoned car lot. Knowing that McKinty was on Cesar Quintero's radar made Solomon a bit more cautious than on his previous visit.

"You're sending me away, aren't you?" Gaby asked. "I heard you tell that man yesterday."

"Yeah, he's gonna help find you a good family."

"Why can't I stay with you?"

"Because that's not possible."

"But I don't want to leave."

"Look, it's all for your own good. You gotta trust me."

"When I go away, does that mean I'll never see you again?"

"No, you won't."

"But you can come and visit me, can't you? Please."

"I can try."

"Promise me you'll come visit me."

When Solomon didn't respond right away, he saw the disappointment in the boy's face. "Let's just wait till you get settled, and we'll see what happens. Right now, I need you to jump in the back and hide on the floor until I come back. I shouldn't be gone for more than fifteen minutes. I need to go check to make sure it's safe. You're gonna do exactly as I say, right? Not like at the gas station, okay."

"Yes."

"Yes what?"

"Yes, I'm gonna do exactly as you say and stay here."

"Okay, thank you."

As Gaby moved toward the rear, he unexpectedly hugged Solomon. After a few seconds, he released him, then climbed between the two seats and curled up on the floor in the back.

Solomon adjusted the rearview mirror and stared at the small figure. He could still feel the warmth of the small boy's arms wrapped tightly around him. Aisha had been the last to hug him, the last to leave him feeling that he truly mattered. It was now the smile and hug of a relative stranger that moved him in a similar way. He sat silently for a minute more, watching the boy in all his stillness, before exiting the vehicle and locking the doors.

Solomon walked the back alley behind the office building. He climbed on a dumpster and lifted himself to the fire escape. He walked up the three flights to the window in McKinty's office, which was open, as it had been the day before. He carefully peeked around the corner of the window frame and through the billowing sheers. Because his view was partially obscured by a post, all he saw of McKinty were his legs dangling eight feet above his desk with a pool of blood beneath him.

Solomon took his gun out and attached his suppressor. He peered again through the open window and saw the ambush that awaited him. There were three men, two at opposite sides of the office, hiding behind partitions, and the third near McKinty's corpse. All three had their guns drawn and were so focused on their anticipation of Solomon coming through the front door that they never heard the menace in the soft breeze behind them.

The first of the three men found out firsthand why Solomon was nicknamed the Black Reaper, the Darkness, and even on one or two occasions the Winter Ghost. The man neither saw nor heard the approach of death. It was just suddenly upon him like an unexpected storm on a wintry night. By the time his two accomplices heard the body fall, the ghost had clipped the bigger of the two in the shooting arm and the younger one in the leg. He crossed to them and kicked their guns away. He dragged the younger one over to the other so that they were now side by side. Solomon said nothing, just glared at the two men, sizing them up. He watched them as they bled. The older man was much more hardened. The other was no more than twenty. Solomon saw menace in the eyes of the older man and fear in the younger one. Still, he said nothing as he pointed his gun at the elder of the two and killed him. Blood sprayed on both Solomon and the young man, who jerked back and started visibly shaking.

"What's your name?" Solomon asked.

"Michael."

Solomon pointed at the dead body. "Michael, I'm hoping that helps eliminate any doubt about what I'll do to you if you don't tell me what I need to know. Do we understand each other?"

The terrified young man nodded.

"I need to hear you say it," Solomon demanded.

"I…we understand each other."

"Good. What does Cesar want with the boy?"

"He needs him for the Skinny Lady."

"What are you talking about? Who the hell is the Skinny Lady?"

"Santa Muerte. She's the one Cesar prays to. A lot of the narcos do. He says she protects him and made him rich. I heard he's followed Santa Muerte for a long time, but they say that six months ago, after his son died, Cesar went crazy and started thinking that somehow the Skinny Lady could bring him back."

"What does that have to do with the boy?"

Michael hesitated, afraid to tell.

"I said, what does that have to do with the boy?" Solomon pressed.

"Cesar thinks that if he offers the Skinny Lady the right thing, she'll bring his son back to him. He said something about finding a pure soul that he could trade for his son. He thinks it's the boy."

Now that the truth had been bared before him, Solomon still struggled under the heft of making sense of what he viewed as nothing more than the mumbo jumbo of black magic.

"Take out your phone," Solomon commanded.

Michael writhed in pain but complied.

"Now call your boss. FaceTime him," Solomon said.

After the third ring, Cesar Quintero's face appeared on the phone. "Do you have the boy?"

Solomon bent over and took the phone.

"No, he doesn't have the boy, but just like you, he's got a world of problems coming his way. I wanted to see your face so that I know who I'm looking for," Solomon said.

"You're only making me think of more creative ways to kill you," Cesar responded calmly.

"Well, whatever you come up with, you should hope you're more successful than the men you've already sent, including your brother."

Though it took considerable effort, Cesar managed to control his temper. He resisted being baited by Solomon. "You have something that belongs to me," he said.

"All I have for you is a lot of pain and a little bit of advice. The dead stay dead. I don't care whatever black magic nonsense you think can change that fact. You're mistaken. When I come for you, you'll know just how right I am."

He hung up the phone, powered it off, then smashed it underfoot.

"How do I find him?" Solomon asked a terrified Michael.

"You don't wanna go after him. He's very dangerous."

"So am I. How do I find him?"

"I only know that he lives in Del Mar just outside San Diego. I've never been allowed to go there, so I don't know the exact location."

"The only reason you're still breathing is because I need information. Is that all that you have to offer?"

As Solomon pointed his gun at Michael's head, the young man wet himself. He panicked and nodded at the dead man next to him. "I overheard Victor say that Cesar goes to the All Saints Cemetery in Del Mar every morning to visit his son. Victor also said the boy is in the biggest mausoleum he's ever seen. Cesar's always got a lot of guards with him though."

Solomon stared at the young man as though he were trying to decide the manner in which he wanted to kill him. As far as the rules of engagement went, Solomon kept them simple. Paramount among them was to leave no enemy standing. Michael knew what little use he was had now expired.

Solomon looked back at McKinty's corpse, which hung from a steel rafter. He finally saw the totality of the torture done to his body. The broken bones and multiple stab wounds. He saw the horrible death of yet another man who had tried to help.

"Did you help them kill him? And don't lie to me," Solomon demanded.

"No, I didn't, but they made me watch because they said I would have to help do the same to you. I had no choice. One of my brothers got into trouble with some really bad people. When Cesar threatened to kill him I promised I would do anything to work off what Cesar says he's owed. I couldn't just stand by and let him kill my family."

Solomon heard the pain in the young man's voice. He thought back to when he was a child and the fate of his entire bloodline was in the hands of callous men with a violent disregard for the sanctity of life. He survived his childhood by making the choice of becoming what he hated in them—a taker of lives. It was possible that Michael was there simply to save his brother. It was also possible that he was there as a result of untenable choices he had made in some desperate pursuit of manhood. Whatever the reason, both roads led to his impending death.

As Solomon looked at Michael, he saw in his eyes the same thing he had seen in the scores of men he'd killed. The all-consuming fear. Much like Michael's dead accomplice with the defiant eyes, Solomon had never been afforded the humility of fear. It was simple mathematics to him—in order for one to fear dying, one had to first value living. He couldn't even remember what fear was until he met Gaby. He was more afraid for the boy's life than he had ever been for his own. Solomon was around

Gaby's age the last time he could recall believing in the purity of a soul.

He held his gun in Michael's face. "I'm just curious. If you could somehow do everything over, what would you do?"

Michael looked at Solomon and the gun pointed toward him. He answered with the only thing he could think of.

"I'd always choose to do whatever I had to do to protect my family. I'm just sorry that I didn't get to make it back home to them," Michael said.

"We don't all get to go home. Close your eyes."

"Please don't…"

"I said close your eyes. It is what it is for men like us. We make our choices, and we live and die by them."

As Solomon looked at him blankly, Michael began weeping. "Please, I have a family. I have parents, brothers and sisters. Please, my wife, Isabel, and son, Mateo, they need me. I'm begging you for their sake."

Solomon still showed no emotion. "This is the last time I tell you to close your eyes."

Michael did his best to stop crying, to die at least with a rumor of dignity.

As Solomon stared at him, he saw the young man more for what he used to be than what he was. Michael was no longer the son to his mother and father or the brother to his siblings. He was no longer the husband to Isabel or the father to Mateo. When death claimed a victim, it did so with no regard for title or designation. There was only the remembrance of all that they were and all that they ever hoped to be. Solomon knew the same would be true the day death came to claim him.

When Michael finally opened his eyes, he was all alone in a room full of the dead. The Black Reaper's disappearance was no different from his arrival. He was the silent breeze that was there one moment and gone the next.

Not that Solomon needed any more motivation to hunt down and kill Cesar, but the murder of McKinty definitely stoked the fire within him. Nothing could stop him from avenging Doc Callan as well as McKinty. If need be, he would kill an army for his claim of retribution. He'd done it before and was certainly up to the task of doing it again.

Solomon knew everything there was to know about revenge. Over the years, it had become a part of his DNA. He had been weaned on it since the tender age of seven.

16

The Warrior

UGANDA 1972

ACHOLI REGION

At seven years old, Solomon was forever stained with the blood of his parents on his hands. After the soldiers took him, it was two days before he learned the full name of the man with the thunder voice who commanded the massacre of his entire village. The soldier who made him kill his mother and father was named Jaffar Okello. The twelve soldiers under his command addressed him simply as Sergeant O. He was a large man in both carriage and character with an unwavering loyalty to Amin, the Lord of All Beasts. Similar to his hero, he had a soul that was endlessly dark. His cruelty knew no bounds. He delighted himself most in the misery of the Acholi people. He regarded the boy as nothing more than an amusing stray.

Okello used every opportunity there was to remind Solomon that he was no king but rather a pet, a dutiful creature that had to readily do his masters' bidding. Solomon fetched their food even as his stomach cramped in hunger. He shined their boots even as the shoeless soles of his feet cracked from their calluses. The boy was beaten with no provocation. He bled but endured the brutality of their whims. No matter the severity, he shed not one stubborn tear. And then there was the aching isolation. He was so lonely a child that the closest things he had to friends, with whom to share his deepest fears and anguish, were the sun, moon, and wind.

Some of the soldiers placed wagers on being able to break Solomon, whom they often referred to as the boy who had forgotten how to cry. What they couldn't quite grasp was that he had used up a lifetime of tears the day of his parents' murder. He cried until his heart dried; then he wept no more. In the weeks that followed, neither nightmare nor vivid recollection of the horrors he saw that day replenished the depleted wells within him.

Solomon spoke no more to Allah. He no longer had use for him or any of his kind. There was no divinity that could offer him what he needed most. He knelt each night, not before a god but rather at the altar of retribution. He was but seven and already godless. Solomon steeled himself with the darkness of his masters. When they beat him for mere recreation, he fed on their hatred. He fashioned himself after their soullessness.

Solomon waited as he learned their ways. He studied what he could from the shadows of his servitude. He cleaned their guns and sharpened their knives. He waited. He lulled them to sleep with bottles of waragi that they guzzled in celebration of their latest massacre. He eavesdropped on their conversations as he washed the blood from their uniforms. As they lay drunk and snoring, he watched over them many a night, much like a young wolf eyeing a flock of oblivious sheep.

He simply waited.

~

After a few months, Okello and his soldiers grew bored of using Solomon as a whipping boy. If nothing else, he had proven himself a worthy servant. He was obedient and submissive, which was the only type of Acholi pet worth having. When they realized that he had neither fear nor feeling, they started teaching him. He learned quickly. They taught him how to hunt, how to fire weapons, how to swing the blade of a machete. They made it clear to him that if he couldn't prove himself in the task of killing, they had no use for him.

In six months' time, they had him shedding the blood of his own people. He learned. He waited. He learned more. It took him a full four years before he felt ready. Before he felt strong enough. Smart enough. Empty enough of the innocence that once defined him.

He waited until the fourth anniversary of his parents' murder, which was also his eleventh birthday. Okello and his men raided a small village of nearly eighty in the hills on the outskirts of Amuru. They killed everything that moved—men, women, children, and beasts. They slaughtered not just the living but the not yet conceived. Both progeny and ancestors were eradicated. All that they had been and all that they would be simply perished in the ether, much like dust in the most violent of winds.

Solomon didn't kill that day. It was the first time in four years that he defied the orders of his masters. When no one was looking, he managed to free a boy and a girl, both around his age, who had run off in the woods when the killings started. He wet his machete with the blood of an old man's corpse in pretense of a kill or two. The soldiers were too preoccupied in the slaughter to notice Solomon's deceit. He did not kill that day, but he knew when night called, he would have his fill. He would honor his parents like a true Acholi warrior and paint the moon red with the blood of their enemies.

They pitched camp just a few miles from the massacre. As they sat by the fire, they regaled one another with stories of the day's events, each soldier trying to one-up the others in their number of kills and sexual conquests. The majority of them were at least a few years older than Solomon, but for the most part, they were mere babes themselves, weaned on raping, maiming, and killing. Soldiers were taught to take. Though they were desperate to be men, they were nothing more than a misguided gang of boys under the tutelage of violent men who never even knew the tenderness of a willing woman.

Solomon filled and refilled their cups, especially that of Sergeant Okello. He plied them all with copious amounts of waragi until their speech slurred and their eyes were nothing more than glassy slits reflecting the fire's glow.

When the soldiers grew too drunk for their own boasting, the night was silenced save for the crackle of the dying flames. Just after midnight, the camp was filled with the drunken snores of monsters.

Of the original thirteen that massacred Solomon's village, only two had been replaced. One had died of sepsis and the other hanged himself in the second winter of his abduction. Solomon had studied the group well. He knew the strongest and the weakest among them. The fastest and the slowest. He knew who slept the hardest and who could hold their liquor the least. They had taught him over two dozen ways of taking lives. Ever the diligent student, Solomon learned quickly the art of the kill. He knew well the delicate construction of the human body. There were just as many ways to kill quickly as there were to prolong the agony of dying. When he gathered their knives and machetes to clean, he knew which ones sliced air and flesh with comparable ease.

He stole the soldier's handguns so when they awoke, it would be to empty holsters. Okello's pistol felt the most natural in his clutch. Whereas the gun had once sagged in the hands of a frightened child, he now held the weapon with the fortitude of a seasoned soldier.

The first four kills required the most precision because he started with the lightest of the sleepers. He covered his victim's mouths and quickly punctured their temples with the blade of a large hunting knife. Although the boy weighed all of seventy-eight pounds, he descended on them like the most brutal of plagues—silent, quick, and fatal. None of the first victims had time nor option to scream.

The next several kills were relatively easier. He positioned himself over his victims and swung a machete down on exposed necks as though he were chopping firewood. Gravity. Precision. One blow per kill. He moved about the camp as silent as moonrise, hovering above one soldier after the next. All that was heard of him were the dull thuds of his revenge, followed by stillness and the steady flow of blood.

He had killed just over half a dozen soldiers when two of the sleeping men stirred from their drunken comas. Solomon discarded the blades and pulled Okello's stolen handgun from his waistband. The two targets the boy aimed for most were heads and hearts. As the soldiers woke and scurried for defense, Solomon dropped them one by one until he and Sergeant Okello were the last of the living.

Solomon shot his former tormentor once in each leg and each arm to render him immobile. He then took his time exacting his revenge. The student became the teacher, the servant the master. The boy showed Okello all that he had been taught about pain. He started with the blades, then tools, then fire. Each act of torture was worse than its predecessor. When the man was beyond resuscitation, beyond enduring any more agony, when only a crumb of life remained for the boy to take from him, Solomon shot him first in the head, then the chest, more precisely in that vacant labyrinth of where a heart may or may not have once dwelled. Okello died that day in a variety of ways.

~

By the time the embers had cooled in the nascent light of sunrise, Okello and his soldiers' corpses were already stiffening. Their cold bodies warmed under the first rays of early morn when the sun and moon shared the sky in equal parts.

Solomon looked out toward the hills at the dawning of a new day. His clothes and skin were stained with the blood of those who had defiled his mother and dishonored his father. He stood among the butchered remains of murderers and rapists. Solomon came to his enemies as an orphaned boy but left them as a man of vengeance. He left them as the son of proud Acholis.

Wisps of dust trailed behind him. The boy trudged many a grueling mile under an unforgiving sun that baked his dark skin until he glistened like crude oil. Solomon heard the desperate echoes of weeping widows and fatherless children. He passed the burned fields and aphyllous branches of charred trees. The air reeked of the rotting carcasses of livestock and the defenseless farmers who had tended them. Beyond the hills, the skies were made gray from the smoke of distant fires.

Although much of the arable lands had been scorched and ravaged by Amin's soldiers, Solomon thought the Acholi region was still inexpressibly beautiful. He walked the endless landscape by way of the emerald-colored fields and down the dusty slopes of untarred roads. When his feet blistered and he grew too tired to continue, he rested under the cool shade of a tamarind tree. Solomon's eyes scanned the valleys of the majestic hills that were blanketed in lush flora. He took in the pastoral vistas that stretched far beyond the limits of his eyes. He marveled too at the trees that were taller than his imagination.

He reached the banks of the Ayugi River just after noon. There he washed his clothes and bathed himself in the waters of his ancestors. Even though it had only been four years since the death of his family along with Akika and Dembe, it seemed like a lifetime ago when he had played naked on the very same shores. Everybody and everything of importance to him was now gone. There on the banks of the Ayugi, Solomon knew he had to leave the only world that he had ever known. He had no village to return to. No loving arms left to welcome him back to his former life. No parents to teach him how to be but a carefree child again. At the ripe young age of eleven years old and the last of his bloodline, Solomon had to leave the land that he loved and go as far away as he could to escape the long reach of Amin's wrath.

Although Solomon's only skill set was soldiering, Okello had taught him that there was never a shortage of wars in the world. There would always be need of men who could kill.

At eleven years old, Solomon was five foot two and not yet eighty pounds, but he was still every bit the ruthless soldier. He traveled for miles caked in mud, blood, and dust, always in search of more warfare. The theater of war was plentiful throughout the lands of Africa. Solomon followed the blood, for where there was blood, there was money to be made. The lonely boy traveled from one African nation to the next, killing for the highest bidder. He was bound not by honor nor allegiance. He was slave to neither religion nor politics. Okello and his soldiers had robbed the boy of all the things precious to him and left in their stead a trade for killing.

There was no conflict too small for him. Solomon killed in tribal wars as readily as he did infamous coups d'état. He fought for idealistic secessionists as easily as he did for avaricious warlords. He fought on the side of the oppressed one month and the side of kleptocrats the next.

The money wasn't much. Human lives were quite cheap in times of war. He saved what he could of his meager earnings. Although his soldiering and mercenary work didn't pay much, it at least gave him something to build on. Though it took him six years and numerous wars, he managed to scrape together half the smuggler's fare on a cargo freight ship owned by the Russian underworld. He made a deal to work off the other half once he made it to America. At seventeen years old, he left his beloved Africa for what he hoped to be a more normal existence.

The cargo ship was huge. To a skinny farm boy who'd never seen anything quite like it, the vessel felt like a world unto itself. The giant containers, the steel bowels of the ship, and even the beefy men who served as the crew all easily dwarfed him. After two and a half weeks of seasickness and grueling labor, they finally made it to New York. After the right bribes were paid and the right customs agents looked the other way, Solomon walked off the huge ship, wide-eyed and sporting a tattered T-shirt, dingy shorts, and a set of ashen knees, eager to start a new life.

17

Land of Opportunity

NEW YORK 1982

Unlike most immigrants who came to America, Solomon did so with no disillusionment. He held no outdated fantasy of landing on the banks of Ellis Island and being welcomed into the benevolent arms of Lady Liberty. He never felt entitled to such dreams, knowing that he'd snuck into America through the back door. He came to the United States indebted to the Russian mob. He came not because of aspirations of wealth and success or because of a desire to stake a claim in the American dream. Solomon's reasoning was much more rudimentary. America was the other side of the world. He came with the hopes of putting as much distance as possible between himself and the ghosts of his victims. Solomon knew as long as he stayed in the land of his crimes, the hauntings would continue to come for him as they had from the beginning. Though he had lost count long ago of how many he had killed, the ghosts came en masse every night to make sure he remembered each of their shining, black, tear-streaked faces frozen in anguish. Solomon came to America because he would never have peace in the land of his father. He came to disappear.

~

In the '80s, the streets of New York proved to be paved not in gold but rather in the rainbow-colored caps of empty crack vials. Though he knew not a soul in Brooklyn or the whole of New York for that matter, Solomon migrated to Bedford-Stuyvesant, hoping to live an anonymous life in the segregated neighborhood populated by descendants of the motherland. He immediately enrolled in night courses and worked hard to lose his heavy accent. All he wanted to do was fit in, so he did what he could to assimilate. His efforts were in vain, though, because even in a sea of melanated people, Solomon was still the darkest among them. In his homeland, the shade of his skin was the celebrated norm, but in America, it was just an excuse to treat him like an alien, particularly by many of his African American counterparts. None of them even bothered to learn his name; they simply called him "the African." He was laughed at and teased as though he were an oddity of color and culture. He found insult wherever he turned. Even the old men on the corner, drinking away their souls, looked upon him with scorn as they chuckled aloud about "the boy who was as black as half past midnight in the bleakest of winters." It stung him to no end that the most virulent discrimination he encountered came from those whom he considered distant kin.

The one exception was the landlady who rented him the SRO above a fish fry spot she owned on Nostrand Avenue. Her name was Ida Gant. A cantankerous, foul-mouthed woman from Alabama who told him that the people who mocked him were *ignant ass niggas* that had no pride and knew nothing of their own ancestry. It wasn't that she was especially kind to Solomon; she just wasn't as cruel to him as the rest of the world.

In between the menial errands he ran for the Russians to pay toward the rest of his passage fare, he did odd jobs for her around the building. Solomon was a quick learner who in no time became her personal plumber, electrician, and all-around maintenance man. Several times a week, she gave him the leftover fried fish that languished in warming bins at closing time. She invited him the first Sunday of every month for an actual home-cooked meal. She made him soul food and introduced him to ginger beer.

Despite the fact that she was technically old enough to be his grandmother or even that most people dismissed her as nothing more than an ornery old cuss of a woman, Ida became the closest thing to a friend that he had had since he was seven years old. Solomon got to see parts of her that the rest of the world couldn't. She exposed him to all types of books and authors and helped him to develop a voracious appetite for reading. Although he loved how she was both witty and irreverent, his favorite thing about her was that she was absolutely fearless. He'd witnessed on several occasions her verbal evisceration of tenants, cops, neighbors, and even local drug dealers with some of the most colorful language he had ever heard. The objects of her ire learned to simply avoid her as much as possible. All except a young Jamaican named Cappy.

He was a drug dealer with long dreads and thick, gold jewelry. He and his crew started selling crack in front of the fish fry four months after Solomon moved in. Ida clashed with them frequently. She argued with them, threatened to throw hot fish grease on them one moment and then called the cops on them the next. She even stood in front of her place of business with a bullhorn, chanting for all the neighborhood to hear that they were drug dealers peddling death to the community. They left but always came back. Cappy threatened her, and when that didn't stop her from publicly haranguing him and his crew, they resorted to violence. First by smashing the windows of the fish joint, then one night by actually assaulting her. Though the perpetrators hid their faces with balaclavas, she knew without a doubt who they were, especially the one with dreadlocks peeking out the sides of his hoodie. After she was backhanded a couple of times and thrown to the ground, he was the one who stood over her and warned her of even greater violence if she didn't learn to keep her mouth shut.

"Me not care dat you're an old woman. Ya feel me? You open your mouth against us one more time, it will be the last ting ya ever say. Trust dat."

Two days later when Ida was released from the hospital with a broken collarbone and bruised ribs, Solomon refused to let her go unescorted whenever she ventured outdoors. She and the drug dealers immediately went back to doing what they each did best—them selling drugs and her publicly harassing them for doing so. Both sides were vehemently undeterred. For her part, Ida even stepped it up a notch. She not only loudly harassed the drug dealers but their customers as well. A few of the other neighbors even joined in, which eventually slowed the transactions by half.

Cappy countered. True to his word, the next time he approached Ida and Solomon, it was with far more violence. Cappy and five members of his crew ambushed Ida and Solomon walking home from the local laundromat one evening. Solomon fought, but he was poorly outnumbered and outmuscled. As they held him down, the figure with the dreadlocks knelt before him. Solomon recognized the Jamaican accent right away as well as the voice that called everybody "Star."

"Let me tell ya sumtin, Star. You ever raise your hand to me or my crew again and I'll be sending your black ass back to Africa in four different boxes. Ya feel me?"

Even after he took out a large blade to illustrate his point, Solomon showed no signs of fear. As he stared at Cappy unblinking and unafraid, he refused to respond. Cappy simply smiled and nodded at his boys, who forced Solomon's left hand open while Cappy sliced off both his middle and ring finger. They then beat Solomon unconscious while the other men restrained Ida and muffled her cries.

When Solomon awoke a few minutes later, he found Ida sprawled on the ground face down among the scattered laundry. Cappy and his crew were gone. Solomon saw the woman's hand move as he hurried to her side. The bit of solace that he found in knowing she was still alive was short-lived when he turned her over and saw that her face, particularly the area around her mouth, was covered in blood. Just as the men had taken his two fingers from him, they had taken Ida's tongue from her.

He knew the reason Cappy chose not to kill them. He wanted to send a daily message to the community, reminding people visually what happened to those who spoke against them or dared raise a finger in their direction.

Ida was hospitalized for two weeks. Although her family had flown in from California to be with her, Solomon pleaded that he be the one to pick her up from the hospital, which Ida endorsed. Despite it being hospital policy for an orderly to wheel discharged patients to the exit, Solomon insisted that he do it. Aside from his greeting to Ida, he said very little else as he pushed her in her wheelchair. He needed to be behind her so that he didn't have to look at her directly. Solomon found it difficult seeing her as well as being seen by her. Not because of the heavy bandaging or the thoughts of her disfigurement but more so because of the shame he felt in failing to protect her from the attack. As he wheeled her down the shiny halls, he listened to the doctor's instructions for Ida's care and rehabilitation. After thanking the doctor, Solomon said nothing as he and Ida made their way toward the exit.

As soon as their cab pulled away from the hospital, he placed a *New York Post* in her lap. The front-page story was about six decapitated Brooklyn drug dealers who were found in an abandoned building in Bed-Stuy. Their tongues had all been removed. Solomon didn't speak to her the entire ride home; he just rested his one good hand on hers and looked out the window. Though she couldn't see his actual injuries, he felt her staring at his bandaged hand. When he finally turned to her, he saw in her eyes the regret of a night that had scarred them both for life. Ida didn't bother to read the article in detail because she knew far more than what was printed. Solomon didn't need to speak or look at her because as far as she was concerned, he had done all that needed to be done.

~

It didn't take long for the lore of the African to take root. Although he never publicly or even privately for that matter claimed the bodies of the drug dealers, Brooklyn made a legend of him nonetheless. He was mythologized through fantastical urban tales quickly born of supposition and weaned on imagination. The stories were told and retold each time with just enough embellishment to cement his folklore throughout the five boroughs of New York for years to come. People feared and respected him without him even having said one word confirming what they steadfastly believed to be true. Overnight, he went from being a boy who was openly mocked because of the blackness of his skin to a giant who was universally feared.

It was a lot having so much hoisted on the shoulders of the then seventeen-year-old. His infamy even got the attention of Clay Freeman, a notorious gangster from Harlem. Clay paid off twice the amount of Solomon's debts to the Russians, then quickly recruited the boy as a bagman, then all-around fixer and eventually his personal bodyguard and consiglieri.

Solomon never wanted the attention. He never wanted the instant reputation. He'd only hoped to live a life of anonymity in America. A quiet, unassuming life where he no longer killed or saw the faces of those whose lives he had taken. He dreamed of living so quietly that if the ghosts came looking for him, they wouldn't be able to find him. He was wrong on all accounts. Once he killed the drug dealers, the ghosts came back.

18

Odyssey

Gaby stared at Solomon as he got back in the van and sped away from McKinty's office.

"Is everything okay? Are you bringing me to another family?" Gaby asked.

"Not just yet."

Gaby looked at the specks of blood on the cuff of Solomon's shirt. "Did you hurt someone?"

"Yeah, people who were trying to hurt me."

"Did you kill them?"

"Just the ones who needed to be killed."

Gaby looked out the window, quiet.

Solomon glanced over at him. "Should I have just let them kill me?"

Gaby continued staring out the window with nothing to say.

When Solomon stopped at a red light, he pulled his phone out and started searching for information until he found the Wikipedia page for Santa Muerte, a.k.a. the Skinny Lady.

Nuestra Señora de la Santa Muerte (Spanish for Our Lady of Holy Death), often shortened to Santa Muerte, is a cult image, female deity, and folk saint in Mexican folk Catholicism and Neo-paganism. A personification of death, she is associated with healing, protection, and safe delivery to the afterlife by her devotees.

Even as he drove, he dug a little more on other sites and found references to unofficial practices of animal and even in rare instances human sacrifices, but that seemed much more an exception than the norm. From all that he had heard about Cesar, the narco definitely leaned more toward the exception than the norm.

Solomon drove down the 118 to the 405 south toward San Diego.

They made a pit stop at a place called the Odyssey Gun Shop in Long Beach. The owner, a lanky Latino sporting cornrows, a pair of surfer shorts, and two prosthetic legs, was assisting another customer when Solomon and Gaby walked in.

"Be with you in a sec," the owner said.

Solomon strolled the two aisles of the small shop as Gaby trailed behind him.

As the owner finished up with his customer, who then exited, he called out to Solomon, "How can I help you?"

Solomon approached the counter. "Are you Raphael?"

"If I'm not, then that means my mother and my old man have

been lying to me all this time. Either way, everybody just calls me Ralph. What can I do you for?"

"I'm a friend of Doc Callan. He always told me that if I was ever out this way and needed anything that you were the one to come to."

"How is Doc?"

"He's, uh… He's not with us anymore."

"Are you kidding me? I just saw him a month ago. How…"

"Let's just say he ran into a very bad situation with a guy named Cesar Quintero."

Ralph took the death hard, the details harder.

"Yeah, I've heard of him. S'posed to be a real evil son of a bitch." He looked at Gaby and said, "Sorry about that, kid."

"I'm on my way to settle up things with him now. That's why I'm here," Solomon said.

"Doc was a good man."

"Yes, he was."

"You tell me whatever you need, and it's yours."

"For starters, how about a McMillan TAC 50 with a scope, suppressor, and ammo? I could also use a couple of magazines for a Colt M1911 and some binocs."

"I like your choices. You and Doc both know good hardware. Give me a sec. I've got some goodies in the back that I think you'll like."

As Ralph disappeared behind a steel-plated door, Solomon looked down at Gaby. "Look, some stuff has to happen that I know you aren't gonna be good with. Whether you understand it or not, no more questions or lectures, all right?"

Gaby just looked at him and nodded.

Solomon added, “This man won’t stop until he finds you, no matter where you go. I need to make sure that doesn’t happen and that you don’t have to worry about that.”

They waited for a few minutes before Ralph came out with a sports bag and the McMillan TAC 50 in a rifle sleeve.

“The rifle is clean, can’t trace it. By the way, I threw in a vest just in case you want or need it,” Ralph said.

“Thanks. How much do I owe you?” Solomon asked.

“I can’t take your money, especially considering what you plan on doing with this. When I got back from Afghanistan almost fifteen years ago with no legs and no job, Doc was the one who recommended I open this place, and he fronted me most of the money. This is the least I can do, trust me.”

“I appreciate it. Thank you. Listen, I’ve got one more favor to ask. I need a quiet crash spot for a day or two, not too far from the San Diego area while I scout things out.”

“The only thing I know of is about an hour outside San Diego.”

“That’s fine. I can make that work. Look, I have to be straight with you. I’m all over the news, so I’ve got some heat on me. I need someone who is reliable and discreet,” Solomon responded.

“I get it. I know two sisters, the Cassiel twins, who run a clean three-star that’s off the grid. It’s out of the way, that’s for sure, but I suspect that’s exactly what you’re looking for.”

“Yes,” Solomon agreed.

“It’s just the two of them, and they’re both pretty discreet. If I were in a jam, I’d trust these women with my life. I consider them family. You'll be good there. I promise. I'll call ahead and give them a heads-up."

Solomon and Gaby ordered a couple of burgers, fries, and shakes from an In-N-Out drive-through. They sat in the nearly empty parking lot, eating their food. Gaby scoffed down two burgers back-to-back as though he were a child who had never been permitted to indulge in fast food. He seemed particularly fond of the french fries.

As he watched Gaby devour his food, Solomon wondered about the boy's childhood. He had clearly been raised well by his father. He was a gentle child who was mature yet innocent. He was bright, sensitive, and polite. Gaby had endured the weight of the unthinkable in the last couple of days, and he seemed resiliently intact. He still smiled with the pure joy derived from downing a chocolate milkshake. The boy drank so fast that he involuntarily belched. Gaby looked mortified as he immediately turned toward Solomon and apologized.

"I'm sorry. I didn't mean to..."

"It's okay, Gaby. It happens."

"But I..."

"It's fine. Really. Did you know that in some cultures, it's considered rude if you *don't* belch after a good meal?"

"Really?"

"Yes, really."

Both to the boy's surprise and amusement, Solomon belched

loudly. He then looked at him as though he were offering a challenge to try to outdo him. Gaby hesitated at first, but after a little goading, he sipped his milkshake and released a belch that would have made even a drunken cowboy proud. They went a couple more rounds before Solomon conceded and declared Gaby the victor.

The simple act of being silly did Solomon good. It had been years since he had laughed as hard. The more he looked at his young sidekick, the more he roared at their childish antics and sheer abandon. The van was filled with the smell of burgers and fries and the bellows of hearty laughter.

~

The afternoon traffic on the 405 was just beginning to thicken. Solomon exited onto Oceanside and made his way to the All Saints Cemetery. He never did a job without thoroughly scouting it first. He slowly drove the property, making mental note of all entrances and exits as well as the vantage points. After driving all the vehicle paths that were open to the public, he parked atop a large hill that allowed him to see not just the main entrance but much of the land below. It was the largest cemetery he had ever seen. As far as he could tell, it was close to two thousand acres.

The cemetery was situated in such a way that much of the property looked toward an unobstructed view of the Pacific Ocean, a design that was clearly more for those still among the living than the sea of those who were deceased. There were acres of flat stones, traditional headstones, mausoleums, twelve-foot statues of angels with extended wings, and even private garden sites behind walls of hedges.

Solomon saw a smattering of mourners at various grave sites. There were couples, singles, and small groups of loved ones paying their respects to their dearly departed. Some came with flowers, some with tears, some with both. The populace was diverse in all ways. There was no racial, gender, or socioeconomic divide. As was the case in the vast majority of cemeteries, death and desegregation went hand in hand.

Solomon scanned the cemetery with his binoculars until he found the largest mausoleum and confirmed it was in fact the son of Cesar Quintero by the brass plaque that hung by the front entrance. He stayed for an hour or so, mapping out the lay of the land. There were three different funerals taking place at various points. He paid particular attention to the thirty or so bereaved who were gathered around the small casket of a child being lowered into the excavated plot.

Gaby watched Solomon as his eyes grew damp and he seemed to drift a thousand miles away.

"Is everything okay?" the boy asked.

"Yeah," Solomon lied.

The truth was that cemeteries were hard on him for a myriad of reasons that pecked at him like a murder of hungry crows. If this was the best opportunity to kill Cesar, then it was a torment worth enduring, because he was more than willing to go to hell and back to protect the boy and avenge Doc Callan and McKinty.

He and Gaby sat in his van high upon the hill overlooking

the valley of the dead. The tombstones looked as if they stretched for miles. Every inch of the place merely reminded Solomon how much he hated cemeteries. Hated the voices of the unliving that cried out to him. He heard not just his mother and father but also the masses of Acholi people butchered so many years ago under the rule of Idi Amin. The most piercing cries of all were from the ghosts whose lives he himself had taken.

19

The Church

As Solomon started the van and headed toward the cemetery's main exit, he looked up at the rain-bearing clouds that hovered in the sky as though they were contemplating when to empty themselves.

Spring was only two weeks young, so the sun was still accustomed to the winter hours that lured its descent in the six o'clock hour. They got back on the freeway at the tail end of dusk. The traffic had worsened. Cars were kissing hood to trunk as they crept like metal snails, progressing more by inches than miles. A stretch of bright brake lights glowed on the darkening roads as far as the eye could see.

After a couple of failed attempts to start a conversation, Gaby played with the radio, trying to find a station that might lighten the heavy mood that Solomon had fallen into when they watched the tiny casket disappear into the ground. The smooth jazz station did nothing. As Gaby landed on an old-school R and B station, he noticed that Solomon lightly tapped his thumb on the steering wheel to the beat of Prince's song "Controversy." It wasn't much, but still Gaby smiled when Solomon glanced in his direction. By the time the song "Jump Around" by House of Pain came on, the two were equally enjoying their private jam session.

As the traffic opened up and started flowing, Solomon was doing just over sixty when he heard the rear passenger side tire blow out. As they swerved into another lane and cars honked, he instinctively reached out his hand to protect Gaby. Once he regained full control of the van, he cautiously made his way over to the shoulder of the freeway.

"Are you okay?"

"Yes, I'm fine," the boy answered.

Solomon put on his hazards and exited the van to inspect the damage. It hadn't quite started raining yet; rather it was still in the misting stage. As he pulled out the spare and started hoisting the rear of the vehicle with his jack, Gaby got out and approached him.

"Get back in the van, Gaby."

"Can I help you?"

"I've got it."

"Please," the boy pushed.

"I would but it's not safe. I'll tell you what you can do though."

"What's that?"

Solomon started removing the flat tire. "Turn up the radio, and leave your door open. You can stay out here with me, but I need you to wait on the other side of the guardrail. Is that a deal?"

"Okay."

Gaby walked back to the passenger side of the van, feeling neither victorious nor defeated. He did as he was told and turned up the radio, then went and stood five feet behind the guardrail as he watched Solomon change the tire. Classic songs of the past played one after the other. Gaby certainly wasn't much of a dancer, yet he moved unabashedly, eyes closed, head bobbing. He danced slightly out of sync with the music, to the sounds of the Average White Band's "Pick Up the Pieces."

As Solomon secured the last of the lug nuts and lowered the jack, he couldn't help but laugh at Gaby's free spirit despite the fact that the boy was rhythmically challenged. When he was done, Solomon crossed over to him.

"You ready?" he asked.

"Can you dance, Solomon?"

"No."

"How come?"

"How come what?"

"How come you can't dance?"

"I don't know, kid. I guess I just never took the time to learn how. Let's go."

"Can I finish first? The song's almost over."

"We should go," Solomon insisted.

"How about if you dance with me first, then we go?"

"I told you, Gaby, I don't dance."

"All you have to do is move. If you give it a try, then we'll go. I promise I won't laugh."

Solomon thought it funny that the boy who had no rhythmic ability was challenging another person to dance under the promise of not laughing at him.

"Please, Solomon," the boy persisted.

Solomon reluctantly made a few barely synchronized moves as Gaby encouraged him enthusiastically. The boy hid his laughter by turning his back to Solomon and twirling about. They moved in their own uncoordinated ways as the headlights and honks of passing cars washed over the two anonymous figures dancing offbeat in the misting rain.

~

As it had to his father and the other namesakes before him, the heavy rain meant more to Solomon than most. He saw life on the other side of the torrent. The storm, although brief, made him think about the gardens and the imminent spring blooms. The showers only lasted for ten minutes, but he welcomed every second, even the pitter-patter of the drops that tapped his van like a used snare drum.

Traffic slowed again, moving only five miles an hour. Solomon felt swallowed by the congestion and the throng of shiny, wet metal all around him. As the van crested a hill, he looked in his rearview mirror at the sparkling city of San Diego to their backs. California was deceptively beautiful after the rains. The cities all seemed to rise up as they basked in the glow of synthetic chasteness. There was the all-pervading illusion that the lands had been thoroughly cleansed of both smog and sin. The white and golden lights glittered like a world made of new jewels.

Solomon took the exit that led him into the wine region of Temecula. Temecula was a sleepy town an hour outside San Diego and forty minutes from Oceanside. Away from the blaze of big city lights and the glare of congested traffic, the night was the color of gun metal. They drove the two-lane road past the silhouettes of the hilly vineyards that surrounded them on both sides.

"I have to go to the bathroom," Gaby said.

"Can you hold it? We'll be there in about twenty minutes," Solomon requested.

Gaby shook his head no.

"Why didn't you go when we pulled over to change the tire?" Solomon asked.

"Because…"

"Don't tell me. It's because you didn't have to go then. Right?"

"No."

"You want me to pull over?"

Gaby looked outside at the darkness, then turned back to Solomon, who could tell the boy was scared.

"I have to go number two." Gaby sounded apologetic for the revolt of the fast food.

"All right, just hold on. I'll find something open."

A mile later, they came across a small gas station, but Solomon continued on when he saw a sheriff's car parked out front. They then passed a modest, two-story white church on the side of the road with lights on and an open door. Solomon made a U-turn and pulled into the dirt parking lot. The clapboard building was old but well maintained.

As Solomon turned off the van, he said, "Go in and ask them politely if you can use the bathroom." As soon as he said it, he realized that he couldn't imagine the boy ever being anything but polite.

"Are you coming in?" Gaby asked.

"No, you go ahead. Try not to take long. I'm tired and just want to go check in and get some sleep."

After Gaby slammed the door behind him and bolted toward the church, Solomon got out of the van and stretched his legs. He walked over to the three steps of the church and sat down. He pulled out his phone and dialed. After five rings, he heard the groggy voice of a waking man on the other end.

"Hello," Tanaka said.

"A good teacher is one who makes themselves progressively unnecessary."

"That's too easy. Thomas Carruthers. I would hope on my deathbed that you would at least send me off with something more challenging."

"Fortunately, rumor has it that you're far from your deathbed."

"Trust me, we're all a little closer than we think. I guess the bright side is that it seems as if the Almighty has decided to let me stay on the earth longer because evidently I still have work to do on the likes of you."

Solomon laughed. "Well then, if you plan to pull that off, you might have to be around for a lot longer. How are you feeling?"

"Like an old man who's been shot. Come to think of it…I am an old man who's been shot. You don't have to worry about me. I'm fine. Is the boy safe?"

“Yes, he’s with me,” Solomon replied.

“Good. That’s what matters most. You did a good thing, Solomon.”

The old man coughed a brief coughing fit.

“You should get some rest. I just wanted to check on you. Sorry I didn’t call earlier,” Solomon said.

“You never have to apologize to me for anything.”

“Even after all this clears up, I don’t know that I’ll ever see you again. I just wanted to…”

“We’ll see each other. If not in this life, then the next,” Tanaka said as his coughing started again.

Solomon could hear a nurse in the background requesting Tanaka end his phone call.

“I’d better go before they take my phone privileges away. You take care of yourself, Solomon.”

“You do the same.”

~

After Solomon hung up, he rummaged in his pockets and pulled out his half-crushed pack of cigarettes. After lighting one and taking a deep drag, he sagged a little from his fatigue. The trip to the cemetery had depleted more things in him than he realized. Solomon closed his eyes, wistfully inhaled, and savored the peace and quiet. He pulled out his wallet and extracted a small photograph of Aisha and a little girl smiling on the ocean’s shore. The little girl was dark like him. The obvious resemblance stared back at him from the photo. Solomon gently ran his finger across it as though he could actually feel the skin of Aisha and the child. After he returned the photo and wallet back into his pocket, he smoked his cigarette and stared out into the black night.

"The body is a temple, or so they say," a man's voice said.

Solomon instinctively reached in the back of his waistband for his weapon. He hesitated when he saw that the stranger was dressed in the tab collar and black shirt of a man of the cloth. He was carrying a small stack of Bibles and looked like no priest Solomon had ever seen. He was built like a heavyweight prizefighter with a rugged, pockmarked face and meaty hands. As he crossed into the light, Solomon saw kindness in the gentle giant's eyes. He relaxed and pulled out an empty hand from behind his back.

"Here's to the chimney of the temple," Solomon offered.

The priest crossed over to him, set his Bibles down, and then sat beside him.

"I didn't mean to startle you."

"You didn't. Just habit."

"I just met quite the impressive young man."

"Yeah, that he is."

"Are you his father?"

"Yes," Solomon lied.

"Did the two of you have a long drive?"

"Yeah."

The priest watched Solomon as he fieldstripped the last of

his cigarette and watched the remains blow away in the night breeze. Solomon felt the man's eyes scrutinizing his every move and detail.

"Are you traveling south or headed the other way?" the priest asked.

"North for now at least until I figure out the shortest route."

"It's been my experience that sometimes shortcuts aren't all they're cracked up to be. Took me some years, but I've learned to appreciate the sure and steady route."

"I'll be fine," Solomon responded.

"You're more than welcome to come inside and have some food."

"No, thank you. I'm not hungry."

"Everybody's hungry for something."

"Yeah maybe, but I'm okay."

"Sustenance of a firearm can't be that filling, can it?"

Solomon looked at him oddly.

The priest just smiled. "You seem like a man who knows his guns. I'm thinking you go for something very reliable. I'd peg you as a Colt man for your weapon of choice. I'm guessing the M1911."

Solomon stared back at the priest, equal parts surprised and impressed. "That's pretty good," Solomon said.

"I'm in the business of reading people. Sometimes I even get it right."

As the man laughed at his own joke, Solomon just continued staring at him. He normally didn't go in much for the garrulous types, but to his surprise, he found the priest interesting to say the least. He also appreciated the man's laugh. It reminded him of Callan's laugh. Deep and full-fledged.

"I apologize. People don't always get my sense of humor." The priest extended his hand to Solomon. "I'm Father Jeremiel. I run the orphanage here."

Solomon shook his hand but never offered his name in return.

Father Jeremiel asked, "Would you mind if I see your weapon? I've always had a fascination with guns."

Solomon hesitated for a moment, then pulled out his gun, removed the magazine, and cleared the chamber before handing it over to the priest. Father Jeremiel cradled the weapon in his hand while carefully inspecting it with the authority of a man who knew guns.

"When I was a kid, my father was a big collector. He taught me and my older brother at an early age how to shoot and clean them. He used to always tell us that a gun was just like a good woman—if you held and treated it just right, it would never let you down. 'Yea, though I walk through the valley of the shadow of death, I shall fear no evil because I'm the baddest son of a bitch in the valley.' Have you ever heard that one before?"

Solomon nodded his head. "Once or twice, but in the version I heard, the noun was even more colorful."

The priest's laughter filled the quiet night like the echo of distant thunder. "Trust me, I know that version as well, but I'm trying to avoid defrocking. My older brother was a career soldier. I was really young the first time he went off to war. He would always end his letters to me with that mantra. I think he thought that was the actual scripture from the Bible."

"I guess depending on how you look at it, it is," Solomon responded.

"Depending on how you look at anything basically becomes what you want it to be. My brother said a lot of the soldiers whom he fought alongside were God-fearing and righteous men. Maybe more accurately, they were mere boys with the *hopes* of becoming men. He said so many of them never made it home from the wars. And some of the ones who did only came back in pieces—literally and/or figuratively. He once told me that all that they found of one of his soldiers was a crucifix that the boy used to wear. I was pretty young, so that was my introduction to the paradox of Christianity. My feeling was what sense did it make to wear the symbol of God if God couldn't even protect them from the very people who didn't believe in Him? My brother saw it differently. He said their deaths were God's ultimate act of protection. He said it was the calling home of angels. Maybe it's not just how you look at things but rather what you choose to see."

Father Jeremiel handed the gun back to Solomon, who snapped his magazine back in and buried the gun in the back of his waistband.

"I didn't mean any disrespect by bringing this to your door," Solomon apologized.

"It's quite all right. It's God's door, not mine. I know you mean me no harm just as I hope you know I mean you none. So which war were you in?" When Solomon looked at him oddly, he clarified. "The cigarette thing gave you away. Some soldiers' habits are hard to die. I was just curious. Which war did you fight in?"

"None that you would have heard of. Some soldiers make a career of fighting in undeclared wars."

"There is no such thing as an undeclared war."

"Spoken like a priest from the safety of his church."

"No, spoken like a sinner who still carries the scars of his own battles."

Solomon turned to see Gaby as he came out of the church followed by four other children roughly his age. They were of different backgrounds. One was Asian, one was white, and two were Latin. The children were all happy. They interacted with Gaby as though they had all known each other a lifetime. The way they innocently giggled among themselves made Solomon think briefly of the long-ago bond he shared with his childhood friend Akika.

"You all set?" Solomon asked as he stood.

"Yes. Solomon, these are friends I made."

"That's good, Gaby. Maybe you'll come back and see them sometime." Solomon turned toward the priest and shook his hand. "It was nice meeting you."

"Same here. The two of you are welcome back anytime you'd like."

The children said their goodbyes as Solomon and Gaby walked back toward the van. Just as they got in, Father Jeremiel approached Solomon and handed him his card.

"You never know when you might need a friend," the priest said.

Solomon smiled and placed the card in his wallet.

The priest then offered him a small Bible. "If you really are open to new friends, you might wanna give God a try. He's the best I've ever known."

Solomon looked down at the Bible but didn't take it.

Father Jeremiel smiled and kept his arm extended with his offering. "Think of it as just a little light reading for the road. Go with God."

"Thanks, Father, but I've already got a travel companion."

Solomon nodded goodbye without taking the Bible. He then threw the van in reverse and backed onto the two-lane road. He turned and headed north.

20
The Twins

As Gaby slept, Solomon pulled up to a small bed-and-breakfast a mile off the two-lane road. The place sat alone with the nearest neighbor a half mile away. A pair of tiger moths flitted about the naked light bulb that lit up the front porch. There was only one other car parked in the small parking lot.

As he turned off the ignition and moved to wake Gaby, he stared at the boy sleeping peacefully next to him. He couldn't help but think about the horrific trauma that the child had endured and the uncertain road ahead. Gaby slept deeply. His dreams transported him far from the threat of being hunted prey. As should have been the natural order of things, the boy slept the untrammeled sleep of the young and innocent. Solomon lamented the painful reality that regardless of whether the boy survived, he would never be the same. He feared that the light he himself had had taken from him so many years ago would also be lost in the child as well. He dreaded the time that the ghosts would come for the boy as they did for him each night. Had he been a praying man, Solomon would have begged first for the child's survival and for the purity of his essence to remain intact. He would have even been willing to compromise with God that if the latter couldn't be granted, that no matter what, Gaby would never grow to become a man like him or Callan, that he would never become irredeemable.

Solomon got out of the van, walked around to the passenger side, and gently lifted Gaby out of the vehicle. As he carried the boy and his dead weight toward the front door, he thought back to the time when he was a child and his father used to carry him as though he were the most precious of bundles. He also thought of the simple delight of holding his own child safely in his arms. Both were memories of things taken from him too soon and much too tragically. Solomon was momentarily saddened by the thought of how easily the most basic joys of life could in the blink of an eye be stolen forever. As Gaby stirred ever so faintly, Solomon pressed the small body of the sleeping child into his chest and held him just a little more tightly.

When he walked through the door, Solomon saw double. The two women behind the desk were seventy-something-year-old identical twins. One was watching an old Ali-Foreman fight while the other was on the phone in a heated conversation. Although not exact, they were similarly dressed. The women were identically plain-looking. Plain features, plain dress, plain presence. Individually, they were the type easily lost in a crowd, but as he saw them together, they were remarkable in how damn near impossible it was to tell them apart. Even though it was after nine p.m., their white hair was still perfectly coiffed in a bouffant style as though they'd each just left a salon. They had the same nose, bone structure, green eyes, and powder-pale skin.

The small lobby seemed obsessively neat. The polished wood shone like wet leather. Three dozen photos in ornate frames hung neatly on the floral-papered walls. The reception desk was bookended by two bouquets of freshly cut mimosa in matching ceramic vases. The place smelled of stew and freshly baked oatmeal cookies. The warm scents of an inviting home reminded Solomon of his mother.

The woman watching the fight stood up as Solomon approached.

"We were beginning to wonder if you were gonna make it. Ralph called this afternoon and told us to be on the lookout for the two of you. My friends call me JoJo, and that's my sister, Ari."

Gaby woke at the sound of the woman's voice. He stared at her even as he hung sleepily with his arms draped around Solomon's neck.

"I'm sorry to get here so late. We ran into a little car trouble," Solomon offered.

"It's quite all right. We don't usually go to bed before eleven. Okay, let's get the two of you checked in."

Solomon held Gaby in one arm and fished in his pocket for his wallet with his free hand. "How much are the rooms?"

"Single or double?"

"Double."

"Since you're a friend of Ralph's, it'll be forty, and it includes breakfast and dinner."

"Arnold said he lost a driver and won't be able to make deliveries until tomorrow late afternoon," Ari said as she hung up the phone and crossed over to them.

"I swear that man loses a driver every two weeks. I'll just go and pick up our supplies from him first thing in the morning," JoJo said.

Although Ari was looking in their general vicinity, Solomon noticed that she only stared directly at him when he made a slight rustling sound from shifting his weight to adjust Gaby. At first, he thought it odd that the woman seemed to look just two or three inches to his left as she spoke until he realized Ari had the vacant stare of the blind.

"So you must be Gaby," she said.

Solomon was completely caught off guard. "How do you know his name?"

Ari smiled. "I know everybody's name. People say I was born with that gift. When God takes something away from you, he gives you something extra in return."

She reached out her hand for Gaby, who looked at Solomon.

"It's okay, Gaby. She's just saying hello to you," Solomon said.

Gaby hesitated at first, then reached out his hand for Ari, who took it and gently squeezed it in both her palms. She smiled at the touch of the boy's hand. "My father used to always tell us to make sure we saw people more with our hearts than our eyes. But even an old blind woman like me can see what a handsome young man you are, Gaby."

"He certainly is, and he has the most gorgeous eyes I think I've ever seen," JoJo chimed in.

"Thank you, ma'am," Gaby said.

"Ooh, and he's polite as well. Somebody's been raised right. Lord knows we don't get enough of that these days," Ari said.

As the women laughed side by side, Solomon couldn't help but stare in wonder at how indistinguishable the sisters were. Not only were they each other's duplicate, but they also sounded and moved alike.

"Evidently he gets his good looks from his father." JoJo winked at Solomon as she playfully nudged her sister. "This house has been in our family for seven generations. We get all kinds of folk come through here now, but nothing's more beautiful than the ones that come through as families. Nope, nothing. Even as crazy as the two of us drive each other sometimes, we still always tell our children and even grandchildren nothing matters more than family."

"Don't talk the poor man's ear off. I'm sure they're tired. We usually eat early, but we knew you were coming so we wanted to wait. Hope you're hungry."

"Actually, we picked up some burgers at a drive-through earlier that didn't agree with Gaby, so I think we'll just go to our room."

"That fast food crap is poison. The boy needs some good old-fashioned home cooking in his system. That'll get him feeling right. Trust me when I tell you that Ari makes the best lentil and chicken stew this side of our grandmother. Would you like to try some, Gaby? It's delicious."

Gaby smiled, then nodded to the woman. "Yes, ma'am."

"Okay then, your room is the third door on the right at the top of the stairs. You're our only guests tonight, so you get the best suite in the house. Why don't the two of you go wash up real quick, and then we can eat," JoJo said.

As Solomon and Gaby headed up the stairs, Ari called after them, "By the way, Gaby, I also baked some homemade oatmeal cookies for you for dessert. How does that sound?"

Gaby broke into a wide smile. "That sounds good."

~

As JoJo ladled out hot stew in large bowls, the aroma instantly made both Solomon's and Gaby's mouths water. Solomon watched Gaby's eyes grow bigger at the sight of the steam rising from the homemade Parker House rolls as they were being buttered and sweet tea was poured. While he waited for the women to be seated, Solomon looked around the room. The heart of the house was exactly what he assumed it would be—emphatically quaint. Lots of gleaming mahogany, bright white linen, knickknacks, lace doilies, and family heirlooms and photos. Solomon thought the place felt a bit archaic but in a comforting way. It was a house of lineage. The twins were the guardians and heirs of their heritage.

Solomon wondered about the seven generations that had passed through the same room he now occupied. He felt their presence. The distant echo of joyous gatherings from long ago still reverberated from the corners of the room. He smelled the meals prepared by not just the twins but their forebearers as well. These were ghosts of a different ilk. They were welcomed. Unlike Solomon's, these came not to haunt but rather to serve as conduits linking the past to the present. Theirs were the spirits of light and ancestry.

When the women had finished serving and finally sat to eat, they each reached out and linked hands with their two guests as everyone except Solomon closed their eyes and bowed their heads in prayer. As JoJo held the left hand of Solomon, which was missing two fingers, he looked at her in anticipation of an uneasy reaction, but instead she held him with affection. Her touch was warm and soft. Soothing. Maternal. Gaby opened one eye and stole a glance at Solomon, then gently squeezed his other hand, coaxing him to join them in prayer. Solomon bowed his head, but his eyes remained open. Ari led them in prayer.

"Dear Lord, we come before you as humble servants begging your forgiveness of our transgressions and weaknesses. Strengthen us, O Lord. Make us worthy of the food you have blessed us with as well as the countless other blessings that you have bestowed upon us. Thank you most of all for our health and for the love of family. Bless and protect our two guests as we welcome them into the fold of our beloved family. Reconcile us, Merciful Father, to each other, to ourselves, and to your loving grace. In the name of your son Jesus, our savior, amen."

As Gaby and JoJo said amen, the boy squeezed Solomon's hand once more, and he muttered an amen as well.

The Cassiel sisters were completely smitten by Gaby. They doted on him throughout the meal as he steadily beamed under their adulation. His eyes lit up when they tempted him with the promise of homemade biscuits with ham, eggs, and grits for breakfast. The house was filled with warmth, delicious scents, and the salve of laughter. The women told jokes and even spontaneously burst into several bars of Whitney Houston's version of "I Will Always Love You" after Gaby told them it was his favorite song.

Solomon's mouth was slightly agape as he listened in awe to the pitch-perfect harmonizing of a chorus of two. Their voices, rich and soulful, surprised him with each note. He was reminded of a bliss he once knew. He thought of his mother and the morning songs she woke him with as well as the nighttime serenades that gently rocked him into the deep sleep of the highly loved.

With all that Gaby had been through and the still lingering threat of harm, the sisters proved to be a pleasant surprise in more ways than one. Solomon thought the twins were funny. He certainly appreciated their sense of humor. He appreciated most of all the way they treated Gaby. There in the house of their ancestors, safe from the likes of Cesar, Solomon watched as the Cassiel sisters afforded the boy the simple pleasure of being a beloved child.

~

The bedroom was spacious yet cozy and smelled of sandalwood candles. Solomon disassembled and cleaned his weapons on one of the two beds as Gaby sat on the other, eating a hot oatmeal cookie and chasing it down with warm milk. After he finished his, he eyed Solomon's untouched cookie, which was on the nightstand between them.

Solomon didn't need to look at the boy to know. "Go ahead. You can have it," Solomon offered.

Gaby grabbed the cookie, broke it, and then offered half back to Solomon, who accepted it and ate it in two bites.

"Solomon, can I ask you a question?"

"What's that?"

"When Miss Ari was blessing our food, do you know what she meant when she said welcoming us into the fold of their family?"

"It just means treating someone like family even if they weren't born into it."

"So you can just choose who becomes your family?"

"Something like that. Sometimes."

"So that means if you and I wanted to, we could choose to be family."

"It doesn't always work the way you think, Gaby."

"Do you have family?"

"Not anymore."

"So if we both don't have—"

"You should finish your cookie so you can get some sleep."

Solomon continued cleaning his weapons in silence as Gaby finished his half of the cookie. When nothing was left but crumbs, he went to the bathroom and washed his hands and face. He then crossed back to his bed and knelt on his knees and bowed his head in silent prayer. He prayed for several minutes. When he was done, he stood, walked over to Solomon, and hugged him.

"Good night, Solomon."

"Good night, Gaby."

It didn't take long before Solomon heard the heavy breathing of a tired child. He put his weapons away and turned off the lights but still looked in the boy's direction, a bit envious of his peaceful rest.

As he lay in darkness, unable to sleep, he thought about the twins and how devout they were about the importance of family. His own bloodlines had been severed, and in return, he too had aborted the legacies of innumerable victims who were now nothing more than a blur of anonymous faces. The Cassiel twins had the familial ties that Solomon had only dreamed of. As he stared up at the overhead ceiling fan, the word that swirled unrelentingly in his mind was *family*.

As he closed his eyes and hoped for sleep, his thoughts were of his woman. Of his child.

21

A New Beginning

TEN YEARS AGO

I know it's been three months, but you told me to let you know when I wanted to live off more than just the memory of our time together in New York. If you're still open to me, I'm ready," Solomon said into the phone.

"You certainly took your time," Aisha responded.

"I needed you to know that I wasn't taking anything you said lightly and that I wasn't making any decisions in haste. I gotta say, this whole missing someone the way I miss you is new to me. I never knew that days could feel like years."

When she didn't respond, he worried that their call had been dropped.

"Are you there?"

"Yes, I'm here."

"I'm not always great at finding the right words that say what I feel, so I'm sorry if things come out a little clunky."

"You're doing just fine. To be honest, your call made my day."

"So what if I told you I've been thinking about coming to California?"

"Should I get you tickets for Disneyland?"

"You're really not going to make this easy for me, are you?"

"I never took you for someone who needed easy."

"Okay, so I'll spell it out. I'm not coming as a tourist. I'm not coming for a week or two. I'm coming to be with you."

"See, that wasn't so difficult."

"Easy for you to say. You can't see how much I'm sweating."

When she laughed, he remembered yet another thing that he loved and missed about her. Another meal for which he'd been starving. As the laughter stopped, he felt her shifting into something more serious.

"I only have one stipulation, and it's nonnegotiable. I can't and won't be with you if you're not able to leave your old life behind."

"I swear to you that I'm done with the violence. Maybe I just needed you to make me realize that it's time to leave behind what I used to be to become what I want to be. Being with you is more important to me than anything in this world."

"I really want to believe you, Solomon."

"If you don't trust me on this, both of us could end up regretting it the rest of our lives. I know for certain I will. Give me two weeks to finish up everything here. I just need to let my boss and his son know that I'm leaving. After that, you and I get to start our lives together. You have no idea how much I look forward to that."

Aisha was quiet on the other end. It felt like forever before she spoke again.

"You haven't exactly been truthful. It's hard to trust a man who doesn't even know what he's capable of."

Solomon was confused. The thought of her doubting him in any way, particularly in his most vulnerable state, left him feeling as if he'd swallowed a hot brick.

"I'm…not sure what you're talking about," he stammered.

"Well, you said you weren't good at finding the right words to say what you felt. That might be the furthest thing from the truth. I think you said what I needed to hear just perfectly."

When she laughed, Solomon exhaled as he felt the sudden knot in his chest untangle.

"You love torturing me, don't you?" he asked.

"What is love without a little torment?"

~

Solomon met with Detective Phee Freeman that afternoon at a Jamaican lunch shack up in Harlem. Phee's partner, Quincy Cavanaugh, was there as well. Solomon had worked for Phee's father, Clay Freeman, for more than thirty years. He had threatened, beaten, and killed many times at his boss's behest. The vast majority of people who encountered Solomon or, as he was better known, the African, feared him. They were nervous not just in his presence but often from the mere mention of his name and reputation.

Solomon had been a constant presence in Phee's life since childhood. Even though Solomon was ten years older, Phee never feared him because Solomon had been his protector since the early years. Theirs had evolved into a complex relationship, one being a known killer and the other a decorated cop. They navigated the murky waters with a "Don't ask, don't tell" understanding.

Phee always felt kinship toward the African. He always had love in his heart for the man he knew without question would lay down his life for both his father and him.

Despite the polarity of Clay being a ruthless former gangster while his son was considered one of the most highly respected homicide detectives in all of New York, Solomon had always regarded both men as the closest thing to family he had. There were always things understood but never spoken between Phee and Solomon regarding the illicit deeds the latter had done on behalf of Clay.

Solomon managed to make small talk with the two detectives until the waitress brought their food. Quincy immediately dug into his jerk chicken patties along with a small mound of cabbage and rice and peas. Phee, who had ordered the curried goat, roti, plantains, and a sweet bread that was called festival, did likewise. Solomon picked at his plate of ackee and saltfish. In between nibbles, he sipped a bottle of ginger beer.

"I had a talk with your father earlier, but I asked him not to say anything to you because I wanted you to hear the news from me directly," Solomon said.

"When you called, you said it was important. So what's going on?" Phee asked.

"I'm leaving New York."

"As in for good?"

"Yeah, that's the idea," Solomon responded.

"Well, I gotta say I did not see that one coming. So what did my father have to say?"

"I could tell he was not happy, but he said he had to respect my decision."

"If you don't mind me asking, is the change because of business or personal?" Phee asked.

"Definitely personal." Solomon smiled like a shy schoolboy.

Phee couldn't recall ever seeing Solomon so happy. Not even the darkest of skin could mute the blush of a man afflicted by an infirmity for which there was no cure. Phee understood it immediately. Solomon was in love. Phee felt a tinge of something approaching shame because he had never considered love an option for a man such as Solomon. Even the slightest of vulnerabilities was a luxury seldom afforded the likes of those whose vocation included killing. Therefore it had never quite crossed Phee's mind that a day would come when love would tame the most dangerous man he knew.

"So where are you headed?" Quincy jumped in.

"California."

"Nice," Quincy responded. "I don't think one has to be a great detective to assume there must be a woman involved," he chuckled.

Solomon smiled. "Of course there is. Isn't that usually the reason for a man's best or worst decisions? If you met Aisha, you'd know this was the best decision I've ever made."

"You're preaching to the choir, brotha. We both know first-hand the sway of a good woman. I'll definitely miss you, but I'm glad you found something special. Someone that makes you smile the way I've never seen you smile. You deserve to be happy, Solomon," Phee said.

"Thank you for that, Phee. And thanks for meeting me. I thought I at least owed you a face-to-face with—"

Solomon's phone vibrated with an incoming text. After he read the text, he pulled out his wallet and left enough money on the table to pay for all three meals.

"It's your father. I have to head back downtown. Quincy, do you have a sec? I need to run something by you."

Quincy instinctively glanced in Phee's direction. "Uh…yeah, sure," he responded.

"Phee, I'm glad we got to do this. It means a lot," Solomon said as he stood.

Phee stood and hugged him, realizing that in all the years they'd known each other they had never actually embraced. Solomon wasn't the type of man one hugged.

"Same here. For what it's worth, I really hope the whole California thing works out for you," Phee said.

"It already has, but thank you. I appreciate that."

After Solomon and Quincy stepped out to Malcolm X Boulevard, Solomon turned to Quincy. "I've been sitting on something for a while now that I didn't quite know how to bring up. But before I leave, I think I need to share it with you."

"What's up?" Quincy asked.

As was his habit, Solomon kept one eye keenly on his environment of pedestrians and passing cars while simultaneously engaging with Quincy.

"I didn't want to just drop this on you in front of Phee. I, uh… I was in Chicago a few months ago taking care of some business for his father and I, uh…"

"You what?" Quincy jumped in as Solomon struggled to say what he wanted to.

"Well, I was at O'Hare, and…uh…I saw your brother Liam."

Quincy was confused. "That's not possible."

"Yeah, well, I saw him nonetheless."

"Must have just been someone who looks like him. Liam's been dead for two years now," Quincy objected.

"You know me better than that, Quincy. I don't make those kinds of mistakes. I wouldn't be bringing it to you if I wasn't certain. His hair was longer. Darker. He looked thinner, but just as sure as I'm standing here with you now, it was him. I followed him to a taxi stand and tried to get a couple of shots of him as he was getting into the cab." Solomon pulled out his phone and showed Quincy the first of three photos.

Although none had great angles, there was just enough familiarity to shake Quincy's previous certainty. He felt as though his heart stopped when he got to the final photo, which was of the man in profile with his hand on the car door. He enlarged the image to better see the unique, channel-set Tanzanite ring on the man's finger. It was the exact ring that Quincy had custom made for Liam several years ago.

22

Aisha and Miremba

Solomon settled his affairs and left for California two weeks later. Three and a half months had passed since he'd seen Aisha in New York, and he immediately thought that she was even more beautiful than he remembered.

He felt the same way about Los Angeles. After she picked him up from the airport, Aisha drove out just north of Point Dume in Malibu to picnic on the beach. Solomon was welcomed by the lapping of the sea as it approached and receded from the shores. New York living was congested, claustrophobic even. California, in contrast, was the land of great expanse.

As they sat holding hands and watching the sun's reflection on the rippled ocean, Solomon felt something that he had always hoped for but had long ago relinquished the possibility of ever attaining: the weightlessness of peace. Aisha made him feel that even levitation was possible. There were times he had to remind himself to breathe. He took everything in, starting with her. Her skin looked burnished under the Cali sun. She smiled a lot as he held her hand, which in turn made him smile even more. She made him feel like a born-again child.

Of all the wondrous spectacles he took in, nothing was more beautiful than what he saw in her eyes when she stared at him. She looked at him as though he was the arrival of something good in her life. Something needed. Solomon vowed to himself that he would always do any and everything to be both muse and beneficiary of such a look. He breathed in the ocean air and sifted sand through his fingers as she prepared their lunch.

"I wanted this to be one of the first of our new memories. This is my favorite beach," she said. Aisha turned around and pointed to the top of the bluff. "There are five amazing gardens up there. The botanical garden is the one just above us. It's got a bunch of beautiful statues and a great view of the beach. The next time we come out here, I'll take you there to see for yourself."

Solomon smiled at the suggestion as she fed him Brie on baguettes along with old-fashioned chicken salad and jalapeño-flavored kettle chips. He was pleasantly surprised when she opened the cooler and pulled out cold bottles of ginger beer.

"My grandmother once mentioned how much you loved these."

Solomon laughed appreciatively as he devoured the food and downed two of the fizzy beverages.

~

They got to her hometown of La Verne just past six p.m. She lived in a modest three-bedroom house with a big backyard and a small pool. They walked a few blocks in the neighborhood just so that he could get a feel for his surroundings. He loved it all: the tree-lined streets, the friendly neighbors, the peace and quiet that New York never offered him. They ate a light dinner at a local Japanese restaurant. Solomon was never much for drinking, but he did enjoy the bottle of Sancerre that she ordered with the pork and ramen special.

"I have to warn you not to get used to eating out a lot. I prefer cooking more than dining out," she said.

He thought to himself that if she cooked half as well as her grandmother, then he was starting off his new life with unanticipated bonuses.

Between the early morning flight, the long day, and the wine, Solomon assumed that by 11 p.m., he would have been fading from exhaustion, but to his surprise, he was still wired. She took him up to the bedroom and gifted him a gray, Turkish cotton bathrobe with the letter *S* embroidered on the front. He took a long, hot shower, then stared at his reflection in the mirror after the steam cleared.

The thought of actually being with her made him insecure. When he finally exited the bathroom and watched her prepare for bed, he realized that his unexpected energy was fueled in part by the anxiety of them making love for the first time. The most they had done was hold hands and kiss publicly. From their third date on, he had the feeling that she was waiting for him to initiate sex, but Solomon was reluctant because he was ashamed of his body. He couldn't help but see himself as a disfigured remnant of war. His wounds were a tapestry of burns, keloids, and gashes on the front and back of his torso, and then of course there were also the missing fingers, which were *unhidable*. He regretted the bodily trauma the most because he knew that despite his vows to Aisha, the physical scars of his violent past were simply impossible to leave behind.

As she crossed to him in a cream-colored silk teddy, Solomon felt the stirrings of feelings and thoughts in ways that he hadn't before. She left him feeling as though he were treading in uncharted waters. Sex in the past had served much more as a reprieve than an act of pleasure. Intercourse for him, be it sexual or emotional, had at best been nothing more than sporadic. Although he had on occasion indulged in the carnal comforts of an available lover, Solomon had never been with a woman who was even remotely like Aisha. He may have known the primal act of bodies colliding, but he had never experienced the tender touch of a good woman. The good women feared him. Understandably so. But Aisha was a different kind of good woman. Despite his dark past and how the rest of the world saw him, her loving ways reminded him that he was in fact a man, not a monster.

He had never desired to please a woman so much. His only wish was to be everything he felt she deserved. As he reached over to the lamp on the nightstand to turn it off, she stopped him.

“There can be no secrets between us, Solomon.”

She took off her teddy and stood naked before him. He was instantly made weak by what he saw. She waited patiently for him to disrobe. When he did, he found it difficult to look directly at her. He was afraid of the possible disappointment in her eyes or, even worse, repulsion.

Aisha gently turned his head so that their eyes were perfectly aligned as she touched his skin and traced the web of scars with her fingertips. She kissed his body until he felt whole and unsullied. As they pleasured each other, Solomon was humbled by the mere taste of her. She was the type of blessing that was usually reserved for much more virtuous men than himself. He couldn’t help but wonder why fate had finally been kind. The more of her he took, the more he felt dominion over his self-loathing. When she finally received him inside her, he was overwhelmed by thoughts, feelings, and pleasure. She made it easy and even necessary for him to relinquish darkness for light. Solitude for union. There in the sovereignty of her arms, Solomon surrendered all preconceptions he had that he was incapable of love. She welcomed him home to a place he’d never been.

They made love three times on their first night together. When they were awakened by the warmth of the morning light, they made love again, then cuddled in the languid repose of spent lovers. Aisha rested her head on Solomon’s chest and listened to the drumming of loud heartbeats. They were both damp with sweat and sex. As she lay on him, Solomon played with a handful of her hair, all the while trying to steady his heavy breathing.

"For a woman so opposed to violence, why do I get the feeling you're trying to kill me?"

She lifted her head and looked at him. "Trust me, there would be no sweeter death, but I actually have other plans for you," she said and smiled.

Solomon laughed as he gently twirled the strands of her hair around his finger.

"Are these plans anything I should be afraid of?"

"That depends on your tolerance for pain and pleasure."

"Maybe I should just wave the white flag now."

"We both know that you're not one to take the coward's way out."

Solomon tilted his head and kissed her and watched the morning sunlight glisten on the back of her thigh. Even as their bodies intertwined, he barely felt her weight on him because she was as much a part of him as his own leg, arm, or heart.

They spent the lazy Saturday morning lying in bed and talking about matters both big and small. They even spoke of things that Solomon had never previously claimed: the future.

He sat up in bed as the conversation turned more serious.

"The beauty is we can go wherever we want. Do whatever we want," he said.

"What exactly does that mean?"

"It means money won't ever be an issue. I've saved up more than enough for us to be happy the rest of our lives."

"This is money from what you used to do?"

There was a slight hesitation before he answered, "Yes."

Aisha now sat up, held his hand, and looked in his eyes.

"Solomon, whatever future we make, we make together. If we have to struggle, we struggle as a team, but the one thing we will never do is live our dreams off the blood of others."

"But—"

"I make decent money. My house is paid for. We don't need much."

"I can't and won't live off you."

"I'm not expecting you to. You'll get a job and—"

"Doing what? I only know how to do one thing."

"That's not true. You're smart. You can learn. I'm not saying things will be easy, but we'll work it out. If we're really going to create this bright future, we can't build it on the foundation of a dark past. So let's just figure it out together."

He decided not to protest. The uncertainty of the future was a bit daunting at first, but knowing that she was in his corner fortified him. She left him feeling that he could do anything. Whereas "respectable" women had in the past stayed clear of what he deemed a void in his soul, he felt Aisha pouring goodness into the abyss.

He kissed her and was quiet as he continued watching her skin glowing in the sunlight.

He married Aisha six months later to the day of moving to California. She convinced him to start a handyman service. Her grandmother had always bragged about how meticulous and hardworking he was when he did odd jobs for her. Solomon started booking more and more small gigs right away mainly because of glowing Yelp reviews and the impressive website Aisha got one of her students to create for him.

Per California law, until he was eligible for his general contractor's license, which would take four years, he could only do individual jobs that didn't exceed five hundred dollars in cost. Even with the restrictions imposed by law, he was on average bringing in fifteen hundred dollars a week. It may have seemed like lunch money compared to the two million plus dollars he had saved up working for Clay Freeman, but Solomon had never felt richer.

From time to time, he couldn't help but think of the irony of how he'd finally found life after having met and fallen in love with Aisha as a result of her grandmother's funeral. It was the only time he could recall something good that came from death. Life was now simple but beautiful in ways he'd never expected.

Solomon took speech and diction classes at night at a local community college. He worked diligently to lose the final hint of an accent. Unlike when he first arrived in New York, it wasn't to assimilate but simply to bury all traces of the man he was before Aisha. She gave him a new beginning. A life unimagined. The ghosts no longer came. He slept each night in the arms of a good woman. He worked hard each day and actually relished the grind of an honest living. A living that didn't involve the blood of other men.

On the day that Aisha was promoted to the department head of African American studies, Solomon took her to their favorite beach in Malibu. Just as she had done on the first day he arrived in California, Solomon prepared a picnic. He brought turkey and Swiss paninis with bags of chips along with two big slices of red velvet cake and a bottle of Veuve champagne to celebrate. He raised his red Solo cup to toast her.

"To the smartest person I've ever met. Not to mention the sweetest, kindest, and funniest. You are without a doubt the best thing that's ever happened to me."

He noticed that although she toasted, she seemed distracted when she brought the cup to her lips but didn't drink.

"Is the champagne not cold enough?" he asked.

As she set the cup down on the blanket and reached in her beach bag, she said, "No, it's fine. I just…I wanted to give you something."

"You're not supposed to be giving me anything. We're celebrating you, not me."

"I know, but I wanted you to have it," she responded.

Aisha handed him a small, scrolled paper with a red ribbon tied around its center like a diploma or commendation of some sort.

"What is it?" Solomon asked.

"Open it."

Solomon untied the red ribbon and unfurled the scroll. To his surprise, he found himself looking at three sonogram images of a fetus.

"I think my champagne days are on hold for a while," she laughed.

Aisha waited for his response but was only greeted by his silence. All she heard was the sound of the steady splashing of waves at the shore. Because she was in her late forties and knew the inherent risks of an older pregnancy, she was insecure about how her news would be received.

Solomon was quiet, his blank expression a tough read. He looked frozen like an inanimate object. A sand sculpture made in the likeness of a man.

As he sat there with his eyes fixed on the scroll, Aisha couldn't tell if he was disappointed by her announcement or not. "You have to say something, Solomon."

When he looked up from the scroll, she noticed that his eyes were moist.

"I can't. Not that I don't want to, but I just know words will only come up short trying to describe how I feel and how you keep making me happier than I ever thought possible."

Aisha reached out and touched his face. "That says it all."

Solomon moved even closer and kissed her long as though that in itself would forever archive the moment. He savored her, the joyful news, and even the taste of the salt air on her lips. When he finally pulled away, it was only to change his position so that he ended up sitting behind Aisha and holding her in an embrace.

Emboldened by the peace of her in his arms, he found some of the words he'd been searching for. "Your grandmother once told me that not all storms come to destroy. Some simply come to clear the debris that we too often cling to. Aisha, you're…you're the needed storm that I never saw coming. This beautiful hurricane that blew right through me and broke all that needed breaking but somehow at the same time mended the pieces of me that I thought were unmendable. I don't think there's a day that goes by when I'm not somehow reminded that you're everything I never expected."

As she leaned her head back on his chest, he held her firmly so that she could feel how loved and protected she was. He never let go, even as he fed her cake while looking out at the ocean and beaming at the thought of their unborn child.

~

Being the descendant of a long line of farmers, Solomon appreciated that the birth of his daughter happened in spring. Though he used to be the most feared and violent of men, he was rendered utterly powerless by the inconceivable beauty of a six-and-a-half-pound newborn who comfortably fit in the palm of his large hand. The first time he held his daughter, his heart was reminded that there was still in fact great innocence in the world. That the purity of his love for her was like a seed of hope blooming even in the most barren of fields. She was born healthy with a head of oil-black hair along with his dark skin and Aisha's doe-like eyes. Solomon hadn't cried since the death of his parents, but on the day of his daughter's birth, he wept enough to flood the Ayugi River.

"I think we should name her Miremba after your mother," Aisha suggested.

Solomon cried even more. His tears flowed freely at the thought of his two greatest miracles. He sat for hours in total amazement, just staring at the two loves of his life. He may have had very little faith in religion or even God himself, but he deeply believed in the divinity of his woman and his child. One was a savior and the other a seraph.

Miremba's birth left him feeling forgiven by the universe. After years of taking lives, he had finally helped to create something perfect and redemptive. It was the love of Aisha and the birth of Miremba that made him reevaluate a lifetime's worth of pessimism in regard to whether it was possible for him and God to forgive each other.

Shortly after Miremba was born, Aisha pleaded with Solomon to start attending church with them. Although he eventually relented, he only went on occasion, two to three times a year to be exact.

Miremba's fourth birthday fell on a Sunday, and her parents planned a full day of activity for their princess. Early church service, then a picnic brunch at the beach.

"Blessed is the protector of angels," said the preacher as he stood before the small congregation of mostly Black and Latin churchgoers.

Solomon had no idea whether the reference to angels was actual scripture or conjecture. He just knew it made him gently squeeze Aisha's hand and hoist his daughter to his lap. Although Solomon had in the past had a few philosophical differences with the preacher, his main issue was much more secular. The cleric, although a nice enough man, seemed to love the sound of his own voice more than the content of his speech. Solomon may not have thought much of the preacher's self-proclaimed enlightenment, but now that he had two angels in his care, the thin man's sermon resonated much more than usual. He certainly felt more fortunate than anyone could ever know. He was honored to be a husband, father, and protector. As the rest of the churchgoers bowed their heads in prayer, Solomon gave praise to the angels that he called wife and daughter.

Miremba made it through most of the sermon before falling asleep. When the service finally ended, Solomon carried the still-sleeping girl as he and Aisha walked toward the exit.

"Excuse me, Solomon, do you have a minute?" a voice called out from behind them.

Solomon and Aisha turned to see the preacher, whom everyone called Pastor Blake, heading down the aisle in their direction. Blake was tall, thin, and lithe with a salt-and-pepper hairstyle that was Afro adjacent. When he was just twenty feet away, an older woman momentarily intercepted him.

As Solomon waited, he whispered under his breath to Aisha. "Oh no. He must have seen me steal the quarter from the collection plate. We'd better run for it while we still can."

Aisha laughed and playfully elbowed him, causing Miremba to stir but not wake.

After the preacher said his farewell to the older woman, he approached the couple. "Hello, Aisha. It's always great to see you, Solomon. I heard that your contractor's license came through a few months ago. Congratulations."

"Almost a year now," Solomon said.

"Wow," the preacher responded. "See, if you came to church more often, I could get my facts straight," Pastor Blake joked.

Aisha smiled. “Don’t give up hope. I’m still working on him.”

“So the board and I decided to add another twenty-five hundred square feet to the building, and I personally think you would be the best person for the job. The handiwork that you’ve done for us in the past has always been stellar, and we love the idea of using someone we already know and trust. We just got our final permits approved last week. All in, the job could easily be six to eight months of steady work. I think you would knock this out of the park. That is, of course, if you’re interested.”

Solomon lit up. “Absolutely!”

“Great. Swing by Tuesday morning, and we can talk more in detail.”

“I’ll be here first thing. Thank you, Pastor Blake.”

After Blake walked off, Solomon and Aisha smiled at each other like two giddy children all alone in a pie shop. Solomon carried Miremba to the car as if she were the most precious of bundles. Poppa Bear and cub. He kissed her on the forehead when she woke while he secured her in the car seat.

After he got in the car and started it, Aisha looked at him and smiled. “I know you choose not to believe, but despite your cynicism, you gotta admit God keeps finding ways to bless us.”

When he didn’t respond, Aisha started laughing as they pulled out of the church’s parking lot and turned on to Bolling Avenue.

“What’s so funny?” Solomon asked.

“You. You’ll never give God credit, but you gotta at least ask yourself who else could have come up with the perfect plan that will make you go to church every day for six to eight months straight?”

Although her contagious laugh was always his undoing, he did all he could to remain unflappable.

"Yeah, well, let's just hope I'm spared from any spontaneous combustion," Solomon coolly replied.

Aisha laughed so fully that it in turn made Miremba giggle even though she had no comprehension of what her parents were discussing.

When they stopped at a red light a few blocks from the church, Solomon, who was still attempting to play the role of the stoic, looked in the rearview mirror at Miremba, who was sitting behind Aisha on the passenger side. "Mir-Mir, are you laughing at Daddy?"

Miremba giggled even louder. "Yes, Dada."

That was all it took to make Solomon finally break character and join in although he was the butt of the joke. One of the things he loved most in the world was the beautiful sound of their happy voices. He thought about what Aisha had said. Although he didn't outwardly protest her claim, he disagreed with her vehemently about who the author of their good fortune was. He gave the glory not to God but rather to her. She was the one responsible for the continuous stream of blissful days. As far as he was concerned, Aisha was both temple and goddess, the one most deserving of praise. She was, after all, the one who transformed him through the alchemy of her love.

It was a picture-perfect day for his daughter's birthday: endless California sunshine, a big job offer, and best of all a car filled with laughter from the two greatest joys of his life.

As the light turned green and Solomon made his way through

the intersection, he never saw the speeding SUV that blindsided them from the passenger side. He was immediately knocked unconscious on impact. He never heard the grating collision of metal collapsing metal, the shattering of glass, or the screeching of tires. He never heard the heart-wrenching sound of his entire world being destroyed.

23
The Driver

Solomon woke from a coma three days later. Everything was a blur. His eyes fluttered at the bright fluorescent lights embedded in the white tiled ceiling. His vision went in and out of focus like the broken lens of a camera. It was a bit of a struggle for him to fight through the fog and recognize Aisha's parents, Audrey and Marvin. Although they stood at his bedside, he couldn't see their faces as plainly as he wanted. The weight of anguish in the room, however, was obvious. When he could finally see more clearly, he saw the tragic masks sculpted on their faces. Aisha's mother held his hand firmly as if she were trying to protect him from the overwhelming pain she was about to inflict. He already knew. The rivers in his eyes overflowed before she uttered a sound.

"They're both gone, Solomon," she finally said.

Her words were shards of glass that tumbled from her mouth,

wounding both receiver and sender. Audrey broke down in her husband's arms as Solomon struggled to stay afloat in the throes of his own torrent. Marvin consoled his wife as best he could until she found enough composure to excuse herself and leave to fetch the doctor.

Marvin was a man's man. Still fit even in his seventies. A big, southern redbone who was the salt of the earth. He was an ex-con who had found God in prison. Unlike Audrey, who was slow to warm up to Solomon in the beginning, Marvin hit it off with his future son-in-law the first day they met at Ida's funeral. The more the men got to know each other, the more Solomon suspected that the simple reason he and Marvin got along so well was that every father, good or bad, wanted to feel that they could entrust their princess to the care of a man who would love, protect, and make them happy.

Solomon couldn't look Marvin in the eye. He looked instead toward the ceiling and cried for many reasons, paramount among them that he'd failed in his role as the protector of angels.

Marvin moved a chair closer and sat beside Solomon. His words were as listless as leaves falling from a dying tree. "It was a drunk driver. Some spoiled-ass trust fund baby. The cop who spoke to us said he had enough alcohol in his system to get a ship full of sailors drunk. Even though the son of a bitch already had two prior DUIs, his rich daddy's lawyers got him out on bail within twenty-four hours. Nobody cares what he took from us. If you've got money, nothing else matters. We're just..." Marvin broke down in tears before he could finish his sentence.

When Solomon finally turned toward Marvin, he still found it difficult to look directly at him. It took quite a bit of effort for him to speak, and even then, his words were stillborn.

"I…I'm…so—"

Solomon closed his eyes in frustration as his attempts to communicate fell short and the sound of his voice withered just out of reach of his father-in-law. More tears ran down the sides of his face. There were intermittent beeps from the machine in the corner. Although its function was to monitor his heart, it could never measure his heartache.

Marvin leaned in even closer and held his hand. "It's okay, Solomon. I'm right here, and I'm not going anywhere."

Solomon kept his eyes closed until he finally mustered the strength to speak the two words that he never imagined having to say, even under such unimaginable circumstances.

"I'm…I'm sorry."

The words hurt Marvin as much to hear as they hurt Solomon to claim. There were heritable vows made by old-school men like Solomon and Marvin, both spoken and unspoken. Loved ones, especially children and women, were to be protected at all cost.

"You don't have to apologize for anything. You did nothing wrong." Marvin attempted to assure him, but it was as impossible a task as scaling an unclimbable mountain. Both were men unaccustomed to the feeling of such helplessness. They were wrapped in pain from which there was neither cure nor lessening. Marvin grew quiet because he knew that nothing he said could adequately comfort either of them in their mutual brokenness. Aside from the faint beeps of the monitor, there in the quiet of the sterile hospital room, the only sound was that of the two big men crying.

"I am the resurrection and the life. The one who believes in me will live, even though they die: and whoever lives by believing in me will never die. Do you believe this?"

Pastor Blake's head hung low as he stood over the caskets of Aisha and Miremba and offered the eulogy. Although the man had officiated many funerals, there were parts of his benediction where the words choked him as though he were a mere mourner instead of the spiritual leader charged with helping all those gathered through their collective heartbreak. The saddest thing in the world had to be the sight of a child's coffin being lowered into the ground.

Unlike the two hundred or so students, fellow professors, and family members who turned out to mourn, Solomon didn't cry at the funeral. Instead, he buried the ocean of tears deeper than any grave that had ever been dug. He was not in the least bit comforted by the preacher's words, which rang achingly hollow to a man who had now lost two entire families under the blind worship of two separate gods. All he could do was sit in his wheelchair and watch as the earth slowly swallowed the casket and a half.

He was numb. Not at just the loss of his wife and child but from the call he had received the day before from the DA's office. The voice on the other end of the line informed him that the results of both mandatory samples of the breathalyzer taken from the defendant had mysteriously been deleted from the police database. Without them, they had no case. It was possible but unprovable that the defendant's father, who was a very wealthy land developer, had paid off a cop to lose the evidence.

As Solomon looked around, he saw the abundance of love and pain on the many faces of those whose lives Aisha had impacted. He couldn't help but wonder about the scope of impact that Miremba would have made on the world. The scripture that Pastor Blake had recited played over and over in his mind. The concept of life after death was just that—a concept. An unsubstantiated theory. What Solomon needed as he watched the loves of his life being entombed in the dirt was something much simpler. Primal. More tangible. His need was in fact biblical, albeit decidedly more Old Testament. Although he had never been a man of scripture, one did come to mind: "An eye for an eye."

"Lemme get…another Jack and Coke," the young man said, slurring his order to the bartender.

He sounded like a cottonmouth who had just gotten out of a dentist's chair and didn't have full control of his oral faculties.

"I'm sorry, sir, but we're gonna have to cut you off," the bartender responded.

"Whatda hell are you talking about? I only had a couple a shots."

"You've had seven, sir."

"What…difference does it…make? I'm not drunk."

"Still, we could be cited for serving you past your limit."

As the young man stood to confront the bartender, he wobbled side to side like a penguin. "You don't know my fuckin' limit, so just do your job and serve me another…drink."

"I'm sorry, but I can't. I'm calling you a cab."

"Fuck you and your cab! You know who my father is? He knows enough people…that he could make one phone call and have this shithole shut down."

Solomon sat at the far end of the bar, watching the man intently as he argued with the bartender. The man's name was Austin Walls III, a perpetual frat boy locked in the body of a thirty-eight-year-old trust fund baby. An arrogant rich boy, deeply seated in the spoils of privilege. Solomon decided that after he was done with Austin Walls III, a visit to the man's father was also in order.

In many ways, Solomon thought of himself as a simple man. He lived his life under the dictate of uncompromisable codes. Although nothing would bring his loves back, there were still things that had to be done. Revenge was much more for the living than the dead.

After throwing his glass at the bartender, Austin stumbled out of the bar. Solomon waited a few minutes, then followed him into the parking lot. He scouted the area and made sure no one was around and nor were there cameras. The night was quiet with only the sounds of an occasional car passing by.

When Solomon confronted the man, he used neither words nor weapons. Just his hands.

~

Wendell P's, the small creole eatery, was packed as usual. The scent of jambalaya, catfish, and even fried alligator greeted hungry patrons at the door. The tablecloths and curtains were the purple, green, and gold colors of New Orleans. The same-colored beads dangling from the ceiling gave the place a Mardi Gras–themed decor.

Solomon still walked with a slight limp as he waded through the crowd and made his way over to his father-in-law, who was seated in the back at a corner table. Marvin's sleeves were rolled up just enough to partially see some of the bloody claws of a black panther tattoo from his prison days. He was wolfing down a fried oyster po' boy and chasing it with a Munchie's pineapple pop drink.

"I was hungry, so I started without you. I ordered you a ginger beer," Marvin said.

"I'm sorry I'm late. Had a meeting that ran longer than I thought it would."

The server stopped by and put a bottle of ginger beer as well as a glass of ice water in front of Solomon. "I'll be back to take your order," he said before walking off.

"I was gonna get you some étouffée, but I didn't want it to get cold."

"It's okay. I don't really feel like eating."

"Isn't that kinda the whole point of meeting up for lunch?"

"I just wanted to talk to you."

Marvin sipped his pineapple pop and studied his son-in-law.

"It wouldn't by chance have anything to do with them finding Austin Walls beaten to death in a parking lot, would it? I also heard his father was found dead at one of his construction sites," Marvin commented.

"Yeah, I saw both stories on the news. Maybe the father crossed the wrong person in one of his business deals. At least that's what I heard the cops were looking into."

As Solomon sipped his ginger beer, Marvin looked down at his bruised and scraped knuckles.

"Who knows? I'm sure men like that had their share of enemies."

The two men simply stared at each other. Even over the din of a crowded restaurant, their unspoken conversation was the loudest in the room. Solomon was the first to break the silence.

"I came by to let you know that I put the house on the market last week, and the real estate agent just told me that I've already got two offers over asking."

Marvin was bothered by the news more than he was willing to show.

"So what are your plans after you sell it?"

"I'm gonna donate all the money to the school to set up a scholarship in Aisha's and Miremba's names."

"And where are you gonna move to? What are you gonna do?"

"Tell you the truth, I haven't thought that far in advance, but I just know it's time for me to move on. Everything around here reminds me of them too much."

"I know if I asked you to stay, it would just be me being selfish.

It would be because of the exact same reason you feel you need to leave. You remind me of them."

The server returned. "What can I get you?" he asked.

"Actually, I'm not eating, but another ginger beer is fine."

When the server walked off and Solomon turned back toward Marvin, he saw the downcast eyes and a hollowness in his father-in-law that he hadn't noticed before. Solomon had been so consumed with his own grief he hadn't fully absorbed the toll exacted on Aisha's parents. Marvin's skin was sallow. Although he put up a good front, Solomon saw that he'd been reduced to nothing more than the impostor of a once strong man.

Solomon reached over and patted Marvin on the back of his hand as a small gesture to remind him that he wasn't alone in his grieving. Marvin's eyes got wet. He pushed his plate aside, having suddenly lost his appetite.

The server dropped off another ginger beer in front of Solomon.

"None of it makes sense," Marvin said as he fought the tears. "Aisha and Miremba were two of the sweetest and purest souls I've ever met. I can't help but think about some of the bad shit I did when I was younger, and it just makes me wish God had taken me instead. I know my past pales in comparison to yours, but I've known blood on my hands since I was sixteen years old. Lots of stuff I'm not proud of. Just like you, everything changed when I fell hard for a good woman. It just happened for me a whole lot earlier in life than you. Even though I made promises to my wife and for the last fifty-something years dedicated myself to being a good Christian, everything changes when you have to bury a child, especially because some asshole had no respect for their life. This thing has just shown me that no matter how much I've tried to convince myself that I've changed, men like you and me never really escape from who we truly are. I mean down deep. The vows I made to God Almighty don't even matter anymore. Maybe I'll burn in hell for feeling this way, but I'm glad you did what you did. Those pieces of shit excuses of humans didn't deserve to live. If I were younger, I would have killed them myself."

Solomon took a sip from the fresh bottle of ginger beer before speaking.

"I've never been the type of man to try to tell anyone what they should or shouldn't believe. Maybe there's a hell, and maybe there isn't. I guess the only thing we know for certain is that what you call God Almighty is the one who let this horrible thing happen in the first place." Solomon stood. "I'll call you before I leave."

As he turned, Marvin said, "Thank you."

"For what?"

"For loving my daughter the way you did. The time that she was with you was the happiest I've ever seen her."

24

Bernael and Kimaris

Solomon's eyes fluttered open at the faint dawn light seeping through the slots of the half-closed blinds. It was just before five thirty, and he was still tired and a bit disoriented from the dream. It took him a moment or two to realize that he was still at the bed-and-breakfast run by the two nice old ladies. He looked over at the crumpled sheets of Gaby's empty bed and then to the open door of the bathroom. When he heard nothing but stillness, he raised himself onto his elbows and scanned the room with growing concern.

As Solomon threw the covers back to get out of bed, he discovered Gaby curled in a fetal position next to him. It reminded him of the countless mornings when he woke to find his daughter snuggled similarly between him and Aisha. The more Solomon stared at Gaby, the more he was reminded that there was nothing about the boy that hinted of fear. He didn't see a single trace of him being haunted by the danger that pursued him. As Solomon continued gazing down upon the boy, all he saw was a child nestled in the peace of knowing he was supremely protected. After a few minutes, Solomon eased the covers back over him, leaving him undisturbed.

By the time Solomon had finished showering and exited the bathroom, Gaby was wide awake and smiling as he greeted him.

"Good morning."

"Morning," Solomon responded. "Are you hungry?"

Gaby's eyes brightened as he nodded. "Yes."

"Okay, remember Miss Ari said that food would be ready at six since we have to get on the road early. As soon as you get dressed, we'll go down and grab breakfast."

Solomon laughed to himself at how quickly Gaby bounced out of bed and made a beeline for the bathroom.

As they came down the stairs, Solomon heard no movement, and neither did he smell the savory scent of the previously promised biscuits and ham. He called for the women as he pushed through the swinging door of the dining room. He was blindsided by a blow to the face that put him on his back.

Gaby let out a scream and knelt by a dazed Solomon's side. Two armed men roughly pushed a bleeding Ari through the swinging door, putting her next to Gaby and Solomon. Solomon instinctively eased his hand to the back of his waistband, only to realize that he had left his gun behind in his room.

The larger of the two intruders was a burly man with long hair and a lazy eye. He sported a prominent tattoo of the name Bernael on his exposed bicep. He looked like a wannabe extra in a B-rated motorcycle movie. His accomplice, a lean, tall man in a vintage Metallica T-shirt, had a shaved head crowned with a collage of tattoos.

Mr. Metallica kicked Solomon. "You shoulda slept in today. Get on your knees." When Solomon didn't move quickly enough for his liking, he kicked him again and yelled, "I said get up."

The burly man pushed Gaby aside and yanked Solomon to his knees. "My name is Bernael. My associate here is Kimaris. You know, there's a whole lotta money on your head, especially if we bring you and the boy to Cesar alive. Don't look so surprised that we found you. You're not nearly as smart as you think you are." Bernael snickered.

As Solomon wiped blood from the corner of his mouth, he stared hard at the two men.

Bernael kneeled down with his gun pointed at Solomon and tossed a black plastic bag before him. "Open it up. Cesar's got his regular crew out looking for you, but we were the only ones smart enough to track down known associates of Doc Callan that you might have reached out to. Go on. Open the bag."

Solomon opened the bag and saw half a dozen fingers as both intruders laughed.

"Took some convincing, but the gun dealer finally came around to seeing things our way. He gave you up about six fingers in."

"What about the old lady?" Kimaris asked.

"We do her, Cesar might pay us extra for making an example out of anybody who helps his enemies."

"She doesn't have anything to do with this, doesn't even know anything about me or the kid. She can't identify you or be a threat in any way."

"Makes no difference. You should have thought about all that before you came here," Kimaris said as he stood up and crossed over to Ari.

"She's got money. She can pay you. Just take me, the kid, and her money, and leave her alone," Solomon implored.

"You don't tell me what to do," Bernael yelled.

"How much money we talkin'?" Kimaris asked.

"I don't know exactly how much, but a lot. I saw it in the floor safe behind the front desk when her sister gave me change after we checked in last night."

Bernael grabbed Ari roughly. "Where's your sister?"

"She went out to pick up supplies."

"He tellin' the truth? You got a bunch of money around here?"

"No, I don't. I don't know what he's talking about," Ari cried.

Bernael shook her roughly. "Don't lie to me."

"I'm not lying," she pleaded.

He pushed Ari hard, and she hit her back against the wall. He placed his hands on both her shoulders and shook her as though she were nothing more than a load of damp laundry. The man saw neither a daughter, sister, mother, or even grandmother on the other end of his cruelty. Save for the potential windfall he imagined her having, he considered her life otherwise inconsequential. Solomon had a flashback of the day the soldiers came and treated the females of his village with such violent indifference.

As Bernael took a long hunting knife out of a belt holster and jammed the blade into the paneled wall just inches from Ari's face, the vibrations made her jump. He grabbed her hand and ran her fingers over the knife's serrated grooves for dramatic effect.

"I ask you one more time, and then I start cutting," Bernael threatened.

"I swear I'm telling the truth," Ari pleaded.

The more he saw how Bernael manhandled the woman, the more Gaby cried as well.

"Please don't hurt her," the child begged.

"You'd better worry about yourself, boy. You don't shut up, I'll stomp you," Bernael barked.

When Solomon stood to intervene, Kimaris punched him from behind, then immediately restrained him as Bernael stood a few feet away with his gun pointed in Solomon's face, taunting him.

"You a hero now? 'Cause if you step at me, you'd better be badder than God. Is that what you're thinking? You got some disasters in your pocket? 'Cause that's what you gone need."

"I'm just telling you that she's lying. She's got money," Solomon said.

"I don't know what he's talking about," Ari proclaimed.

"Shut up. Show me the safe," Bernael snapped. "Keep an eye on him. If he even breathes hard, cut his fuckin' hand off."

He grabbed Ari by the arm to lead her to the front desk area. As he lowered his gun and stepped away to investigate, he left his knife sticking in the wall.

As soon as he turned toward the doorway, Solomon seized the opportunity and headbutted Kimaris with the back of his head, breaking his captor's nose. Kimaris's eyes watered, and blood flowed freely down the lower part of his face and the yoke of his T-shirt. In one fluid motion, Solomon grabbed the knife from the wall, spun around, and stabbed Kimaris in the soft dimple just above his windpipe.

As Bernael turned around, Solomon hurled the blade with such force that he buried it four inches deep in the center of the man's chest. Bernael's finger reflexively squeezed the trigger while he was falling backward. Two shots rang out, and one of the bullets hit Ari in her midsection. She fell and bled.

Solomon quickly crossed to retrieve the gun as Gaby hurried to the woman's side. Bernael was on his back, still alive, breathing as if he were sucking air through a clogged straw. Unfortunately, he was conscious enough to see Solomon standing over him with the gun aimed down at his face. Not that it would have made any difference, but he was too injured to even plead for mercy. Bernael helplessly stared at the infinite darkness of a gun barrel pointing at him as well as the equally black skin and soul of the man who did the pointing. All he could do was lie prostrate and gaze up at death's beckoning.

One bullet did the job, but Solomon shot him twice for good measure.

"Gaby, go get in the van. We've gotta leave."

"What about Miss Ari?"

"She's not our problem. We can't be here when the cops come. I'll grab our stuff from upstairs. Go get in the van."

Solomon took the stairs two at a time. Gaby didn't move from the woman's side. He held her hand and felt her warm blood on his skin. As he hovered over her, his tears fell on her cheeks and rolled down the side of her face. Although she held his hand and muttered words he couldn't quite make out, Gaby knew she was praying. He threw in a silent prayer of his own as Solomon hurried back down the stairs, carrying the duffel bag as well as the rifle in a case.

He barked at the boy, "Gaby, I told you to go get in the van. We have to leave now."

"But she's still alive. We have to help her," the boy pleaded.

"We don't have time. Let's go."

"We can't just—"

Before Gaby could finish his sentence, Solomon swooped him up and carried him over his shoulder. Gaby kicked and fought him as best he could but to no avail. Solomon carried the flailing boy outside to the van and put him in the passenger-side front seat, then put his gear in the back. As he slammed the door and walked toward the driver's side, Gaby quickly jumped out. When Solomon came back around to the passenger side, Gaby threw himself underneath the van.

Solomon kneeled and pleaded, "What are you doing? We talked about this. You have to do what I tell you to do. It's for the best. Now get in the van so we can go."

Gaby rolled out on the other side, keeping the van between them.

"We can't leave until we help her," he demanded.

"Gaby, listen to me. It's not safe for us to stay here. Please, we have to leave."

As Solomon moved around the hood of the van, Gaby quickly countered by moving toward the back. The boy was on the verge of hysterics. "How can you just leave her? She didn't do anything to anybody. She needs you to help her. You can't just leave her."

Solomon finally exploded. "Who the hell do you think I am? What do you think I do? I'm sorry the nice lady got hurt, but whether she lives or dies, it's got nothing to do with me."

Gaby exploded back, "It's got everything to do with you!"

~

The two paramedics were young. One was male and the other was female. The man had sandy-brown hair, and his partner had shoulder-length tresses that were as black as a raven. They worked on stabilizing Ari as best they could while Solomon stood nearby with his gun dangling at his side.

As the female paramedic stole a nervous glance over her shoulder at Solomon, he gestured for her to turn back around. "Don't worry about me. Just do your job, and everybody will be fine."

Ari was now in and out of consciousness but seemingly doing much better than she was before the paramedics arrived.

"She's lost a lot of blood, but we have her stabilized," the man said.

They lifted Ari onto a canary-yellow gurney and started wheeling her toward the door.

"If I were a gambling man, what would the odds be on her?" Solomon asked.

"I'd say sixty-forty."

As soon as they exited, Gaby met them on the porch. He grabbed Ari's hand as they wheeled her down the four steps. When her eyes opened at his touch, he saw the pools of tears and tried to comfort her.

"They're gonna take care of you, Miss Ari," Gaby reassured her. "Please don't cry."

The woman's voice was soft and weak, but Gaby bent closer to her to hear.

"I'm just crying because I wish I could see your eyes."

Gaby held her hand until the paramedics hoisted her into the back of their rig.

Solomon addressed the male paramedic. "So what's the story?"

"We got a call that a lady thought she was having a heart attack. When we got here, this is what we found." When Solomon tilted his head at him, the young man got even more nervous and corrected himself. "I'm sorry. This is *all* we found."

"Both of you are young and have your whole lives to look forward to. Make sure you remember that and don't change your story. I'm not the kind of man you want to have looking for you. Give me your driver's licenses," Solomon demanded.

The two paramedics looked at each other before both of them fumbled with their wallets and handed over their licenses, which Solomon promptly pocketed. He looked down at Ari, then put his hand on Gaby's shoulder and led him away to the van.

"Is she going to be okay?" Gaby asked.

"There's a good chance she'll be fine," Solomon responded.

"Thank you."

"Yeah, I, uh… Let's go."

Just before Gaby climbed in the van, he turned and looked once more at Ari as the paramedics tended to her.

~

The freeway was spotty. Traffic flowed one minute and then became congested the next. When they slowed, Gaby glanced in Solomon's direction a couple of times as the two rode in silence. Solomon stared straight ahead at the road and the phalanx of cars before him. Gaby finally turned and spoke. "Are you mad at me?"

"Why do you ask?"

"Because you haven't talked since we left."

"What do you want me to talk about?" Solomon asked.

"I don't know. I just thought…"

"Do you have to go to the bathroom or anything?"

"No, I—"

"Because if you even think you have to go, you should say so now. There won't be time later."

"I don't have to go," the boy responded.

Solomon finally turned toward Gaby. "Look, I'm not mad. I just…you know sometimes two people can disagree on something and both of them can still be right. I understand you wanting to help the old lady. You were trying to protect her, and I even admire that. It's just who you are, and I have to understand and accept that. Just as you have to understand and accept that the biggest priority for me right now is trying to protect *you*. I'm sorry I yelled at you, but I'm not sorry that I'm willing to do anything to make sure you're safe."

"So what happens after I am safe?"

"I don't have all the answers, Gaby. I'm trying to figure out a lot of this stuff as we go, but you have to trust me. My hope is that all of this ends today and you'll find another good family to raise you, and you have as close to a normal life as possible."

"And what about you?"

"Not everybody was meant to have a normal life."

"Why do you say that?"

"It just is what it is."

"Are you…are you going to kill the bad men?"

"Yes, I am. I'm going to kill them all."

25
The Tomb

Solomon parked again atop the hill overlooking the cemetery. The sky was a perfect blue with fat, cottony clouds that looked painted by the master of masters. It was a beautiful day, one that would soon be marred by blood.

Solomon looked through a pair of binoculars as he leaned on the hood of his vehicle, surveilling the mausoleum of Cesar's dead son while Gaby sat inside, staring at him. The structure was the size of a single-car garage and was bookended by two rows of young, manicured cypress trees. As far as he could tell, it was the largest in the entire cemetery. It was a massive, ornate tomb constructed of thick stone and a wealth of grief.

At seven thirty, there were no visitors, just the dead. It was quiet enough to hear the grass yawn. Solomon's van was obscured by a bosky patch of land under a quartet of mature oaks whose leaves swayed back and forth on the unseasonably breezy day. The morning was perfectly quiet other than the unfamiliar chirps from a species of bird that Solomon had never heard before. All around him were stillness and the permanence of peace among the dead.

He crossed to the rear of the van and removed the Kevlar vest as well as the rifle from its sleeve. He put on the vest and zipped his jacket over it. As he assembled the scope and suppressor, Gaby exited the van and stood next to him. They were both quiet. Off in the distance, a worker arrived and started pruning a row of hedges near the cemetery's entrance. Gaby just stared at Solomon, who seemed to be in a zone. The boy looked on much like a wide-eyed apprentice studying the meticulousness of a true craftsman at work.

Although Solomon finally spoke, his eyes stayed focused on the preparation of his weapons.

"When I was around your age, Gaby, there were choices in life I never got to make because bad men came and made them for me. The only decision I was afforded was to either become like them or be killed. My biggest wish for you is that you're able to walk a path of your own choosing. Hopefully one day, you'll put all this behind you. All of it: the bad men, the pain and fear you feel, and even me as well. Regardless of all that you've been through, you've still got a shot at happiness and a good life. Because in the end, that's the only way you turn all this around. Do you understand what I'm saying?"

Gaby nodded. "I think so."

Solomon looked toward the field of tombstones for a moment and then continued, "Someone very dear to me had to teach me that if you let your enemy dictate who and what you become, then they get to defeat you all over again every day for the rest of your life. I just don't want you to end up like me, wasting years you never get back before you realize that simply being happy is the greatest victory. If you make the right choices, you can survive all this in the long run. I still don't know and guess I never will why I went through the things that I did, but maybe somehow if it helps me to stop you from going through it, then that might be the closest I ever get to making any sense of it. I just need you to promise me…actually yourself, that you'll live your best life and try to be as happy as you can be."

"I promise. Do you think you've ever really been happy, Solomon?" Gaby asked.

"Yeah, I was, a time or two. At least for a while."

"You think you'll ever be happy again?"

Solomon had to think before he answered. The smiles of his woman and child flashed in his mind.

"I think I've had my share. Maybe there was a little more to be had after that. Maybe there wasn't. At this point, just knowing that you'll be safe from the men who want to hurt you would make me happy."

"Do you still think you're like them?"

"I am what I am, Gaby. I've accepted that, and so should you."

"What if you're wrong? What if God sees you the same way I do? No matter what happens today, in the end, God will protect you, Solomon, because you have good in you. My father always said that if there's good in a person's heart, then they can be forgiven anything."

Solomon stared at the boy blankly. "I think the kind of

forgiveness your father was talking about is more for boys like you than men like me."

~

After Solomon bade Gaby to hide in the back of the van, he grabbed his rifle, his two handguns, and the rest of his gear and moved a hundred yards closer to the mausoleum, where he took up position behind a dense cluster of blue elderberry bushes. As he lay in wait, he thought about Gaby and why he persistently tried to see Solomon for more than what he really was. The fact that the child could still see the world through the prism of hope and innocence confirmed that he was not yet lost to the type of indifference Solomon had experienced when he was the boy's age. The thought warmed Solomon more than he knew how to admit to himself. He did think about what the boy said, even though God, forgiveness, and redemption were neither his priority nor consideration. Killing Cesar and protecting Gaby were the only two things that mattered to him. Both goals were intimately intertwined.

He waited an hour. And then another. Fortunately, just a smattering of visitors came and went; none lingered for long near the mausoleum. Evidently Monday mornings were not popular times for mourners. Solomon was somewhat relieved because he hoped that there would be no collateral damage. No bystanders in the wrong place at the wrong time. One of the last things he wanted on his hands was the death of another innocent.

At just past nine thirty, a caravan of three black Escalades arrived and parked in tandem in front of the mausoleum. Eight men exited the vehicles as the three drivers remained in their respective seats. The bodyguards were dangerous-looking men with the lumps of concealed weapons beneath their jackets. Six of the men took up strategic positions around the building, four in front and two toward the rear. The two remaining men opened the back door to the middle SUV and stood sentry as Cesar Quintero emerged from the vehicle. The guard who walked behind Cesar was as wide as a billboard, making it impossible for Solomon to hold Cesar in his scope long enough to get off a clean shot.

After the two men escorted their boss to the door of the building, he entered alone, prompting them to take up position with the rest of their associates.

Although Solomon hadn't anticipated the kill being easy, once he saw Cesar disappear into the mausoleum, the degree of difficulty rose exponentially. There were two choices: He could wait and gamble that a better shot would present itself as Cesar exited, or he could go in after him. The latter choice meant that he would have to give up the advantage of his surprise. He would have to kill the other eleven street soldiers, who he assumed were skilled in their own right. Needing to guarantee that Cesar wouldn't escape, he opted to go in after him.

The first thing he needed to do was to separate the men into sections as much as he could. The three Escalades were at least ten yards from the nearest guard as well as being positioned slightly out of their direct view. The three drivers were the easiest, so they would have to be first.

Successful snipers required a special skill set that demanded of them the ability to make second-nature mathematical equations. Distance times velocity times atmospheric influence such as weather and topography. The wind was blowing against him at about eight miles an hour, so Solomon adjusted his calculations accordingly. Since the SUVs were parked in tandem, he made the choice to start with the one in the rear and work his way toward the lead vehicle. The silent kill from a suppressor would buy him a little time, but he knew he would have to be quick and accurate. The tempered glass would crack like a spiderweb and crumble after being penetrated by a bullet, so Solomon allotted himself no more than three seconds per kill. Three seconds to shoot, calibrate, shoot, calibrate, shoot.

As he looked through the scope, he saw that the first target was texting on his phone. Solomon positioned his weapon so that it was shooting at enough of an angle that the bullet's exit would land in the passenger-side metal doorframe. He took out his target before the man could read the incoming text.

The second was reclining his head on the headrest. Solomon fired a through-and-through shot to the temple. Although he couldn't see the exit wound, he could see where the bullet embedded itself in the side of the passenger's headrest.

He wasn't sure if the driver of the final vehicle saw or heard something behind him, but the man suddenly opened his door and was in the process of getting out when Solomon shot him in the groin to make sure the bullet didn't exit the opposite window. The man was dead before he crumpled to the ground.

Solomon studied the remaining guards, intently searching for vulnerabilities to exploit. So intent in fact was his focus on them that he never noticed the man in a black denim jacket with a gun thirty yards away behind a dense stand of trees, watching *his* every move.

Solomon crouched and quietly moved in closer, using the vehicles to shield his advance. The two guards on the north side of the mausoleum were standing three feet apart, directly in front of each other, having a quiet conversation. They were within an inch of being the same height. Solomon clicked on the red laser finder to better line up his shot. He had to be perfect if he was going to be successful pulling off the two-for-one kill he was attempting. He set the laser dot on the back of the head of the guard facing away from him. When he squeezed the trigger, the bullet ripped through the nape of the neck of the first man and then through the trachea of the man facing him. They both fell like marionettes with severed strings.

When their two colleagues who were guarding the south corner of the structure saw the two men fall, they reached for their guns. Solomon dropped one before he was able to pull his weapon. The other managed to fire before being felled by a headshot.

Solomon dropped his rifle, pulled out both of his handguns, and readied himself for the assault on the four remaining guards. He placed his back against the wall of the mausoleum and waited to pick off whichever of the guards came first, no matter from which direction. Solomon was quite a skilled sniper, but his true talent was small arms combat. He was both a master and a terror with handguns because he was the trifecta of speed, accuracy, and mercilessness. Though many a nickname was born from his storied career—the

Black Reaper, the Wraith, the Winter Ghost, the Blood Wind, and, most famously, the Darkness—there in the cemetery among the sea of graves, he was simply the Cold Wrath of Death.

Two of the four remaining guards came for him from both the east and the west. Although the two men got off several rounds, Solomon killed them both with two shots each.

He used the row of cypress trees to shield himself from the final two men. The men hesitated out of fear for just a second when Solomon exploded from behind the trees and came at them in a full sprint, firing both weapons simultaneously. Although they fired back and tried to retreat, their initial hesitation gave Solomon the advantage he needed. He shot one in the hip and the other in the rib cage. Neither died right away. He finished them off as one tried to crawl away and the other tried to plead.

Solomon reloaded both weapons and then moved toward the entrance of the mausoleum. He knew as he approached the door that although he may have leveled the playing field numbers wise, he had also sacrificed the element of surprise. The gun battle had announced his arrival, and he now suspected that Cesar was waiting for him on the other side of the door, armed with weapon in hand and the irrefutable fact that one of them would soon be left among the dead.

He flung the door open and hid behind the doorframe, expecting to be greeted by a hail of bullets, but none came. As he cautiously peeped in, he saw that the room was aglow with the flickering flames of at least three dozen lit candles, which cast dancing shadows on the stone walls. Cesar had his back to Solomon, facing an altar as he knelt beside a gold-plated casket. The interior of the mausoleum was twenty by twenty feet with three-foot-wide columns in each of the four corners as well as the altar, which was near the far wall. Above the altar was a large painting of a female skeletal image in a corset and shroud with a ring of light behind her head and a scythe in her hand. Although Solomon had only heard of Santa Muerte for the first time a couple of days ago, he assumed that this was the image of the one they called the Skinny Lady. Cesar knelt in silent prayer before not the casket but rather the image of the female deity.

Solomon kept both of his guns trained on Cesar's back as he took a step into the tomb. Cesar didn't bother to turn and face Solomon. Instead he spoke with the calmness of a host welcoming a tardy guest.

"Based on your reputation, I assumed it was just a matter of time before you came. I'm glad you didn't disappoint."

"Turn around," Solomon ordered.

"I'm sure for a man like you who prides himself on principles, you'll find no honor in shooting me in the back."

"That's up to you. You don't turn around, you'll find out the hard way how much getting to kill you trumps any and all principles."

As Solomon kept both guns trained on Cesar, he continued looking around, first behind the two columns closest to him, then toward the two farthest from him. He saw, tucked in one of the corners, what looked to be two rolled-up sleeping bags and a few discarded water bottles. He knew something was off right away. As he quickly did the math, he saw a figure suddenly come from behind one of the farthest columns, firing at him. Although Solomon was able to put the man down with two shots, he realized just a fraction of a second too late that the shooter was a decoy. A second figure who emerged from behind the opposite column shot him twice center mass.

The vest saved his life but didn't prevent him from getting the wind knocked out of him from what felt like two rapid blows from a baseball bat. As he was falling backward, he managed to squeeze off two shots in the direction of the shooter. One found its mark in the man's neck. When Solomon's back crashed to the floor, he lost both of his guns.

Cesar crossed and stood over his fallen nemesis as Solomon writhed on the floor sucking air, trying to get his wind back.

"Knight takes all pawns but still loses," Cesar gloated as he retrieved the two guns, then casually shot Solomon in both legs. "That's just a warm-up. I'm curious to see exactly how many bullets I can put in you before your body gives up. Hold that thought."

He crossed to his henchman, who was trying his best to speak but could only muster desperate, gurgling sounds as he writhed in pain. Cesar looked at the man as indifferently as he would a wounded bug and shot him, putting him out of his misery. He then knelt over Solomon. "You're the only one who gets to suffer here. So where were we?"

He placed the muzzle of the gun underneath Solomon's vest and shot him point-blank in the stomach. Solomon screamed out in agony.

"Don't worry; you don't get to go so easily. There's a lot more pain to come. The thing I love about a good gut shot is that it's a long, hard way to die. Gives you plenty of time to think about how stupid you were to think you could ever cross me and there would be no consequences. All you had to do was give me what was mine and walk away."

"He was never yours and never will be yours," Solomon said defiantly.

"That's where you're wrong. Do you realize that only light can replenish light? The boy is my hope of seeing my son again, and you thought, what? That you could deny me that by playing the role of savior?"

"No matter how much your try to convince yourself, Gaby doesn't belong to you."

"If he can bring my son back to me, he does."

"Are you really so deluded that you think killing the boy will somehow bring your son back?" Solomon demanded more than asked.

Cesar smirked. "We all make choices in the name of love that others can't understand. How many people would condemn you for things you've done that they consider unimaginable? I heard the cops couldn't prove it but that you beat a father and son to death for the people you loved. That wasn't going to bring them back, but you did it anyway. So I just have to ask you what you would be willing to do. I mean, how far would you go if you felt there was a chance, even the slightest possibility, of bringing your family back?"

"I told you before, the dead stay dead. There's no coming back."

"There are a few billion Christians on this planet who would disagree with that. It's all about faith. You and I just serve different gods."

"I don't serve any god," Solomon retorted.

"Hate, love, fear, greed. We all serve something. Mine is just beyond your comprehension."

Solomon forced himself to smile. "No matter what you think or what you serve, you still lose. You'll never see the boy again. He's long gone. I made sure he was safe before I came for you." Solomon winced.

"Really, that's interesting. I was hoping he was here with you."

"I'm glad to disappoint you."

"You don't disappoint me at all." Cesar smiled back at Solomon.

The silhouette of a person appeared in the doorway, casting a shadow over Solomon. He strained to tilt his head enough to see a man in a black denim jacket entering the tomb. As the figure stepped forward, Solomon noticed that he was limping. When the man was no longer backlit by the sun, Solomon saw his face. It was Michael, the young man whose life he had spared at McKinty's office. Michael had a gun in one hand and held on to a terrified Gaby with the other.

Gaby tried to run to Solomon but was held back. The boy's cheeks were gleaming with tears, and his small body trembled from stress.

"Do you mind if I say something to him?" Michael asked Cesar.

"Just make it quick," Cesar said.

"The last time I saw you, the situation was flipped. You told me that people like us live and die by our choices? I'm here because I made the choice to protect my family. To make sure they're never harmed or threatened again by—"

"All right," Cesar interrupted. "We need to—"

Michael turned toward Cesar and, without warning or hesitation, pumped four bullets into his boss at point-blank range.

Gaby jumped, startled by the sudden gunfire. When Michael released his hand, the boy hurried to Solomon and knelt beside him with tears in his eyes. Solomon looked at Michael, shocked, then at Cesar's dead body, which was slumped at the side of his son's casket. Gaby saw the blood that pooled beneath Solomon and cried even as he tried to comfort him.

"It's okay, Gaby. It probably looks worse than it is. Don't worry. I'll be fine."

Gaby did his best to put up a brave front. He wiped away his tears before speaking to Solomon. "See, I told you. I told you in the end, God would protect you."

"Do me a favor. Maybe next time, ask him to protect me *before* I actually get shot."

The boy laughed in spite of himself.

"We gotta go before the cops get here," Michael said.

26

Father Jeremiel

Michael drove the van as Solomon lay in the back on a pallet of fertilizer bags with his head resting on Gaby's lap. Gaby used the sleeve of his shirt to wipe the sweat from Solomon's forehead. As they left the cemetery, the sound of approaching police sirens could be heard in the distance. Michael's jean jacket, now slick with blood, was snugly tied around Solomon's abdomen, offering needed compression.

Michael looked in his rearview mirror. "The nearest hospital is twenty minutes away."

"We're not going to the hospital," Solomon protested.

"But if we don't get you to—"

"I said we're not going to the hospital. Just stay on the 405 until I tell you to get off. Gaby, reach inside my jacket pocket, and take out my wallet and cell phone. I need to take care of something."

The boy hesitated, seemingly paralyzed by fear and sorrow.

"It's okay, Gaby. Everything's going to be fine. You trust me, don't you? I told you that I would make sure you were safe, didn't I?"

Gaby nodded his head and wiped his eyes.

"That's exactly what I'm doing. I'm going to make sure you're safe and taken care of, and that's the most important thing right now. Do you understand that?"

The boy nodded his head.

"I need to hear you say it, Gaby."

"You making sure I'm safe and taken care of is the most important thing right now."

"Good. Now grab my phone and wallet for me, okay?"

~

Michael turned off the main road and pulled into the small parking lot. The church was quiet. Like the air around it, everything was still. The winds were no more. The stark white stucco glowed in the bright morning sun like the subject of an Ansel Adams photo.

Solomon raised his head but struggled to lift his body.

"Michael, would you go ask Father Jeremiel to come out here? He's expecting us. Do me a favor, and help me sit up first."

Michael got out and opened the side panel of the van, then helped Solomon up to a sitting position. As Solomon winced from a sharp pain, he saw panic in Gaby's eyes.

"It's okay, Gaby. I'm fine."

"Are you sure?" Michael asked.

"Yeah, I'm good," Solomon replied.

Gaby stayed in the back with Solomon. As Michael walked toward the church, the boy looked sadder by the second.

"You're gonna leave me here?" he asked.

"Yes. The priest will take good care of you. He'll help you find a good home."

"But I want to stay with you," the boy protested.

"You can't."

Gaby turned away and looked out the open door. "I'm never gonna see you again, am I?"

Solomon hesitated before he spoke, sensing the boy's fragility. "No."

Gaby was quiet for a few moments, then turned back and looked Solomon in his eyes.

"You're going to die, aren't you?"

"At some point, we all die, Gaby. To tell you the truth, I always assumed it would have happened to me a lot sooner than now."

"Maybe I can help you to get better like I did before."

Solomon couldn't help but smile. "Not this time. It's okay though. I'm fine with it. I really am. Might not make sense to you now, but one day, it will. I promise. Ever since I was around your age, all I've ever done was fight and hurt people. Truth is I'm tired, Gaby. I'm just…tired. You're the only thing in this world that I don't regret fighting for. If I had to do it all over again, I would. Just knowing you're safe makes everything worth it, so please don't be sad for me. Maybe I don't have a right to, but I'm just asking you to make sure that the rest of your life matters. I mean really matters. Because then that means my life meant something too. And don't forget what I told you about being happy, okay?"

"I won't. I promise."

Gaby tried as best he could to remain strong in the eyes of Solomon, but he was unsuccessful. He turned again to look out the open door in an effort to hide the breach of tears and any evidence of his undoing. His heart broke into far too many pieces to put back together.

Although the boy did his best to conceal his face, Solomon looked at his profile and saw his dark skin shining from the wet streaks that began falling like the start of a spring rain. Knowing that he had nothing to stop the sadness, Solomon rubbed his own palms on the front of his pants in an attempt to wipe away as much blood as he could before reaching out and holding the small child's hand in his. They sat without words that would have only proven to be insufficient. It was their simple touch that spoke the things that neither could say. Their hands bonded together, not just by the stickiness of drying blood but more so by all that the boy and man had come to mean to each other.

Despite what he told Gaby at the cemetery, Solomon knew that he had lied to the boy. He had in fact hoped that he would forever live on in the heart of one so pure. In the short time that they'd spent together, Gaby had become like the earth that grounded Solomon. He thought about how meeting the boy not only gave him purpose but also reignited a light that had all but been extinguished. Despite the pain and the nearing of his end,

Solomon was at peace because the boy with the amber eyes still gave him life even in the shadow of imminent death. They sat hand in hand perfectly quiet until they saw Michael limping as he and Father Jeremiel rushed toward the van.

Father Jeremiel crossed to the van and stared through the open door at the bloody sight. He made the sign of the cross and kissed the silver crucifix that hung from his neck. "Holy Father! When you called, why didn't you tell me you were hurt?"

"Doesn't matter."

"Of course it does. We have to hurry and get you inside and do what we can to save you."

Solomon made a hand gesture, stopping Jeremiel's efforts. "It's too late for all that. That's not why we came."

"I've already tried to talk to him, Father, but he won't listen," Michael declared.

Solomon looked in Michael's direction. "Michael, do me a favor. Take Gaby inside and wait for the Father."

Michael didn't move; he just looked at Jeremiel, who finally nodded to him to do what he was asked.

"Come on, Gaby. Let's go," Michael said.

As Gaby got out of the van and turned to follow Michael, he didn't look at Solomon. He said no goodbyes.

Solomon called out to him, "Hey, Gaby, you're forgetting something, aren't you?" When Gaby moved back toward him, Solomon pointed down at the floor of the vehicle at the Dodgers baseball cap and the trumpet in the case. "You can't get great at something if you don't practice."

Gaby picked up the trumpet case and the cap, nodded at Solomon, then followed Michael toward the church. He looked back over his shoulder twice before disappearing into the building.

~

The priest loosened the compression to inspect the severity of the wound. The look on his face simply confirmed what Solomon had already inferred.

As the two men locked eyes, Solomon spoke. "There's nothing you can do for me, Father. The only thing that matters now is that you promise me you'll take care of Gaby and find him a good home."

"Of course I will, but we still need to—"

"No buts. He's all that matters," Solomon said.

"You have my word, Solomon."

"Good." Solomon was quiet for a few seconds, sucking in air as though he were trying to manage his pain through breathing. His eyes glassed over in a vacuous stare while his mind floated in a distant space.

When Father Jeremiel gently placed his hand on Solomon's shoulder, the contact brought him back. As he looked around, it seemed to take a moment or two to recognize the priest as well as his surroundings. His mind was racing in a desperate effort to remember the final pieces of business that he deemed most important.

"Did your bank reach out to you?" he asked.

"Right after you called. They informed me that someone had wired more than two million dollars in donation to the church.

You have no idea how much help that will be for the kids and the work we're doing here."

"Would you do me a favor and use some of the money to hire Michael to help you out here? He's a good kid just trying to do right by his family."

"I don't need any convincing. Lord knows I could use the help."

"Let me ask you something, Father. Do you think that good things can come from bad?"

"I'm an old-school priest who still believes that light trumps darkness."

Solomon contemplated the priest's words, then responded, "I've known all kinds of people. Mostly bad. You're a good man doing good things. I even saw it in the faces of the kids who I met last time. They were happy. I mean, really happy."

"Thank you. That means a lot. Maybe I can still do something for you. Are you sure you won't come in and let us see? Rumor has it that I've ushered in a few miracles here and there."

The two men regarded each other with the ease of two old friends.

Solomon laughed. "I'm sure you have, but I'm good. Truth is I just wanna go home."

Jeremiel nodded. "I understand," the priest conceded. "You know, I've met a lot of people too, and for whatever it's worth, Solomon, I see that there's genuine goodness in you. And no matter what you might or might not think of God, He knows there's goodness in you as well."

"Thank you. And thank you for everything that you're doing for Gaby. He's a special kid."

Father Jeremiel smiled and held Solomon's hand. "I know. I knew it the minute I met him. You don't have to worry. Just trust that God and I will both take good care of Gabriel. He'll be just fine."

27

Home

A few of the angel statues in the botanical garden were tethered with the yellow tape of a crime scene. Michael helped a weakened Solomon to the garden's edge overlooking the beach below. Solomon sat in the soft earth, resting his back against the statue of his favorite seraph. Michael sat beside him. They had a panoramic view of the sea before them as well as the garden behind them. As Solomon looked down at the ocean's bluff just twenty feet below, he saw that his beloved stretch of beach was empty. The only sounds were the rolling waves and squawk of gulls. The sky was a late-afternoon spectacle of deep blues and a golden sun that looked inexpressibly perfect. The sinking orb glittered over both sea and sand as though they had been sprinkled with crushed diamonds.

Solomon's skin was gray and clammy. Though it became

incrementally more challenging for him to breathe, he still smiled at the beauty of the ocean.

"This was the beach my wife brought me to the very first day I came to California. After she died, I started working here at the gardens so that I could see this view every day."

"This place is beautiful, in a heaven kind of way."

"Thanks for bringing me back here, Michael. I'm okay now. You can head back."

"I'm not gonna leave you here by your—"

"It's fine. I'm good. Trust me."

"You shouldn't be left alone."

"It doesn't really make a difference, does it? Whether I'm alone or not doesn't change what's coming. Don't worry. I'll be fine. I'm home, Michael. I prefer it this way."

Michael looked out to the water, disappointed, as though he had somehow failed.

Solomon rested his hand on the young man's shoulder. "I wanna thank you for everything you've done, but it's time for you to go back home to your family. You need to be there for them. That has to always be first and foremost in your heart. The measure of a man is how he takes care of his family. Always remember that. You got a second chance to be the best version of yourself, Michael. You gotta live up to that. You owe it to your family and to yourself."

"I will, Solomon, and I promise to work hard for Father Jeremiel."

"I know you will."

Michael didn't move. He just sat quietly watching the waves of the ocean advancing and retreating, his thoughts seemingly held captive by something unseen and unspoken. Solomon knew there was more on the young man's mind than the current predicament. The more Solomon looked at him, the easier it was to recognize the familiar load that weighed heavily on him. It was the same type of weight that he himself had shouldered since the age of seven. It was the unforgivable burden of having taken a life.

"You did what you had to do to protect your family. You're old enough to learn to live with that choice but young enough to put all this behind you. The fact that you feel bad right now is a good thing. It means you've still got a heart, and if you listen to that, it'll keep you away from the kinds of choices I made. Trust me, it's not the kind of life you want."

Michael considered Solomon's words, then nodded at him as he stood and wiped dust and specks of mulch off the back of his jeans. He took in the garden and the ocean one last time, then turned back to Solomon. "Thank you. And you were right. Gaby is definitely special."

"Yeah, he is."

"I swear to you that I will look out for him like a big brother should."

"Thank you. He's been through so much."

"Don't worry. I'll always have his back."

Solomon flashed a weak but grateful smile. "That really means a lot. Would you do me one last favor?"

"Of course, anything."

"I left my phone in the back of the van. The password is 0672. Look up the name Margaret. Call her and tell her that I said she and the girls are safe now. Let her know that her brother was avenged. And tell her I'm sorry I didn't make it to tell her in person."

~

Once he was alone, Solomon was comforted by the memory of his wife and daughter. He thought of the countless picnics on the beach that the three of them shared. He thought of how much his daughter was like her mother in their mutual love of the sea. The image of them dancing in the sand and splashing about in the water not only made him smile but somehow diminished the pain of his wounds. He loved the beach as much as they did but for very different reasons. For them, it was a deeper connection to God. For him, it was the overwhelming sense of freedom. Whereas New York had often left him feeling confined both physically and mentally, the quiet beach reminded him that life was to truly be lived with no such constrictions. Much like the view, he felt infinite. The nearness to the water also reminded him of his time as a child spent with his parents on the banks of the Ayugi River. His father would often sit him in his lap and point out toward the horizon and instill in him the idea that his dreams should be as vast as the sky and with the depth of a bottomless sea.

Solomon breathed the ocean air in deeply. He filled his failing lungs with swigs of life and a few more precious minutes. He felt the weight of his past wrongs lifted and replaced with the peace of self-forgiveness. As he stared out at the water, there was neither judgment, shame, nor regret. No failures. No defeats. No hauntings from the unsummoned. There was only substantiation. Proof of life and a reminder of the abundance of his prosperity. The times Solomon spent with his wife and daughter on the ocean's shores always left him feeling like a king of immeasurable wealth. This was the place that left him feeling whole and cleansed. The place that let him shine like sun on water.

The lids of his eyes grew heavy. Solomon faded in and out of consciousness a couple of times. The fugue made it more and more difficult for him to differentiate in which realm he languished most. He floated on the edges of indeterminate space and time. He was neither fully of the living nor fully of the dead. It was just a few days ago when he found himself bleeding in the very same spot among the stone archangels. His mind flashed an image of him lying helpless in the firm clutch of death. Just as he had then, he offered no resistance. He was only thankful that now that death had come full circle, the place of his fatality was ultimately of his own choosing. Besides the lands that birthed him, the gardens and the beach were the two most peaceful places he had ever known. The lapping sounds of the ocean brought even more memories of his wife and daughter. He could think of no better place for his final submission.

As he sat with his back against the base of the stone cherub, Solomon simply waited. While he waited, he heard his mother's voice singing to him the songs of his childhood. He saw her looking at him with forgiveness in her eyes for the man he had become. He heard the dulcet whistling from his father as he tilled the fields.

He felt his father's unconditional love for him still intact despite his violent course. Solomon even heard the childish giggles of the first girl he had ever loved. He smelled the land of his birth. He smelled his mother's cooking. He smelled home. Cradled there in the soft earth of the garden, he thought of long-forgotten memories before the soldiers came and took from him all that mattered.

Eyes closed, Solomon listened as the waves quieted and he heard the buoyant laughter of his daughter. After much effort, he opened his eyes and looked below onto the shoreline and saw Miremba playing in the sea-foam with Aisha. Both their faces were made moist from the faint spray of the ocean's spindrift. Solomon watched intently as the two loves of his life darted in and out of the water with giddy abandon. He then noticed that Ida stood nearby, waist-deep in the sea, softly singing to her granddaughter and great-granddaughter. Their wet skin shone like polished gold as they looked up toward him, waving, then pointing toward the arrival of others.

Solomon turned his head and saw his parents walking hand in hand as they did when he was still a child. He saw Akika, Dembe, and even his former teacher Mr. Mukasa laughing with Doc Callan. Mr. Tanaka was there sitting on a wet boulder sipping from a cup of tea. The twins from the bed-and-breakfast arrived with Raphael, the owner of the gun shop, fingers intact. Father Jeremiel and Michael were there with the children from the church, as was Cesar Jr. with a headful of thick, curly locks. He, like the other children, shone, but none as gloriously as Gaby, who was front and center, beaming brighter than sunshine while sporting his crisp white Dodgers cap. When they all turned and cried out the boy's name, he raised his horn to his lips and grinned at Solomon. Gaby's cheeks swelled like water balloons on the brink of bursting.

As Solomon watched the boy straining with unbridled effort, he found himself smiling and rooting for his young companion. His heart raced as he tried his best to will Gaby to success. Even from his elevated perch, he could see the veins in the young boy's neck boldly pronounced from the sheer exertion of him attempting to bring forth sound.

Gaby tried again and again, but each time, all that came out was the hiss of wet air. Father Jeremiel crossed to Gaby, placed his hands on the boy's shoulders, and whispered in his ear. When he took a step back, Gaby raised the horn once again to his lips and blew with such fervor that Solomon thought he felt the statue on which he leaned shake ever so slightly. And then Solomon heard it. An absolutely indescribable sound. One unlike any beauty he'd ever known. It was a pitch so pure that it stilled the ragged tides and opened the skies like parted sheers. It was a sound that carried with it revelations of things neither seen nor known. A sound of impossible clarity.

While Solomon continued listening to the swell of the mesmeric harmony, he saw past sun and sky. He saw ever so clearly the shores of his motherland. Solomon saw through even the portal of time. As had been the way of his people since the dawn of man, the pounding of talking drums welcomed the arrival of life. Dark figures came en masse. Hundreds of beautiful Black men of varying ages with heads held high, shoulders back, and broad chests bulging with pride as they strolled forward. They were all proud kinsmen, who glistened with sweat from having been kissed by the sun while toiling on the land from first light till last. They were generation after generation of stewards of the land. Their black skin shone so luminously that Solomon had to squint as he watched them in awe. Each of them moved like a god. The men arrived with outstretched hands that were calloused and had been made strong by Mother Earth. They came bearing the truths of untold secrets. Secrets of the universe that Solomon had long been blinded to were now displayed before him. The men beckoned to him with their open arms and sang in his native Acholi Luo dialect the very songs that his father used to sing to him as a child while they worked the fields.

Despite never having met the men before, Solomon recognized them nonetheless. They were Nangobi landmen, his paternal ancestors. They were his clan, his spirits of light and ancestry. All the Nangobi men who came before him now came to collect him. They came to call him home. They bade him, the last of their bloodline, to take his rightful place beside them. Solomon was uncertain whether his mind deceived him, but he thought for just the briefest of moments he even saw Allah, the god of his kin, standing tall among the tribe.

The world shook under the rhythmic echo of beating drums as the men clenched their fists and lifted the sky with their songs. Their voices were so deep that they raked the floor of the ocean. Solomon's ancestors danced in celebration of his return. When their songs came to an end, their voices roared and filled the skies with the mighty rumble of tribal chants. "Alkebulan, Alkebulan, Alkebulan." Solomon wept with pride as he listened to them bellowing the indigenous name of the motherland before the colonizers renamed it Africa.

He locked eyes with Gaby, who was now standing in the center of the circle surrounded by the multitude of Nangobi descendants. It was in that moment that Solomon truly understood his father's words and the meaning of Ubuntu—"I am because you are. You are because I am."

As Solomon stared raptly at the boy with swollen cheeks, blowing his horn louder than thunder, he knew why the child had looked so familiar to him earlier. Solomon looked up at the face of the onyx statue on which he leaned and realized Gaby was the spitting image of the stone angel with a trumpet pressed to his lips.

When they looked at each other, both Solomon's and Gaby's faces were wet with joyful tears as the boy blew ceaselessly and the ancestors filled the shores with calls beckoning their progeny home. The sound of drums continued to fill the air with syncopated booms that moved both earth and sea. The ancestors continued dancing and chanting. "Alkebulan, Alkebulan, Alkebulan."

Dear Reader,

Solomon Nangobi began the Martyr Maker series as a secondary character. A former child soldier who grew into a ruthless assassin: complex, flawed, and dangerous. And yes, beloved by my readers. I loved him too. After the first book, it was clear that Solomon had endless layers that demanded deeper exploration.

Solomon's story explores a broken man faced with the possibility of his own redemption and whether that redemption is something you earn or something you choose.

Of the four books in this series, *Laws of Solomon* is my most vulnerable and personal. Solomon's journey mirrors questions I believe many of us wrestle with: Are we forever defined by our mistakes? Or are we allowed to be forgiven and grow beyond them?

I hope that you have walked away with a reflection that impacted you as deeply as it impacted me whilst writing.

Thank you, most sincerely, to all my readers. You inspire me to push through.

Eriq La Salle

"Bracing, emotionally complex... An amazing read!"
—S. A. COSBY, NEW YORK TIMES BESTSELLING AUTHOR OF KING OF ASHES
LAWS
OF
SOLOMON
A MARTYR MAKER NOVEL
AWARD-WINNING AUTHOR
ERIQ LA SALLE

Enjoy this excerpt from *Laws of Wrath*, another Martyr Maker thriller

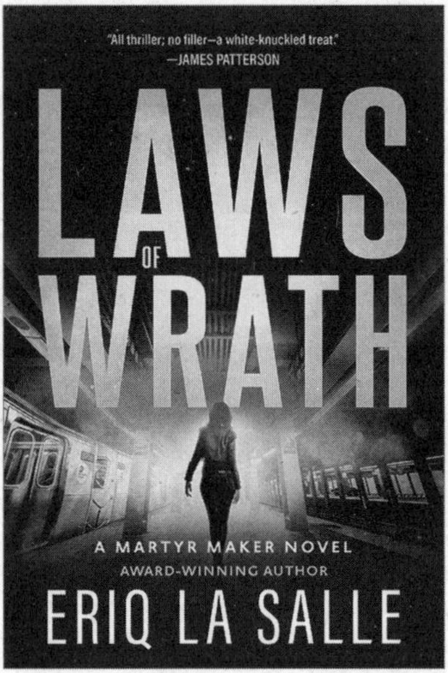

57

The African turned down the street that Jelly's house was on. They drove past two crows feasting on the carcass of a smashed squirrel. As the car neared, the birds hopped on the curb as if they were in a sack race. Just as he and Phee got to the end of the cul-de-sac, they both noticed the guard posted in front of the house. As the guard looked in the direction of their vehicle, they both caught a glint of metal in his right hand. The African calmly made a U-turn and headed back up the street.

"What are you doing?" Phee demanded.

"Easy Phee, we don't know what de situation is in dere; no need to announce our arrival."

The African cut off the lights and pulled over half a block up the street. He reached under the seat of his car, pulled out a handgun, and attached a silencer. He handed the weapon to

Phee with an extra clip, and then grabbed a gym bag from the back seat.

"What about you?" Phee asked referencing the gun.

"Don't worry about me; I've got what I need. You take de front I'll go in through de back."

Even though Phee had his own gun, he took the offered weapon and turned to exit, until The African stopped him with a firm hand on his shoulder.

"Dere are things dat I'm gonna have to do when we're in dere Phee, and I can't be worried about you being a cop," The African said.

"You don't have to worry; I'm not a cop tonight. Just do what you do," Phee said as he exited the car and made his way back toward the house.

Phee made a quick jog through neighboring yards. His vision blurred a couple of times from the burst of energy. He hid behind a bank of snow-covered hedges, taking a second to clear his head. The last ten feet to the house was completely open terrain. The crunchy, thick snow beneath him made the thought of an unannounced arrival impossible. He burst from behind the bushes and ran as fast as he could toward the guard. As the guard turned and raised a nickel-plated .38, Phee popped the man twice before he could get off a shot. Pffft, pffft, the two bullets knocked the guard off the porch and deposited him with a thud in a mound of snow. The imaginary bees that Phee heard in his head returned, seemingly angry at having been awakened.

The African was a living myth. A fantastical legend that was embellished upon each time tales of his exploits were told. There were those that labeled him a ghost. A man killed at least a hundred times or so who repeatedly refused to stay dead. Some said that he sold his soul to the devil at the tender age of eleven. Others said that he was the devil. However blurred the lines of fact and fiction, there was one indisputable truth: The African was the purest of killers. The guard at the back door had probably never heard the urban mantra that proclaimed, "Bad boys moved in silence and violence." He never saw death coming. One second the guard was standing and sucking on a cigarette; the next he was facedown in bloodied snow. He looked like he was lying on a bed of cherry-flavored snow cones. The man died terribly confused.

Reading Group Guide

1. Why do you think Solomon finds peace in tending to the garden? Do you like to garden? What feelings does it evoke in you?

2. What in Solomon's past makes him uncomfortable with children? How does Gaby begin to break through those walls?

3. For what reason is Cesar chasing Gaby? Do you believe this is a legitimate and logical reason?

4. Do you believe a person's past necessarily dictates their future? Was Solomon destined to be surrounded by violence, or could he have chosen a different path at some point?

5. What kind of discrimination did Solomon face when he first arrived in the United States, and how did he react to it? Do you see this discrimination in society today?

6. Gaby suggests that he and Solomon could choose to be family. What do you think Solomon's idea of family is? What kind of chosen or found family do you have in your own life?

7. What do Aisha and Miremba give to Solomon that he'd lost? How do their deaths affect him?

8. Whom does Solomon see before he dies? Why do these people bring him comfort? Are there figures from your life you would like to see at your end?

9. What do you think Gaby meant to Solomon? Did he represent or symbolize something Solomon had always longed for?

10. Do you think Gaby's life was worth the amount of death and violence done to save him? Was his life more valuable in some way than that of Doc Callan's, McKinty's, or Solomon's? Why or why not?

11. Compare Solomon's childhood to Gaby's childhood. How are they similar, and how do they differ?

A Conversation with the Author

Where did the inspiration for this story come from?

This story has shadowed me for a long time. Over twenty years ago, I wrote an unproduced screenplay about a hit man who saves a little girl. The idea never left me. I kept wondering what kind of man becomes capable of such extreme violence, and what kind of love could redeem him? I think I grew into the story. Twenty years ago, I wasn't at the place where I could tell the tale with the honesty I can today.

I was also influenced by two characters from two of my favorite films: Luca Brasi from *The Godfather* and John Creasy in *Man on Fire*. I took Brasi's reputation for violence and unshattering loyalty to his bosses and blended that with Creasy's circumstance and need for redemption.

What is your usual writing process like?

I wake up early, usually around 6 a.m. (on good days, 4 a.m.), and attempt to write. I do my best thinking in quiet spaces with a view of nature. My zen garden has become a sanctuary for me, a peaceful place where my characters can visit me and I can listen.

Some days the words come easy—eight hours of work done in two. Other days I get two hours of work done in eight. Writing humbles you. It reminds us that we are not in control of our muses. One must remain disciplined enough to show up and hope that inspiration comes to visit you.

Like most writers, I've wrestled with doubt and severe writer's block that last for days. The key is to always return to my laptop whether I feel inspired or not.

What kind of research did you do for this book?

The research mainly focused on Uganda in the 1970s under Idi Amin's rule. I wanted Solomon's memory of his youth to feel as authentic and lived-in as possible. I wanted my readers to smell the air, see the dust on the road, and feel the heat of the African sun.

Beyond the historical fabric of the time, I also explored faith, the symbolism of archangels, and the structure of parables. I wanted *Laws of Solomon* to read like a parable—blending the real world with the spiritual realm.

Do you have a favorite character?

Solomon has always been a favorite of mine. Even when he was introduced as a secondary character, there was something unresolved about him. Something that always made me gravitate toward his quiet power.

The more I wrote about him, the more I understood that he needed his own story. A story not just about his role as a feared hit man but about his inner world. His longing. His loneliness. And about his subsequent search for peace, meaning, and dignity.

Gaby is dear to me as well. He represents innocence but never weakness. He carries a lightness with him and impacts every character he meets positively. He is the moral center of the story.

What would you like readers to take away from this story?

The book asks difficult philosophical questions:

Can the most violent of men become the most peaceful?

Can even the most corrupted soul be redeemed?

Can a man with a dark soul still choose light?

Above all else, I hope readers are moved and that they're absorbed in the story. I am a storyteller who believes in engaging characters. I want readers to fall in love with them, cry with them, and cry *for* them. And then chew on those questions I underscore throughout the book. Wrestle with them. And then maybe believe, as they reach the last page, that redemption—no matter how costly—is possible.

Acknowledgments

Thanks foremost to God.

My agent, Rockelle Henderson—you are an amazing strategist who is not afraid to take chances. You keep raising the bar and challenging me in ways that have made me a better author. I'm very glad we have taken this journey together and continue to do it on our terms.

My editor, Anna Michels. Thank you for helping to elevate this novel while protecting my voice and vision.

Mandy Chahal—thank you for being such a passionate advocate for this book. So great having your support and resources. From our very first marketing meeting for *Laws of Solomon*, I knew the book and I were in great hands. Thanks for thinking outside the box.

Wren T. Brown—the walks and talks matter.

My nephew Eugene Haynes IV. You never hesitate when it comes to helping me in any way you can as I continue on this literary journey. I love our strategy sessions. Our angel Ada would be proud that we are doing great things together as a family.

A special thanks to:

Orsayor

Danny

Kim

Lisa

Storm

D. H.

You all know why.

About the Author

© Allister Foster

Actor. Director. Producer. Author. Eriq La Salle is best known to audiences for his award-winning portrayal of Dr. Peter Benton on the groundbreaking medical drama *ER*. He attended Juilliard and NYU's Tisch School of the Arts. La Salle's career spans Broadway, film, and television, with notable roles in *Coming to America*, *One Hour Photo*, and *Logan*.

Beyond acting, La Salle has built a prolific career behind the camera, directing and executive producing for HBO, Showtime, NBC, Fox, and CBS. Some of his numerous credits include *Law & Order: SVU*, *Law & Order: Organized Crime*, *On Call*, *FBI*, and *Chicago P.D.*

After decades of success in the entertainment industry, La Salle turned to publishing. He launched his highly personal and award-winning Martyr Maker series, beginning with *Laws of Depravity* and followed by *Laws of Wrath* and *Laws of Annihilation*.

With these novels, he brings an unusual new depth and emotion to the traditional procedural thriller.

These days you can find Eriq planning his next television/film projects and writing happily in his zen garden in Los Angeles.

Find Eriq online at iameriqlasalle.com, on Instagram @eriqlasalle, and on TikTok @eriqlasalleauthor.

Don't miss a single gripping thriller from Eriq La Salle!